250

MOHUNE'S NINE LIVES

MOHUNE'S NINE LIVES

*Being the Peregrinations of
Squadron Leader* PETER ST. MAUR
BEVERLEY DE L'EPEE MOHUNE

*(which is, of course,
pronounced Moon).*

By PELHAM GROOM

BOOKS INC.

DISTRIBUTED BY

LIVERIGHT PUBLISHING CORPORATION

c. 8

HR

CONTENTS

MOHUNE'S NINE LIVES

CHAPTER ONE

IN WHICH PETER MOHUNE MEETS THE BLITZ

"Seen this picture of Grubby getting his D.F.C.?" demanded a Pilot Officer.

"Looks quite Byronic, doesn't he," agreed another, pausing in his letter writing, "You know I've simply nothing to put in my diary."

"It certainly has been quiet to-day," admitted the first speaker. "Wonder what Jerry's up to. Haven't heard a plane take off all the afternoon. I don't like it ... much."

"Oh, he's just waiting for us to come to Readiness. You mark my words, just as soon as we get over to the dispersal point, Convoys will pour through the Straits, bombers will roar over the coast, we'll bog about the sky getting cold and miserable ..."

"Throw a book at him someone," put in a third voice, "he's making me cry."

The Ante Room in the Officers' Mess at Marsden, the Headquarters of a Fighter Command Sector in the South-East of England, was full: pilots were everywhere, some sprawled in the deep leather armchairs, some unashamedly lay at full length on the wide settees in an attempt to liquidate their overdraft of sleep. Two Squadron Leaders rested their elbows on the high mantelshelf and discussed the merits of different forms of aerial attack.

In one corner a Flight Lieutenant played Shove Ha'-penny with an Army Officer. "Fan me," ejaculated the Flight Lieutenant as he wiped the chalk marks from the board with languid despair; "I repeat, 'Fan me.' You've done it again. I mean I ask you how can innocence prevail against the Licentious Soldiery. I mean, it isn't skill, it's ... well, just misspent youth and what not, not forgetting of course the sedentary life you Army Birds lead. Actually the Yanks have a word for such as you, you're Bums on the Plush, positively Bums on the Plush. You sit back in a nice warm room, and just draw in the boodle. I mean compare the two of us. I wear myself out from dawn to dusk, while you just practice these Bar Room games so that you can take drinks off me at night. It's unfair actually."

The Searchlight Control Officer grinned. He knew his Batchy Salter. "So it's lazy we are, is it?" he demanded. "Ye gods, have you ever been in an Operations Room when we've had a show on?"

"Never, and that's the point. I've been in there and seen you playing nap in a corner, or ogling a ravishing W.A.A.F., but so far as work's concerned, I ask you a question: 'Do the Army know the meaning of the word WORK?' Answer—definitely not."

"Batchy, you lie; through those horselike teeth of yours, you lie." The Captain pulled the metal discs towards him with a circular sweep and sent one skimming up the board. "Let me give you an example," he continued, "just a short sketch of what our job can mean ..."

"Fan me, I know that. All you do is to waggle search-lights about the sky, and it's not as though you did that yourself. As I say, you sit in our nice warm Operations Room and make some poor devil out in the cold do your work for you. Furthermore, I have the conviction, a deep-seated conviction I might add, that you and 'Guns' are in cahoots, when I fly overhead you tell them that I'm hostile: they fire at me, ruin my nerves and you cash in at this futile game when battered and weary I finally come to earth. Through you, soldier, our days become purple purgatories and our nights nasty nightmares. I hope you appreciate the alliteration, and anyhow," Batchy Salter stretched his long body over the board, "that halfpenny is not in that bed. You're perpetrating a swindle, but don't mind me, go on with your little line."

The S.C.O. scored the point, despite Batchy's wail of protest. "You may laugh, young Salter, but a night shift is no joke. By the time I have asked the Controller whether he intends to put aircraft into the sky, and he's asked the Met. people what the weather's going to be like and argued with the Group Controller about it, and has told me there won't be any flying, and I have told the Searchlight Posts of his decision, and told them they can Stand Down, and having listened to the Controller grumbling about Group, and having told the Posts to Stand To again because the Observer Corps think there's a hostile craft approaching, and having listened to the Station Commander's eulogies on the W.A.A.F.s, and having stood the Posts down again because the Observer Corps have changed their minds, and had an argument with Operation "B" about the way he notifies us of the movements of aircraft, and having stood the posts to again to illuminate a runaway balloon, scrounged a cup of tea from the canteen, listened to the usual mush from Brigade, and helped to home a friendly bomber, and having mopped up the tea sent flying in exasperation at being told there will be night flying after all, it's all that I can do not to start all over again by Standing Down the Controller, illuminating the Station Commander and homing the W.A.A.F.s. It's a grand life..."

Whatever qualification the Captain might have had in mind it was stifled by the preliminary gurgle of a loud speaker situated over the Ante Room door.

"Attention everybody." The room was instantly quietened. "This is the Operations Room calling. Will Squadron Leader Mohune report to the Controller immediately. I will repeat that. Will Squadron Leader Mohune report to the Operations Room immediately. That is all." The loud-speaker gave a final click and was silent.

"My cue," murmured the taller of the Squadron Leaders, and forced himself away from the mantelshelf. "I'll be seeing you, and if I get a chance I'll certainly try out that attack of yours, although I think it's too dangerous."

"That coming from you, Peter St. Maur, is pricelessly funny."

"So that's the great Mohune, is it?" announced the Army Officer.

"It certainly is," agreed Salter, "the one and only, but surely you've met him before?"

"No, I've always just missed meeting him. He was M.I.20 or something before the War, wasn't he?"

"Soldier, Peter St. Maur has been everything."

Batchy's voice fell into the monotonous intonation of a museum guide—"Peter St. Maur Beverley de L'Epee Mohune, M.B.E., D.F.C., A.F.C., the gem of the Royal Air Force Collection, international swordsman, crack pistol shot, brilliant pilot, and the pride of the Air Force Intelligence Department, only son of Sir Robert St. Maur Beverley de L'Epee Mohune. Six feet in his socks. Eyes a peculiar shade of violet blue, lashes Greta Garbo would envy, although in many ways he is as ugly as your humble servant. First saw the light of day in April 1910, now the Leader of the finest Squadron in the Service, and is furthermore a Controller of unmatched skill. Hobbies—locks and wire puzzles. Distinguishing marks a small hole in the left ear. Fan me, that's Mohune."

The subject of this oration, Squadron Leader Peter Mohune (which is, of course, pronounced Moon) made his way towards the jealously guarded precincts of the Operations Room. A sentry at the gate of the compound presented arms smartly, and the salute having been acknowledged, demanded the Squadron Leader's credentials. Obediently Peter produced his pass and was allowed through the gates. At the outside door of the Operations Room he was stopped again, and again had to prove his identity, then he was past the last barrier and striding along the softened corridors and since no red light was glowing above the door giving access to the holy of holies, he pushed the heavy steel-covered defence aside and, stepping into the Operations Room, halted and saluted the Dais. Saluted as a naval officer will salute the Quarter Deck, and with some reason, for this was the abode of the Oracle, the Sector Controller whose word is Law. No aircraft may take off, no aircraft may land in that wide stretch of England under his control without his permission, and furthermore while aircraft are airborne they are under his direct control. Such is the miracle of the Radio Telephone. It is the Controller who informs the Fighters of the presence of hostile aircraft, and it is the Controller who maps out the plan of campaign and places the aircraft in the best position to carry out their attack. Without his sanction no enemy aircraft may be engaged. The safety of the pilots and of the English countryside are in his care. His word is Law and it is a law which is both admired and respected.

Entering the Operations Room, as he has done at the far end of the long rectangular chamber, Mohune had the scene laid out vividly before him. To his left, running from end to end of the room, ran a gallery of some twelve feet from the floor. In the center of this gallery was a balcony in which sat the Sector Controller. On either side of this gallery sat the Operations Officer and the Army Liaison Officers. Beneath and in front of the Dais was the plotting table, a vast skeleton map depicting the South-East of England with its guardian straits and channels, and about the table were the Plotters, W.A.A.F.s with earphones clamped to their ears, connected to the neighboring Observer Corps Centres and to other secret sources of information. No aircraft, hostile or friendly, could approach that Sector of England without its course and height being plotted on that pale green map.

With a lithe spring Mohune mounted the steps, strode

along the Dais and stood behind the Controller. "You want me?"

Squadron Leader Bell, the Controller on duty, swung round in his chair. "Oh, hello, Peter. The Old Man wants a word with you. He'll be over in a minute."

"Jamake. Doesn't seem to be much doing."

"Very quiet. Distrust it. Looks as though there's something piling up over point Z though"; the speaker indicated a point in the South-East corner of the map, and as though his words had been a signal, a telephone operator seated beside him just off the balcony and who was connected to Fighter Group Headquarters, began to scribble down an order, repeating the words aloud as he wrote.

"Serial 76. Two Squadrons patrol point B at fifteen thousand feet." Action was rapid but unhurried. The Operation Officer further along the Dais pushed two telephone keys forward on his switchboard. "965 Squadron Dispersal? . . . Good . . . Stand by. 879 Squadron Dispersal point . . . Order for both Squadrons. Serial 76 . . . Both Squadrons patrol point B at fifteen thousand. 965 Squadron to lead. 879 Squadron above and behind . . . O.K. 965? . . . O.K. 879?"

Switching off the telephone connection the Operation Officer pushed another switch forward, a switch which by means of a broadcast system would connect him with every building on the Station. "Attention everybody," he began. "Operations Room calling. 1320 Squadron is to come to readiness. 1320 Squadron is to come to readiness. That is all."

"I'll get back now," suggested Mohune. "I'll look in and see the Old Man later."

"You'd better hang on, he was insistent that you should stay whatever happened."

"Jamake. Batchy can lead the gang if they should be ordered off. Mind if I use your 'phone?"

"Have 'em all."

There was no doubt that a fine collection of telephones presented itself for Mohune to make his selection from. There were two green handsets and two red ones for speech with aircraft in the air and a blue instrument which was in direct connection with the Group Controller.

A switchboard with twenty-seven two-way keys with attendant standard microphones for communication with the Squadron Dispersal points and the outside world as represented by the Station itself.

Mohune sank into the vacant chair beside the Controller, a chair which incidentally was marked 'Station Commander only,' but as Mohune's broad shoulders quickly obscured the inscription it caused him little discomfort.

"Hello 1320 Dispersal?...Flight Lieutenant Salter there? Squadron Leader Mohune...That you, Batchy? ...If the Squadron takes off you're to lead them.... No, blast your eyes, I'm not losing my nerve; I'm just encouraging the young idea....The Form? The form at the moment is quite promising; there are about twenty bombers over point Z, heading North-West. There's another raid way to the West of 'em, fighters probably, but they're miles away. That's all for the present...negligible chicken feed."

A loud-speaker on the wall behind the balcony gave tongue in the voice of the look-out situated on a hangar roof—"Twelve Spitfires now taking off, initial letter P."

"That's 965 off," commented the Controller; "haven't taken long about it either."

"Pretty smooth," agreed Mohune. "Might be worse. Four-and-a-half minutes. There will be plenty for them to do by the look of things."

"Yes, they're certainly going to make a Blitz of it. I'll have to get my Stand-By Controller in, if your boys take off. I suppose you wouldn't care to look after them for me. Bill was on last night and I think the strain is beginning to tell. . . ."

"Nothing I'd like more," replied Mohune eagerly. "In fact I was going to suggest it."

"Twelve Spitfires now taking off. Initial letter Z for Zebra," announced the look-out.

"You're off in good time," was Peter's comment as he watched the plots of the oncoming raiders, which had now increased to two separate raids of approximately thirty aircraft each, and which were all steadily approaching the coast.

"Looks good to me," agreed Bell, as he picked up a red microphone. "Hello Tallow Leader, Tallow Leader, Priskin Control calling. Let me know when you have reached required Angels. Priskin Control over to Tallow Leader . . . Over."

Tallow Leader, in other words, the Squadron Leader of 965 Squadron, whose call sign was Tallow, replied, and the answer in Bell's receiver was loud enough for both Controllers to hear.

"Hello Priskin Control Priskin Control, Tallow Leader answering. Your message received and understood. Beeswax has joined me. Tallow Leader listening out to Priskin . . .Out."

A voice announced that 1320 Squadron had come to readiness.

The wave of raiders moved on across the board.

"Time for a cigarette before the fun begins," suggested Bell. "It will take my crowd ten and a half minutes to reach their height and objective."

"Thanks," said Mohune, making a selection from the proffered case and flicking his lighter into action. The few minutes rest before the action began were welcome. In a short while the strain would be intense, sweat would stream from them, and at the end they would be limp and exhausted.

"Yes, Mayson?" the Operations Officer was standing at Bell's shoulder. "An aircraft from practice flight wants to do an engine test, sir." "Nope. In fact we'll have the light on now."

"Very good, sir."

A red light which signified that an interception was in progress and that the Controller was not to be disturbed by any matter not connected with the approach of the incoming raiders, winked into life. Duplicates of this lamp flashed in the Intelligence Office, while illuminated panels which enjoined the strictest silence glowed outside the doors of the Operations Room.

"Marsden here." The Operations 'A' was taking down another order from Group.

"Serial 82. 965 and 879 Squadrons intercept Raid number 124 . . . yes . . . Serial 83 One three two oh Squadron patrol point B for Beer at twelve thousand feet."

Squadron Leader Bell crushed out his cigarette and

reached for his handset. Group had now selected a raid for him. Raid 124 was his objective and the two Squadrons under his control must now be steered to intercept the enemy. Quick thinking and decisive orders, there is no time for mistakes when two formations are moving at four miles a minute and the fighter pilots have quite enough to do without being confused by a succession of contradictory orders. From now on Raid 124 would be the personal property of Squadron Leader Bell; it would be his responsibility that this particular section of the Luftwaffe did not reach its objective.

"What's the form?" whispered a voice in Mohune's ear, a voice that Peter recognized only too well as that of Group Captain Mitchelor, the Station Commander of Marsden, alias the Station Master or the Old Man.

"All squadrons ordered off, sir," replied Mohune without taking his eyes from the board, for already he was studying the position of the raiders in preparation for the moment when the Squadron under his control would be given their interception orders.

"Quite a Blitz," murmured the Old Man. "Haven't seen anything like this for a long time."

"Certainly has the makings of a nice party," agreed Peter.

"Twelve Spitfires taking off. Initial letter M for Mother," announced the look-out.

"Three minutes dead," declared Peter with a note of pride in his voice. This was his Squadron which he had nursed from the beginning, training them, transforming them from a bunch of keen youngsters into a perfect fighting machine, a Squadron whose record was one to be proud of. The "rest room" at their dispersal point was decorated with a hundred and forty-five swastikas, and their roll of honor consisted of but four names. A record that no other Squadron could approach.

"Damned good," commented the Station Master.

"Serial 87" Group were at it again "... 1320 Squadron intercept Raid 133."

Mohune's glance flashed to his particular raid block on the board, gauged their course and speed in a split second, and picked up his microphone.

"Hello Pimpernel Leader, Pimpernel Leader, this is Priskin Control calling you. Vector one five zero, Vector one five zero. Thirty Bandits approaching you from the South-East. Increase Angels to fifteen, increase Angels to fifteen. Priskin over to Pimpernel Leader. Over."

Those few words conveyed to Batchy Salter who was leading the Pimpernels that he was to steer on a course of a hundred and fifty degrees, that his objective was thirty bombers, and that he was to increase his height to fifteen thousand feet.

His answer came back promptly. There was no airy persiflage now. "Hello, Priskin Priskin. Pimpernel Leader answering. Message received and understood. Listening out. Out."

By now the South-East corner of the board was littered with raid blocks and in the slight pause which Mohune was allowing himself he was interested to note the skill of the Controller beside him, whose obvious intention was to manipulate his two Squadrons so that they would be between the enemy and the sun, an obvious move to the layman, but one that requires the utmost skill, for once let the fighters get too far behind, let the Controller give his order thirty seconds late and

they will be behind the bombers, which will necessitate
a stern chase before action can be joined.

A voice crackled in Mohune's ear. Batchy again. Not
talking to Peter this time but to the members of his
squadron, "Blue One, Blue One." Batchy was patiently
plaintive. "Don't you realize that you've let your flaps
down instead of pulling your wheels up ... Close up,
Green One, close up ... Pull your finger out Green One
and close up ... Keep together, boys, keep together ...
Get off my tail, blast you, Red Three, get off my
tail ..." Batchy was enjoying himself.

Mohune nudged Bell's arm. "Take a look at Raid 64,"
he urged, "coming up from the South. Looks as though
it intends to look in on us for a drink."

"Certainly does," conceded Bell. "Let's hope that
Group have got their eye on it."

"We can rely on them to do that." Mohune depressed
his transmitter switch and picked up the handset ...
"Hello, Pimpernel Leader, Leader Priskin Control calling. You are now approaching your objective. Bandits
will cross you from starboard to port. Be prepared to
change Vector to zero one zero. Keep look out for Hawks
above. Priskin over to Pimpernel Leader. Over."

The warning about the presence of Hawks, the code
word for German fighters, was a general one, but none the
less necessary. It is so easy in the stress and excitement of
aerial combat to overlook the fact that there may be
other aircraft in the sky besides yourselves and your
prey. The bombers appear as a sitting target and then
hey presto! down come a swarm of Me 109s and Hell
is set on fire about your ears.

"Hello Priskin Priskin, Pimpernel Leader answering.

Your message not understood ... intercommunication interference ... say again please, say again ... Over."

"Hello, Pimpernel Leader, Priskin answering. I say again ... You are now approaching your objective. Bandits will cross you from starboard to port. Prepare to Vector zero one zero. Look out for Hawks. Is this understood?"

"Hello Priskin, Pimpernel Leader answering. Message received and understood. Listening ... Hello, Priskin Priskin." Batchy's tone had adopted an urgency ... "Bandits three miles to North-East of me flying West Angel's twenty. Can I investigate? Over."

"Hello Pimpernel Leader. NO, you may not investigate. They are not for you. Continue on present Vector, continue on present Vector. Is this understood?"

"O.K., spoil sport. Listening out."

"Raid 64 seems to be proceeding unmolested. He'll catch us bending if he does get through."

"Verily, *mon vieux,* he will do all that ..." Mohune was interrupted by a light flashing over the direct line to the Group Controller. Replacing his microphone he picked up the blue handset. "Marsden Controller," he announced.

"Group Controller here. Have you noticed Raid 64?"

"Noticed it, sir? That's hardly the word I would have used. It's positively thrusting its presence upon us!"

The Oracle laughed. "Yes, I'm afraid it is. What's the form of your Squadrons now?"

"965 and 879 should be in the thick of it at any minute and I reckon to intercept with 1320 in about two and a half minutes."

"Splendid. I'm sending reinforcements to cover you

as soon as I can, just in case 64 gets through. Saltlock are trying to intercept them now, but I rather fancy they've missed them." The line went dead.

"My squadrons have sighted," announced Bell.

"Smooth work," replied Peter. "I'm allowing Batchy another thirty seconds. If he isn't in touch then I'll change his line . . ."

"Hello Isis." Batchy was jubilant and was using Peter's nickname in the Squadron. "Hello, Isis! Batchy calling. We are engaged. Over."

"Hello, Batchy Batchy. Isis answering. Well done, well done. Slap 'em down. Listening out. Out."

Peter reached for the Group 'phone. "Marsden Controller here. Thirteen-twenty have engaged and the other squadrons have sighted their objective."

"Good show, Marsden. Good show. Oh, by the way, your reinforcements will be late. You'll have to do the best you can. They're on their way, but that's the best I can do for you. Best of luck."

"Thanks" . . . Raid 64 was getting uncomfortably close. "Look here, Bell," suggested Mohune, "I'll take over 64, you've got your hands full."

"I certainly have. My boys have lost touch in the clouds."

With no apparent haste Mohune made his way to the broadcast microphone and the Station Commander who had been an interested spectator faded silently away.

"Attention everybody. Operations Room calling. All available pilots report to Practice Flight, take off independently and patrol base at fifteen thousand feet. Officer in charge of practice flight to get all available aircraft up. This message to be treated as urgent. That is all."

Mohune returned to his chair fully aware that the few pilots left on the station would have but little chance of stemming the oncoming attack if even they could get to the necessary height in time, but at least it meant there would be no fighter left on the ground for the raiders to bomb.

"Attention everybody." The Operations Officer had taken Mohune's place at the microphone on Peter's signal.

"Action Stations. Action Stations. That is all."

Mohune snapped his fingers above his head and a runner sprang to his side. "Tell the Gun Control Officer to warn his guns to look out for friendly aircraft that may be coming in to land."

"Hello Pimpernel Leader, Pimpernel Leader." Raid 64 was uncomfortably close now—there was no doubt whatever as to its destination. "Priskin Control calling. How are you getting on? Over."

"Hello Priskin..." there was a languid note in Batchy's voice now but most of his message was distorted by interference; in fact, the only two words which Mohune could catch were two which he had hoped to hear, and they were... "Two Jerries."

"Well done, Batchy, well done. As soon as you have finished your party return to base as I am being menaced. Over."

"Hello Priskin Priskin Pimpernel, Green One calling. I have lost the Squadron. Can you tell me where they are? Green One over to Priskin. Over."

"Hello Green One. They are engaged over point A for Apple. Over."

"Thank you, Priskin. Listening out."

"Hello Isis." Batchy's voice seemed more languid than ever. "I think you must be under a misapprehension. I did not say that I had shot down two Jerries. I said that two Jerries were trying to shoot me down, although while you were nattering to Green One I have decreased that number. The Squadron is split up now and still engaged. I will come and cure your headache as soon as I can. Over."

"Hello Priskin Priskin, Pimpernel Blue Three calling. I am out of ammunition. May I come back and re-arm. Over to Priskin. Over."

"Hello Blue Three. Priskin answering. No, don't return to this base yet if you have no ammunition. Is this understood? Over."

"Hello Priskin, Blue Three answering. Message received and understood. Listening out."

There was a slight smile playing about Mohune's lips as he lowered his handset. The Pimpernels were doing their stuff. He glanced down at the board and studied the faces of the W.A.A.F. plotters and was pleased to see that despite the fact that everyone of them realized exactly what Raid 64 meant, not a hand trembled and not a lip quivered. He snapped his fingers again and whispered over his shoulder to the runner: "Close the blast-proof doors."

An appreciable tension settled over the room as the heavy reinforced doors were closed and the massive bars pulled into position. A W.A.A.F. directly below Mohune fingered her hair with a nervous gesture and

turned a shade paler, then looking up suddenly she
caught sight of Mohune watching her and turned pink
as he gave her an encouraging wink.

"We're engaged at last," announced Bell.

"Three Hurricanes and two Spitfires taking off," announced the look-out.

"Hello Priskin Priskin, Pimpernel Leader calling
Priskin. Shall not be home yet. Have smashed bombers
but we are now engaged with Hawks. Over."

"O.K., Batchy. Best of luck. Listening out."

"Hello Priskin Priskin. This is Priskin Leader calling.
I am now airborne with composite flight. Have you any
information for me. Priskin Leader over to Priskin Control. Over.

"That's a stout effort, Bell," announced Mohune.
"The Old Man's flying himself." He flicked down the
transmitter key. "Hello Priskin Leader. Gain height as
quickly as you can. Bandits quite close to us now. Control over to Priskin Leader. Over."

Catching the Operations' Officer's eye Mohune
nodded and the Flight Lieutenant addressed the broadcast microphone.

"Attention everybody. Operations Room calling. All
personnel not engaged on Operational duties take cover.
Take cover. That is all."

"Hello Priskin Control, Priskin Control, Priskin
Leader calling. Have sighted Bandits but they are far
above me. Is this understood. Over."

Mohune made the necessary signal that he understood ... understood too well that there was precisely
nothing between Marsden aerodrome and the rapidly
approaching Raid 64, but the realization of the shape

of things to come put no visible indication on his face. The same slightly mocking smile played about his lips, the left eyebrow was quirked quizically. He bent over and whispered in Bell's ear, "This, *mon vieux,* is where we take all that's coming to us."

"And then some," agreed the other and went on with his controlling in the same unhurried manner.

"Twenty-five enemy bombers approaching from the South at about fifteen thousand feet," announced the look-out. "Aircraft identified as Ju 88's."

Everyone in the Operations Room knew that they were enclosed in the selected target, knew that Jerry Hun would try to destroy that building, and would expend his whole energy in doing so. The Operations Room, the heart and brain of the whole Sector, the controlling force behind the three Fighter Squadrons, and everyone knew that there was nothing to hinder him in his ambition.

"Any second now," suggested Bell. Mohune smiled and nodded, and as though that nod had been observed by the leader of the German formation, the attack commenced. Bell had just time to add "Shouldn't think we'll hear much in here, the walls are too thick," when Weeooshercrumpher of the first bomb shook the building. Twenty pairs of eyes looked up at Mohune's, found them smiling and returned to the work in hand. Then everything happened at once. Crumpher, Crumpher, crumpher. The room swayed as though it were a tree in a high wind. The emergency lighting swayed to and fro while flakes fell from the high ceiling in a miniature snow storm.

Another shattering crumph and one of the blast doors

was torn away and sailed across the room, missing the plotters by inches to crash up against the wall at the far end, shattering a glass indicator screen to minute fragments. Clouds of gray dust mingled with acrid blue smoke eddied into the room.

"The enemy aircraft are now bombing the aerodrome," said the look-out.

"You're telling me," grinned Mohune, and a girl laughed as he picked up his microphone.

"Hello Pimpernel, Priskin calling. Exercise great caution when landing at this base. Look out for bomb craters. The attack should be nearly over now. I will tell you when you can come in to land. Priskin over to Pimpernel Leader. Over."

Then Hell cracked. Bombs screeching like tortured banshees dived at the ground which shuddered at their onslaught. Buildings bulged, tottered and collapsed. A lorry lifted by unseen hands cavorted across the aerodrome and came to rest on its nose. Glass and bomb splinters hummed through the unresisting air like a swarm of deadly bees. A hangar roof crackled as flames licked its camouflaged gables, a road junction usurped the appearance of a disused quarry. Noise, brain shattering noise, dominated the world as the Junkers flew over their target unhindered, their perfect formation unruffled. Again and again the Operations Room trembled, although the personnel within its shaking walls remained calm. A W.A.A.F. who found her fingers fumbling as she compiled a raid block, said *damn* loudly and distinctively.

Weeooosh, weeooosh, weeooosh. Peter glanced up at

the ceiling. Near. Unpleasantly near. A second passed
... two seconds passed ... then C-r-r-rumph. In the far
corner of the room a chunk of ceiling as big as a full-
sized billiard table crashed to the floor, broke into small
pieces and enveloped the occupants in a cloud of dust,
enveloping them as effectively as a sandstorm will blot
out a camel caravan. Currumpher. Down the same end
of the room the wall cracked and split. A large V-shaped
section of it fell out and disintegrated into a medley of
bricks and dust. Mohune and Bell stood motionless
straining their ears to hear their pilots' voices in their
handsets, although they both knew that the third ex-
plosion would bring the massive ceiling crashing down
upon them to crush them like corn under a millstone.

"Hello Pimpernel Leader. Hello, hello, hello."
Mohune put the microphone down. "I'm not transmit-
ting. The transmitter's gone west." Bell nodded.

"Sir."

"Yes, Mayson?"

"The Group line's gone, sir."

"Jamake. Test all 'phones, will you?"

"Very good, sir."

"Number three is a long time going off, isn't it,"
queried Bell, in much the same tone as he would have
used to enquire whether the six-fifteen to Brighton was
not running late.

"Let's hope it's a dud. I'm going to evacuate the place
now."

"Think you're wise?"

"A damned sight wiser than sitting here waiting for
that thing to go off. We can do nothing more here. The

R.T. is dead, the 'phones are all phut . . . besides Emergency Operations should be working by now . . ." he broke off as a cloud of dust settled on his uvulva. "Floor Supervisor," he called through a spasm of coughing.

From the billowing clouds below, a corporal, an animated snowman, climbed up in front of the dais.

"Sir."

"Muster the crew and get them out through the Officers' entrance. Duck for cover as soon as you're clear."

"Can't be done, sir. The Officers' door is jammed solid and where the other door was is a pile of rubble that would take weeks to get through."

Peter nodded. "Very well, we stay here till they get us out. Any casualties?"

"No one dead, sir. A signaller has copped it rather nastily, and one of the girls is pretty badly knocked about. They're being attended to as best we can."

Mohune nodded. The dust clouds were subsiding now, revealing the plotters gathered in grotesque and statuesque groups. The girl who had said damn so clearly was still holding the raid block and was staring at it without comprehension.

"Enemy aircraft . . . being attacked . . . by fighters," began the look-out . . . " 'ere you leave me alone. I've got a job of work to do."

"Don't be a blurry fool . . ." broke in another voice. "The whole blurry hangar's afire. Wot you think you are, a blurry salamander or just Joan of Arc. You're coming down with me . . ."

"Leave me alone, I tell you . . . I . . . I . . ."

"That's right, that's right, go and faint on me. I like

to see devotion to duty but I 'ates a blurry martyr.
Hello . . ." The voice became clearer and was obviously
addressing the microphone . . . "Hello Ops. If there's
anyone alive in there we'll have you out in a jiffy, so
keep your chins up."

CHAPTER TWO

IN WHICH HE BECOMES AIRBORNE

A GROUP of Officers stood by a camouflaged touring car discussing the Blitz. Squadron Leaders Mohune and Bell were easily distinguishable by their dust-covered uniforms. A third, Batchy Salter, who still wore his short leather flying coat, was bareheaded, his fair hair was ruffled by the slight wind and, as usual, he had much to say. An Intelligence Officer was taking notes and doing his best to turn Batchy's flowery discourse into the stereotype language of a combat report.

"Fan me! Was it a party? Question: Was it a party? Answer: Verily it was a party. What is it you want to know? Where were the boys of one three two oh? Watching the jerries as they fell below. Right in the pants they aimed their blow. What ho! What ho! What ho!"

"What time did you take off?"

"Oh, you can fill that in."

"What was the patrol ordered?"

"There again you can be useful."

"Well dammit, Batchy, what did you do?"

"Well, we met the blighters, thanks to as pretty a piece of controlling as I have ever seen. They were Dorniers, and we came in from above and behind. Seven of them went down . . ."

"Smooth work, Batchy . . ." put in Mohune.

"Nothing to it, sir, I assure you," deprecated Batchy with an airy wave of his hand.

"All confirmed?" demanded the I.O. who was rather new to the Squadron.

"Oh rather . . . I sent Green One who had a headache down to count them on the ground. We split up and went in again and the rest of them turned and beetled off home. We were about to follow when a swarm of 109's came down on top of us out of the sun, and it was about then that you told me of your spot of bother, sir. Well, a real fight started then, but they soon felt the urge of the Fatherland and stood not on the order of their going but with their yellow noses well down sprinted for home. They left six behind to litter the countryside. Then back we came and those of us who had any ammunition left waded into the blokes who had been brightening up your life. Incidentally there was a solitary Spitfire that went for the bombers head on, like a bat out of hell, ought to have been blown to bitumen but Question: Was he? Answer: He was not. He went slap through 'em like a Scot through a whisky bottle and their formation simply ceased to exist. Just split up and ran like a pack of girls caught bathing without their costumes, if you know what I mean, sir . . ."

"I haven't your experience, of course, but I gather your meaning. Continue . . ."

"There's not much else to say. Our ammo soon ran out but we sort of hovered about as it were and then another batch of Spitfires appeared on the scene and that was the end of Jerry. Not one of the blighters reached the coast but, fan me! that chappie in that Spitfire, he was terrific; he ought to be given a Squadron to lead of his own. No, he was even better than that. I'd say he was good enough to join the Pimpernels ..."

"Must have been outstanding for you to notice him, Salter."

Batchy pivoted to face the newcomer who had joined the party unobserved. It was Group Captain Mitchelor, who looked as though he had just come off a ceremonial parade, so bright were his buttons, so sharp was the crease in his slacks.

"Outstanding, sir?" burbled Batchy, "he was superb."

"Did you notice if he was one of our Spits?" inquired the I.O.

"He was one of ours. The letters were Z R T."

"And you think he ought to lead a Squadron, do you?" continued the Old Man. "A man who loses his formation before the fight begins and goes bald-headed for the first thing he sees does not deserve to lead a Squadron ..."

"But fan me, sir, he broke up the formation and I saw him shoot down ..."

"All right, all right, Salter. But you can take it from me that that particular pilot will never lead a Squadron." The old man turned to Mohune. "I see that you've rendered a report on the Operational damage done to the Station. We seem to have got off lightly, casualties are small too. Nine dead and not more than a score wounded. When I saw the signals block of the Ops. Room, I feared the worst. Transport seems to be the trouble, every blasted tire of every blasted vehicle appears to have been pierced by splinters. I'm informed that upwards of one hundred and seventy bombs, including delayed action, duds and incendiaries, were deposited on us in one place or another. What worries me more than anything else is that I've nowhere to sit down. My office is a shambles and my chair which was lifted out of my room, is up there."

Mitchelor flung out an arm, the group of officers turned in the direction indicated, and there perched on a hangar roof was the Seat of the Mighty. Two more Squadron Leaders joined the party.

"Well?" demanded the Old Man.

"Eight destroyed, nine probable, and six damaged, sir," was the laconic retort from the leader of Marsden's second Spitfire Squadron. "Our casualties," he continued, "One missing but that's Bonzo. He'll turn up sooner or later, he makes habit of it."

"Well done." Mitchelor turned to the other newcomer. "And yours?" he demanded.

Beeswax Leader answered quietly. "Not so hot, sir. We slapped down five. All Me 109's, but we...we lost four."

"Bad luck. That's always the penalty of being the upper guard. Cover Squadron always meets the fighters. Who were they?"

"Fleming, Willersby, that's the new boy joined us yesterday, and Denton for certain and Banks is missing."

Mitchelor stared into the Squadron Leader's eyes, no word was spoken, no word was necessary. They understood each other's inmost thoughts. The Old Man spun round suddenly and strode away, calling over his shoulder for Mohune to accompany him.

"By the way, sir," demanded Batchy of the Commander of the Upper Guard, as they watched the two men walking off across the aerodrome. "Who is the bright

lad who juggles with death in one of your aircraft
Z RT?"

"Z RT? It's . . . Why do you ask?"

"He ought to lead a Squadron . . . he's terrific . . ."

Squadron Leader Clark laughed. "He'll never lead
a Squadron."

"That's what the Old Man said, but who is he?"

"It's the Old Man himself. He gave up leading Squadrons after the last War."

"Fan me!" ejaculated Batchy with some feeling.

Mohune was the first to break the silence. "Bombing
of aerodromes with the idea of putting them perma-
nently off the map is a sheer waste of time, bombs and
energy," he suggested as he pointed out a string of
craters to his Group Captain. "If they hit a runway,
which is unlikely, we can repair it at a fraction of the
cost it took to cause the damage. Admittedly they've
bruised us a bit by hitting the telephone exchange, their
first bomb on the Ops. Room was a direct hit on that,
but the G.P.O engineers are working like niggers and
all communications will be working to-night . . ."

"They're grand fellows," put in Mitchelor, and Mohune continued. "They're certainly that. The R.A.F.
owe them a hell of a lot, but as I was saying, those
bombers with nothing to hinder them should have
been able to wipe us out, but they failed as they always fail. Marsden is still operational. The aerodrome
is safe to take off from and land on, ammunition and
fuel supplies are intact and the Emergency Operations
room is functioning as well as its brother ever did. Furthermore, I'm told that the Ops. Room can be repaired

in quite a short while. So what have they gained, as Salter would say. Answer: Nothing."

"Morale?"

"As good as it ever was, if not better. Everyone now knows how few casualties are caused by air attack. I grant you, sir, that it's not pleasant to know that you are being used as a dartboard by someone who is throwing particularly heavy darts, and that added to the knowledge that if you were outside the perimeter of the camp you'd be perfectly safe. All that is much worse than being bombed in a town, where there is not the urge to run away from your job to a safe spot, because you know that when they're bombing a town they are dropping their stuff with no particular object in view and one place is therefore as safe as another, but despite the knowledge that outside the camp area was a safety zone not one man showed the slightest inclination to leave his post. As for the W.A.A.F.s they were marvellous. In fact they were even better than the men, and when a way was cleared for us to escape from the Ops. Room they moved out as though they were filing out of church."

"There's a lot in what you say, Peter, but you must remember that it was only a comparatively small raid . . ."

"It was the largest they could get through, sir. They must have used nearly five hundred aircraft in order to get that formation through, and they were lucky at that . . ."

"Maybe, maybe, but remember although bomb craters can be filled in, runways can be repaired and telephone wires can be re-laid, had they hit the Emergency Operations Room as well, we should have been out of the fight."

"I still join issue, sir. Firstly, the odds against them ever finding the E.O. are phenomenal, and, secondly, any other Sector could have taken our lads over and controlled them as well as their own."

"That's true enough."

The two men walked on in silence. Already delayed action bombs had been flagged and roped off. Parties of men were at work clearing away the debris, and the work of the Station proceeded on its normal course. They stopped for a second to chaff an irate Equipment Officer who was searching a pile of rubble for his precious voucher books.

"I believe you wanted to see me earlier on," suggested Peter, as they stopped again to examine the wreck of a small building. "You sent for me before the Blitz began."

Mitchelor dabbed at a clot of blood on his forehead. "So I did," he admitted, and then added, "You're posted."

"WHAT?"

"True enough. I've done all I could to scotch it, but without any success whatever."

"But the Squadron . . ."

"I said all that and got snubbed for my pains. Their reply was that there are other Squadron Leaders and they emphasized the word rather nastily. They want you to teach Air Combat at an O.T.U. You go to-morrow."

"An instructor's job!" Mohune was aghast. "I can't do it, sir. There are plenty of older men who are cut out for that sort of life. I'm not."

"Well, Peter, there it is. I'm as sorry as you are, but I'm afraid it's a case of now's your chance to learn."

They had now arrived at 1320 Squadron's Dispersal Point. Inside the hut immediately before him Mohune knew that he would find the members of his Squadron, for the Pimpernels were at Readiness, a state which means that they would be expected to be in the air within five minutes of receiving an order. The thought that he had probably led them for the last time smote him sharply; he shrugged his shoulders. "I'd better go in and break it to them," he muttered. Mitchelor nodded. "Come and see me in my Quarters when the Squadron is put back to Released," he suggested.

Peter saluted and, turning away from the Old Man, entered the Pilots' Room.

For the last two months most of his time on the ground had been spent in this hut, but now Mohune stopped just inside the door, and looked around as though seeing it all for the first time. The boarded-in windows decorated with red paint in the semblance of casements, dummy curtains made of sacking, neatly looped back with rope. The bar in the far corner about which several of the Pimpernels, including the lanky and loquacious Batchy Salter, were grouped, while others lounged, fully clad ready to take off, in Lloyd loom chairs. Candles burning in the tops of whisky bottles—the electric cable had suffered in the Blitz—illuminated the walls which were decorated with the trophies of the chase. A machine gun from a Heinkel, a clock from a Dornier, an oxygen bottle from a J.U.88, a battered airscrew, a wing tip bearing the black cross of Nazi Germany. The pictures by Doumerge and Petit.

The scoreboard with its hundred and forty-five miniature swastikas—there were more to be added now. The
door giving access to his office and the telephone switchboard. It all seemed strange and unreal. Mohune made
his way to the little crowd at the bar.

"Make way for a tired and thirsty man."

"Fan me," began Salter, but catching the haunted
look in Peter's eyes, a look which Mohune had not been
quick enough to mask, fell silent.

"Rye," answered Peter to the honorary barman's enquiry. He threw the drink back at a gulp and turned
to face the crowd which gathered about him. "Well,
me lucky lads," he began, "I've got some news for you
. . . I . . ."

"Attention everybody. Operations Rooms calling.
Green Section one three two oh Squadron, Patrol point
X for Xray. Green section one three two oh Squadron,
Patrol point X for Xray at seven thousand feet. That
is all."

Mohune's news was forgotten. The three pilots of
Green Section made for the outer air.

"That's the Plunk Light Vessel," cried a voice.

"Get my bus started up," snapped Peter, and was
through the door into his own office. Kicking off his
shoes, he thrust his feet into flying boots, thrust his arms
into a short leather fiying coat and shrugged it over
his broad shoulders, grabbed his parachute, snatched up
his Mae West and his helmet and sprinted out to his
aircraft.

Batchy was waiting for him and as Mohune arrived
the Spitfire's engine burst into throbbing life.

"It's only a section to take off, sir."

"I know, Batchy, I know, but I want air. Help me into this damned stuff."

Obediently Salter took up the parachute harness. "You know, sir," he suggested, "I mean to say you don't look any too spry to me. I mean a trifle pale about the gills, a little glassy about the odd optic . . ."

"Stop being a wet nurse, Batchy. I'm all right. Never better." Mohune tugged at the chinstrap of his helmet and sprang up to the open cockpit. "Fact is, Batchy, Old Horse," he shouted above the roar of the engine, "This is to be my last flight with the Pimpernels."

"Fan me! Hi, sir I mean to say, Hi, you can't . . ."

Batchy could neither hear nor be heard. The Merlin's note rose to an angry roar and died away again, and the Spitfire commenced its journey to the runway.

The three aircraft of Green Section were now airborne and climbing rapidly. Mohune adjusted his microphone and turned his plane into wind, his left hand moved forward and the plane gathered speed.

CHAPTER THREE

IN WHICH MOHUNE COMES TO EARTH

GREEN Section were as three gulls against the distant sky line when Mohune turned his Spitfire on to the bearing which would lead him to his objective.

"Hello Pimpernel Green One, Green One . . ." The Controller was passing instructions to the Section warning them that a hostile bomber was approaching the point which they were making for, and giving an additional warning to the effect that German fighter aircraft were to be expected in that vicinity.

"Good Old Bell," murmured Peter, as the wheels of the Spitfire folded under him. "Knows his job, keeps 'em well informed."

"Hello Priskin, Control Priskin," he called. "Isis calling you. I am airborne and will formate on Green Section. Is this understood? Isis over to Priskin Control. Over."

"Hello Isis Isis, Priskin answering. O.K. But who gave you permission to take off? Over."

"No one, sir, she said," answered Mohune unabashed. "I apologize most humbly. Listening out to you. Out."

"Hello Isis Isis, Green One calling you. Will you take the lead? Over."

"No. I'll just weave along behind you. Listening out."

Ahead the clarity of the sky was now smudged with cloud. A layer of cloud at twenty-two thousand feet blotted out the sun, and below that gray roof heavy masses could be seen dark and ominous on the horizon and it was apparent that accurate judgment would be necessary on the part of the Controller if an interception was to be effected. The hounds would be blind and more than ever would depend on the skill of Priskin Control. Green Section disappeared, swallowed up by the angry castles ahead and a minute later that same cold clamminess closed about Peter's Spitfire, cutting down the visibility to nothing, and enshrouding the aircraft in a dismal world of gray twilight. Mohune shrugged himself into a more comfortable position and outside the three bladed airscrew clawed viciously at the mark as it dragged the Spitfire onwards towards its objective.

"Hello Pimpernel Green One, Green One, Priskin Control calling . . ." It was Squadron Leader Bell again. His plan of campaign was now formulated and he was giving his final instructions to the fighters.

"Keep sharp look out," he ordered, "for Bandit approaching from South at your present height. He will cross you from Starboard to Port. You should intercept at any moment now. Priskin over to Green One . . . Over."

"Not much chance of interception in this stuff," thought Mohune, but even as the thought flashed through his mind, he shot out of the cloud, out into a wide circular amphitheatre of clear sky. Dead ahead were the three aircraft of Green Section, and below, far below, the sea green and unfriendly like a glass tray upon whose surface could be seen the minute speck which Peter knew to be the Plunk Vessel, and there, sure enough, approaching from the South and not a hundred feet below Green Section, was the twin-engined silhouette of a Junkers 88, so similar in appearance to the English Blenheim, but so different in purpose. Green Section had seen the bomber and Green One was already giving tongue. "Hello Green Section, Number One attack line astern, line astern ... GO."

Over went the Leader, and following their Number One the remaining two Spitfires dived into the attack. Gray pencil lines of tracers left the leading edges of the foremost Spitfire, then he was away and Number Two was concentrating on the attack. Mohune guessed that the German rear gunner had been put out of action by the first burst, for no answering fire came from the bomber, who forged steadily on towards its target. Then as the second fighter turned away a plume of smoke streamed from the 88's Port Engine, a flash of blue light came from inside the fuselage. The enemy was catching it badly. Mohune turned his attention to the sky above and he did not see the bomber stagger and plunge downwards towards the sea, but he did see the ominous specks, four thousand feet above, approaching from the South.

"Hello Green One," he called as he turned his plane to face the oncoming menace. "Messerschmitts above and behind you. 109's, twelve of them."

"O.K. Isis. Turning now. Hellow Priskin Control, Control. We've slapped your Bandit down. How right you were. A smooth piece of controlling. Your Hawks have just appeared. Going into the attack now."

"Well done, Green One. Listening out."

Already Mohune had pointed his spinner at the sky,

had pointed it upwards until it was nearly vertical to meet the downward rush of the first fighter, his thumb stroked the gun button on the control column, then down it went, home into the shallow socket, eight browning guns, four in either main plane spat at the oncoming fighter. The Spitfire shook with the sudden force of their laughter, then losing flying speed, fell over and away as the 109 quivered, broke and fell in a thousand pieces towards the sea so far below.

Up went Mohune again and out of the corner of his eyes he saw that Green Section were in the thick of it. In that split second Hell had broken loose. Three against eleven, twisting, turning, guns snapping whenever a target presented itself. Round in a steep turn, an Me in the sights, down went Mohune's thumb again. Over went the German on to its back with smoke flame flecked pouring from the cockpit. Then Green One was pounced on, round went Peter, but he was late, late by a fraction of a second; Green One was caught and went twisting down out of control. No time to see what fate befell that pilot . . . the fighting was still on.

Green Two was the next to add to the score. He sent a long burst into his target who fell away disabled. Green Three met another head on and blasted it from his path. In that same second the transparent hood above Mohune's head was pierced by a score of bullets, an unseen finger reached over his shoulder and wiped away his altimeter, he swung violently round to Port and saw Green two pounce on the fighter that had so nearly ended his career. No chance to watch the result, another Messerschmitt was before him asking for trouble, asking for the trouble he quickly collected.

Another aircraft fell in pieces and with a stab of anguish Peter saw the vertical stripes of the R.A.F. markings as the battered plane fell past him.

Two Spitfires left. Mohune swung round looking for another target, beneath him a carpet of cloud had been drawn across the sea, away to the East four Messer-schmitts were streaking for home, but of the remaining aircraft of Green Section, there was no sign.

Mohune was alone. The Germans were too far away for him to chase. He fumbled for his R.T. switch, failed to find it and looked down. There was no wireless set, a jangle of wires like tortured nerve ends jutted out in all directions. A twisted piece of metal and a battered panel was all that was left of the instrument.

"Near enough," admitted Mohune as he turned the Spitfire for home. Bell would have to wait for his news until the plane reached Marsden.

It was at that moment that Peter realized that all was not well with his craft. The mighty Merlin engine was coughing spasmodically, shuddering with spasms which shook the plane badly. All very unpleasant, for Mohune had no idea of his exact position, had no idea of his height or how far the cloud below him was above the surface of the inhospitable sea. But his realization was twofold. Firstly, he had no controller to guide him home, and secondly that he was losing height rapidly and both were facts that were distinctly displeasing, and coupled to all this was the knowledge that he was many miles East of his base and therefore well out across the sea. He patted his Mae West affectionately.

If Peter Mohune had a private fear, it was that of death by drowning, but had anyone been present within the crumpled confines of the Spitfire's cockpit, he would have seen no trace of that fear peeping from the pilot's steady eyes, indeed he would have marvelled at the slight smile which still played about Mohune's lips. Gently the stick was eased forward. Mohune had a natural inquisitiveness and he had decided against baling out before he had satisfied himself that it was essential. He reckoned that the cloud above him was, at its highest point, at least seven thousand feet above the sea and it might be that it was but a thin layer, and that if he was still in his aircraft he might find a ship, or even the Plunk Light Vessel that he could glide towards, and who would give him sanctuary, for strong swimmer as he was he had no intention of competing for Channel honors in that freezing expanse of the North Sea.

The gray carpet came up to meet the Spitfire, and with the Merlin making noises that both King Arthur and the designers of Rolls Royce would have considered undignified, the aircraft nosed its way into the unresisting cloud.

Two minutes of suspense and the danger that the murk might reach down to caress the clutching fingers of the waves was left above. Mohune stared down at the scene stretched out below him in amazement. Something was wrong, radically wrong, there was no ship, there was no sea; green undulating countryside, white roads, neat fields, a few clumps of trees, an occasional house made up the picture.

"Error has crep' in," muttered Mohune. His calculations were sadly at fault, but gravity and the failing engine gave him no time to solve the mystery of his position. The plane was no more than two thousand feet up, and the selection of a field in which to put her down was an urgent necessity. A smooth landing surface was not to be seen and Mohune decided to make a Belly Landing in a field then ahead of his starboard wing.

As calmly as though he was making for the smooth runways at Marsden, Mohune made his approach. He pushed back the framework of the transparent hood which covered the cockpit to ensure a quick getaway, then lowered his flaps and his forward speed decreased. His decision to land with his wheels retracted was a correct one, the ground on closer inspection was certainly bumpy, and a Spitfire does not take kindly to uneven surfaces. For a brief second he skimmed along parallel with the ground, then many things happened at once. A jar as the underside of the fuselage met the unyielding surface, a shuddering jolt as the airscrew hit the ground attempting to cleave its way through as it had done through the clouds, a task which it found impossible and flung the plane aside in disgust, and then everything was strangely quiet.

As Peter scrambled from the cockpit a bird sang from the gaunt limbs of a nearby tree. Peter turned and saluted it gravely, and then as it burst into an even more joyous song, Mohune pulled off his flying helmet and discarded his Mae West, and pulling down the long zip of his jacket, delved for his cigarette case, selected a Player, and flicked his lighter into action.

There was nothing to do now but wait. It would be no more than a few minutes before a member of the ubiquitous Home Guard would appear on the scene. Queer hissing noises were coming from the dormant Merlin and Mohune turned to glance with some apprehension at his damaged aircraft. He stepped on to the wing and glanced into the cockpit and it was as he looked up again that he noticed movement in the hedge at the far end of the field. His first thought was that the Home Guard had arrived in strength but the furtiveness of the newcomers held his attention. The Home Guard were never furtive. In a flash the mystery was solved. His calculations had been correct. He was East, far East of his base, he was in fact over Occupied France, and the figures who were now hurrying towards him were German soldiers. Puffing calmly at his cigarette, he looked about him to find, as he had expected, that he was surrounded by the oncoming soldiers.

A voice shouted in passable English: "You are a prisoner of Nazi Germany."

Mohune laughed. "I knew it was nasty," he shouted back, "but if you know it, too, why don't you do something about it?"

The men were close now and halted at the command of an Officer who stepped up to Peter.

"*Herr Gott,* it's Mohune," he exclaimed in English, and in that language Peter answered,

"*Herr Gott,* it certainly is; but who are you, my little man?"

"Do you not remember? I'm Promft."

"You certainly are quick off the mark, but . . ."

"No, no. I see that you have forgotten but I have not. I will remind you. At Marsden in 1936 you were the Administrative Officer . . ."

"Correct."

"And one day a Lufthansa Air Liner force landed and . . ."

"Upon my Sam you were the pilot..."

"That is so, and you pulled me from the flames. This is now"...the words came very slowly..."a...very difficult situation in which I find myself."

"Much more difficult for me," laughed Mohune, "what's worrying you?"

"You are my prisoner. I who owe a debt to you have to make you captive."

"Forget it. If it wasn't you there seem to be quite a few who are gathered together for that express purpose."

"You will not hold it against me?"

"C'est la guerre. Incidentally the chappie with the bayonet behind my left ear, must he be quite so close?"

"He will not harm you."

"I know that, but...well, he has something that his best friend will not tell him about. Now what do you want me to do?"

"I hardly know," admitted Promft. "I have always wanted to meet you again and now when our two countries are at War we have to meet. If I let you go with these men I will not see you again, surely for an hour we could be together."

"These are not your men then?"

"No." There was contempt in his tone. "My Staffel is some miles from here. I happened to be motoring past when you landed. I know, I have it. I will take you to meet my brother officers. They will be pleased to meet an English Ace and proud to meet the man who saved my life. You will be my prisoner. Come, I have a car at hand."

The journey across the field to the large gray open

tourer was but a matter of minutes, and with Peter and
Karl Promft in the back they were soon speeding along
the uneven surface of the French country lane.

For a few minutes there was silence, both pilots were
fully occupied with their thoughts. The clouds had
drawn away and the sun was sending long shadows
across the bare surface of the field, there was promise of
rain in the air.

Glancing at the German's collar with its three birds
Mohune said: "I see that I call you Hauptman now."

"Yes. Your flying coat disguises your rank. What
is it?"

"Squadron Leader."

"Major, eh?" the German laughed. "In happier days
I should be calling you sir. Have you had any fights
with us?"

"Quite a few."

"Have you . . . have you brought many down?"

"Twenty-seven."

"Twenty-seven. You must head your list."

"I believe I do, and frankly after what I saw in
Norway and later in this country, I can only wish that
I could add a hundred more."

"I understand. This total war is not pretty. I, too,
have seen it. I am . . . you will like me less when I tell
you this, perhaps you will wonder why you took the
trouble to save my life . . . Herr Major, my Staffel is one
of a Kampfgeschwader . . ."

"Bombers . . ."

"Yes, bombers. It was only natural that with my experience with Lufthansa that I should go to the long-
distance aircraft. My Staffel are equipped with Ju 88's,

fine aircraft but there have been many times when I
have hated the work."

"Could you not apply for a transfer?"

Promft shrugged his shoulders. "That would imply
dissatisfaction and all that that would get me would be
a flogging. You see Herr Major, there are few who think
as I do. Many of them, most of them in fact, boast of
their accomplishments. We are nearly there now. I shall
at least be able to offer you a drink before the Interrogation Officers get their hooks on you."

The car drew up before the door of a farm house and,
leaving the car, Mohune followed his captor through
the front door where they were met by another officer
who, by the single bird on his collar, enclosed in a
wreath of leaves, Mohune recognized as a major. Promft
clicked his heels.

"Herr Major," he began in German, "I have to present Major Mohune of the English Air Force." The
Major stared intently. Peter smiled and Promft continued, "He is the star pilot of their Fighter Command.
He was shot down. I took him prisoner. I have met him
before. In 1936 he saved my life . . . took me from my
burning aircraft in England. He was at one time in their
Intelligence Service . . ."

"Herr Hauptman, you talk too much," the Major
turned to Peter. "I am pleased to make your acquaint-
ance," he announced in German, but Mohune, who had
no intention of revealing the fact that he knew any
German, made no reply. Hurriedly Promft translated.

"Herr Hauptman, I said you talk too much. You are
not the only man who can talk that accursed language."
Again the Major turned his attention to the Englishman

and repeated his formal little speech, and now it was Mohune's turn to bow.

"Thank you."

"It is not often that English pilots call upon us. They prefer the safety of their own shores, a safety that before long will be denied to them. But you will drink with me. Take off your coat. Herr Hauptman, order brandy."

Mohune stripped off his short flying coat and, with a sneer on his lips, the Major regarded the six medal ribbons which were now revealed.

"They give baubles cheaply in your country. What are they? One for each time you take the air?"

"No"—Mohune was still smiling—"we get them principally for having a sense of humor and for keeping our temper."

"For keeping your temper? Huh. I thought perhaps one might be for the defeat of Dunkirk, another for the evacuation from Norway, another for the betrayal of the French, Greece, Crete, Malaya, Singapore, and so on . . ."

Mohune's reply was stifled by the entrance of a group of young officers who had come to see their captive and who were followed by an orderly carrying a laden tray. The German Major nodded towards the Englishman who accepted a glass, the Major followed suit and raised his glass: "The fortunes of war."

Mohune's glass rose toward his lips; he was about to drink when an Ober-Lieutenant, a hard-eyed youth with the nervous intensity of a fanatic, thrust himself between Peter and the waiter, and with a flick of the hand, sent Mohune's glass spinning across the hall. Instantly his heels clicked, his arm was raised in the

Nazi salute, and the words "Heil Hitler" brayed across the silence. All eyes were focussed on Mohune, but he was not in the least perturbed. His left eyebrow quirked upwards and quietly he reached over the rigid shoulder of the Ober-Lieutenant, picked up another glass from the waiter's tray, raised it to his lips with a smile and a slight bow, murmured "God Save the King," and then turning to the Major, "I think that it's time for me to go."

The Major smiled for the first time. "I wish I had a medal for you," he declared. "Your sense of humor has won another victory."

Within five minutes the Major had led the way back to the waiting tourer.

"I have to hand you over to the military authorities for the time being. We have no guard room accommodation for prisoners of war. May I give you a word of advice?"

"I would welcome it."

"Keep on the right side of these people. They are not as we are. They have no finesse."

The day had drawn to a miserable end. Long fingers of invisible rain streaked down through the darkness and Mohune could feel the fur collar of his flying coat becoming bedraggled about his ears and it was with a feeling of distinct relief that he climbed from his seat and entered the guard house. Almost immediately he was ushered into a lighted room, a room which boasted of no furniture other than a desk with a chair behind it, and a long form on which the only occupant was seated with his back to the door.

The door slammed behind Peter's back and the Major's footsteps hurried away down the corridor.

The figure on the bench turned at the noise.

"The Bishop," exclaimed Peter. "Where did you come from?" Pilot Officer Parsons rose to his feet. "Hello, sir. By heck, I'm pleased to see you. They got me in the shoulder. I think I could have got back all right, but they'd put a burst through my glycol, so down I came. They picked me up pretty quickly and hustled me along here. What are our chances of escape, sir?"

"Too early to say yet, but we must keep our eyes open. How's your shoulder?"

"Not too rosy. Bleeding's stopped. Smarts a bit. But look sir, if we do get a chance to make a getaway I've got a map..."

"The devil you have. It would have been wiser to have burnt that..."

"It's not one of ours, sir, that went when I burnt Amelia, the poor old bus made a pretty blaze. No, coming along in the car I felt in the pocket and found this." Parsons delved inside his coat and produced a folded map which he handed to Mohune. At that moment the door burst open and Peter thrust the document into his shirt. The newcomer was not a member of the Luftwaffe. His uniform with breeches and polished riding boots proclaimed him to be a member of the Storm Troopers. He was a big man with a low forehead and overhanging bushy eyebrows which were drawn down in a scowl as he looked at the Englishmen. Flinging himself into the chair behind the desk he crashed his fist down upon a bell. Instantly a door leading to a further room burst open and two more Storm Troopers hurried in.

"Take these men away and search them," ordered the man at the table.

The newcomers seized the prisoners and hustled them into the room they had just left, larger room this in which a party of Storm Troopers were lounging. One of them even larger than the man they had just left lounged to his feet and made a remark to his companions, a remark which brought forth a gust of laughter.

"What did he say?" asked Parsons.

Mohune shook his head and the youngster continued: "But you said . . ."

"Silence . . ." bawled the bull elephant in German, and then to Mohune, "Strip."

Peter gazed at him vacantly as though he did not understand and the German, taking a pace forward, gave a vicious tug at the zip fastener of Peter's coat. "Nakid," he barked in English, "nakid." Mohune shrugged his shoulders. "Better humor them, Bish," he suggested, as he pulled his arms out of the coat and threw it on to one of the benches which lined the walls.

Pluckily Parsons tried to follow suit, but his injured shoulder was obviously troubling him, and seeing the beads of perspiration burst from the boy's forehead, Mohune moved across to lend assistance. Immediately his shoulder was gripped and, caught off his balance, Peter was sent spinning across the room to crash against the far wall.

The Troopers laughed uproariously, first at Mohune and then at the pathetic efforts of Parsons as he tried to divest himself of his clothes. The bull elephant, whom the others addressed as Strumm, grinned, preening himself as a master of men.

With a smile still on his lips Peter made his way back to the center of the room and began to undo his tunic. At this moment one of the Troopers left his seat and, crossing to the Squadron Leader, ran his finger along Mohune's medal ribbons. Instinctively Peter looked down and up came the Trooper's balled fist at his nose. A rich jest this which received its due reward of laughter. The tide of Mohune's temper surged against a thin protecting wall, but was saved from overflowing by the swaggering entrance of the Storm Trooper from the other room.

"Get them dressed," he ordered, "get them dressed at once. They are to be interrogated immediately. Get their clothes on."

Mohune's coat was flung at him. "Who's doing it?" demanded Strumm. "Hesse, the staffelkapitane, and the little swine Promft." The words were spat out. The Trooper was annoyed.

"Why can't they leave it to us? Our methods are effective. *We'd* find out everything," complained Strumm. "These aristocratic swine are as effete as the thrice damned English themselves."

"There's a Major from Intelligence coming along later."

"Intelligence!"

"You, Strumm, will take them to Headquarters. Take two men as escort. If they try to escape, shoot, and shoot them in the belly." Strumm grinned and two minutes later the little party was making its way through blinding rain along a cobbled street.

Mohune was still smiling, but those who knew Mohune would have known that smile. They went at a sharp pace, Parsons shuffling, stumbling, half running. Once he nearly fell. Strumm pushed him roughly forward and Mohune's eyes became hard. Deliberately he paused, pulled out his cigarette case, put a Player between his lips and flicked his lighter into action between his cupped palms. Instantly Strumm, who was on Mohune's right, thrust across to strike the cigarette from the Englishman's lips and like a flash Peter's right hand was beneath the German's armpit. The German fell forward off his balance and a toe becoming entangled with his feet upset him completely. He staggered across the road, tripped on the curb and fell to his knees. In a second Strumm was on his feet again and fumbling for his pistol, screaming with rage he rushed at Mohune who stood for him in silence.

"Did you trip, mein Herr?" Peter's enquiry was solicitous. The German waved a fist as though about to strike, then regaining his self-control, he caught Mohune's arm and hurried him on into the night. They trudged on. The rain was a deluge, small rivers burbled in the gutters, large pools had formed in the uneven surface of the road. They turned a corner and ahead a blue light shone wanly in the gloom, a door swung open and a voice called to Strumm to hurry. Roughly the Storm Trooper ordered his men to double and then ran forward into the darkness but yet again that toe was entangled between his feet and Strumm measured his length in a handsome puddle not distantly related to

a small lake which caused a mighty splash at the feet
of the surprised officer in the doorway. Invective flowed
freely and continued even after the escort had ushered
the prisoners into a room in which the Staffelkapitane
and Hauptman Promft awaited them.

It was the latter who spoke. "Herr Staffelkapitane will
see the prisoners separately," he snapped. His voice no
longer held a tone of friendliness but was hard and guttural. A Storm Trooper caught Parsons by the shoulder
to lead him away, but Mohune stepped forward to bar
the way.

"Excuse me," he began, "before Pilot Officer Parsons
is led away, I have a complaint to make."

"You have a complaint to make"—the Staffelkapitane's
voice betrayed his amazement—"very well, we will hear
it." Then in German he ordered the guard to remain.
"Your complaint, Squadron Leader, I trust is not a
frivolous one."

"I can assure you of that, sir. We are English officers.
Our countries are at war, but that does not prevent a
modicum of civility being shown to us."

The Staffelkapitane nodded, then, "But perhaps you
are too squeamish, but continue with your complaint."

"We have received no civility. We have been humiliated and struck."

"Humiliated, that is perhaps a good thing for you
English, although I should have thought Dunkirk was
your humiliation. Is that all?"

"No sir, it is not. My comrade, a wounded man, has
been manhandled. Of course, I must admit that the
Trooper concerned was not entirely to blame, he was
perhaps not quite sober."

"Do your pilots need to be inebriated before they fly?"

"I was referring to the Trooper, Herr Staffelkapitane."

"You infer that the Trooper was drunk?" The German's voice rose.

"I put that forward as an excuse for him, sir."

"As an excuse? Do you realize what you are saying?"

The Storm Troopers having no English had no knowledge of what was taking place. All that they could gather was that the Staffelkapitane was rapidly losing his temper, which pleased them more than a little.

"Are you suggesting this merely because you were manhandled?"

"Not that alone, mein Herr. He appeared sober enough when he was conducting our search, although now I come to think of it I should have realized his condition at the time for, despite the fact that express orders were given for us to be searched, no search actually took place, and I have heard that Nazis always obey orders."

"That is, of course, unquestionable, but if you did not realize that he was drunk when you were in the bright light of a room, how could you possibly have formed that opinion in the darkness of the night?"

"I suppose it must have been that the cold air affected him." Mohune's voice became confidential. "The night air often has that effect; you may have noticed it yourself, and this man stumbled about; once he fell right across me into the gutter and then when we arrived here he fell like a sportive seal into a puddle outside the door."

Promft put up a hand to hide the smile about his

lips and the Staffelkapitane turned his fury on the Troopers. In a few terse sentences he outlined Mohune's accusation, then in conclusion "Is this correct? Did he stumble across the road? And did he fall into a puddle?"

The Troopers were silent.

"Is this correct?" thundered the Staffelkapitane.

A halting admission came from one of the men.

"Where is he now? Where is he now?"

"We left him with the officer at the door."

"What did the officer say to him? Come on, out with it. What did that officer say to him?"

"Herr Staffelkapitane, he asked Strumm if he was drunk."

"Enough. Must I be hindered in my work by you dabauched scum. It's bad enough when you do it in your own quarters, but when you interfere with the working of my Staffel it is intolerable. Bring this man Strumm to me. Bring him here."

Two minutes later a bedraggled and mudstained Strumm was ushered into the room.

"Herr Staffelkapitane?" There was still a note of truculence in the Trooper's voice, a note which was quickly damped by the enraged airman.

"You are accused of being drunk on duty."

"Drunk? Me? Why my comrades will testify that I have had nothing to drink . . ."

"Oh, I have no doubt that they will testify, you all stick together like leeches, but the fact remains that Herr Major asserts that you manhandled prisoners entrusted to your care. You may do what you like with your political prisoners, but I will not have you touching one of my captives. It makes interrogation impossible, it stiffens their stubborn pride. Well, what have you to say?"

"Why I . . . I . . . was detailed to search the prisoners."

"You ordered them to strip?"

"Naturally."

"And you searched them?"

"Of course, Herr Staffelkapitane."

"What was in their possession? Answer me that."

"I . . . I didn't have time to find out . . ."

"You didn't have time to find out. You expect me to believe that? To proceed. It is further asserted that you were unable to walk in a soldierlike manner when you were escorting the prisoners. Your own comrades lend testimony to that assertion."

"It is a lie."

"It is a lie, eh? You didn't stumble into the gutter like a drunken pig?"

"No, Herr Staffelkapitane, I did not stumble. I was pushed there by the prisoner."

"Oh, so you now claim that the Englishman attacked you."

"That is correct."

"A serious charge, one that would bode ill for the Major if it were proved. You took steps to report the matter . . . I say, you took steps to report the matter? Do I have to repeat everything I say? Come, answer me. Has this assault been reported or hasn't it?"

"No, mein Herr."

"I suppose you have not had time?" Rage was giving place to sarcasm.

"I had an accident . . . I tripped and fell . . ."

"That I can well believe, but are you sure that the

prisoner did not pick you up and throw you across the road into the puddle. No, you are wasting my time. You will leave here in arrest and I will report the fact to your Troop Leader. March out!"

As the door closed behind the damped and enraged Strumm the Staffelkapitane, his head bent over the papers on the table, gave an order for Parsons to be removed, and when he looked up there was a twinkle still flickering in his eyes, a twinkle which he tried to hide by another reference to his papers.

"Squadron Leader Mohune," began the Staffelkapitane at last, "It is my duty to interrogate you and I am performing the duty myself instead of leaving the task to a more junior officer, as it is seldom we obtain such a valuable prisoner as yourself ... I'm sorry ... Promft, a chair for the Major ... a cigarette, Mohune?"

"Thank you." Mohune's lighter flicked into action. This was quite in accordance with the best traditions of interrogation. Make a prisoner comfortable and he may unburden his heart.

"Before we start, Herr Staffelkapitane," continued Peter, "I think that so much of your time has been wasted it is only fair that I should warn you that I know there are only a few questions that I am compelled to answer."

"Precisely. Let us finish them off first, shall we?"

Mohune smiled. "My name is Peter St. Maur Beverley de L'Epee Mohune ... I'll spell those for you ... and my rank is Squadron Leader and that, sir, is all that I can tell you ..."

"You know too much about this game for me."

"I have done it myself ..."

"That is interesting. You speak German?"

Cursing himself for falling into the trap of his own making Peter made haste to extricate himself. "No," he laughed, "I've only done the job in peace time. On exercises." He rose to his feet and crushed his cigarette into an ash try. "I think I had better say no more," he smiled, "except to say that I am pleased that it was you who conducted my interrogation. May I be removed now?"

"All in good time, all in good time, and may I suggest that before we go any further you turn out your pockets and leave the contents with me."

In silence Peter complied with this request and placed the articles on the table. The pile was not a large one. Cigarette case, lighter, handkerchief and wrist watch.

"And Herr Major, do I not see a book or something peeping from the opening of your tunic?"

"Oh that," Peter laughed, "as a matter of fact I had forgotten that." He drew out Parsons' map and threw it on to the pile. "It's not my property at all."

In silence the Staffelkapitane opened the map and spread it out before him, then he looked up at Peter and his expression had changed. In that second it had become harder and more purposeful.

"Where did you get this from?" he demanded.

"Oh, I just found it," smiled Peter.

"You just found it. Must I ask where?"

Mohune was about to make a noncommittal reply when the door burst open and an officer with greatcoat buttoned to the neck hurried into the room; halting before the table he saluted. "Herr Staffelkapitane," he announced, "I am Major Von Rinck of the Intelligence." He removed his cap and shook the rain from it vigorously. "This is my man?"

The Staffelkapitane nodded and the newcomer turned to Mohune.

"Sit down, please." Von Rinck perched himself on the edge of the table and continued: "A few questions." He produced a formidable sheaf of papers from an inside pocket of his greatcoat.

"A cigarette? No? Now I won't keep you long. Just routine stuff. You are Squadron Leader Peter St. Maur Mohune?"

"Right first time."

"Of M.I.20?"

"I am the Squadron Leader of a Fighter Squadron."

"Yes, yes, yes, but you are also of M.I.20. Wonderful fight you put up this afternoon. Quite wonderful. I spoke to one of the pilots who did come back. Now you admitted that you were M.I.20 . . ."

"I did nothing of the sort. I am a Squadron Leader of the General Duties Branch of the Royal Air Force . . ."

"Now look here, Mohune, I want to get some sleep to-night. Let's not haggle over trifles. I have put a call through and I have checked you up. We know that you are a member of Colonel—I beg his pardon—Air Commodore Dettmer's Air Ministry Intelligence Department. We have your description. Height six feet, deep blue eyes; what was it the baroness said about those eyes? Ah yes, here it is . . . dreamy as a supine leopard but holding the humor of a modern Rabelais. But to continue . . . small hole large enough to admit the passage of a match stick through the left ear . . . hole caused through sword thrust with German agent in 1935 and which has never completely healed. There you are, you see, everything fits right. Height, eyes and hole.

"You are Mohune of M.I.20?"

Peter made no reply but stepped forward to retrieve his cigarette case from the table, but was halted by the I.O.

"No, no. Don't touch those, please. One of mine ... a light?"

Mohune bent his head over the small flame of the German's lighter and then, looking up at the ceiling, inhaled luxuriously.

"Well, Mohune?" demanded von Rinck.

"Well, von Rinck?" Twin plumes of smoke escaped from Peter's nostrils.

"I can't see what you are driving at," he continued.

"Of course you can't. It's such a small point."

"Then let's leave it, shall we?"

"Mohune, we are both Service men, regulars, not civilians in uniform. We understand each other. I would like to think that your case would be left in the hands of my department ..."

"My case? What case? I am a prisoner of war ..."

The Staffelkapitane leant forward and whispered in the Major's ear. Von Rinck nodded.

"You are an obstinate young man, Mohune," continued von Rinck. "We know that you are the Mohune who worked against us in the Port Richboro affair. You are a Secret Agent ..."

"Pardon me, but I must repeat that I am the leader of a Fighter Squadron ..."

"And once again I repeat that there are several questions for which I must have answers. It would be in your interest to give them to me."

"Really, Major, you surprise me. Is this bribery?"

"Bribery! Why, you insolent young puppy." For a moment it seemed that the Major's choler was about to boil over, then suddenly he regained control. "Listen, Mohune, I am an Intelligence Officer and I am offering you sound advice. I have to obtain the answers to these questions or else..."

"Or else..." Mohune laughed. "Quite a Hollywood gambit. Don't say you'll take me for a ride."

"That's just what I do say. I will take you for a ride. A damned long ride to Berlin and the Gestapo."

"Look here, Von Rinck. I don't know what you're aiming at, but I can tell you this, that I am a prisoner of war and the two questions that I can be forced to answer by International Law I have already answered. More than that you cannot ask of me, and if you do you are doomed, as was the carnally-minded nurse, to a bitter disappointment."

"Is that final?" demanded von Rinck and Mohune nodded.

"Squadron Leader Mohune." It was the Staffelkapitane who took up the conversation. "Will you take my advice and answer these questions?"

"Sir," replied Mohune, "as I see the position, there are no questions for me to answer until I admit that I am a Secret Agent, and since my mother always impressed upon me that it was wicked to tell a fib, I cannot agree to that assertion."

"I am sorry. I have had my orders." This was von Rinck again. "I shall have to take you to Berlin."

Mohune shrugged his broad shoulders. "Very well," he murmured, and then to the Staffelkapitane. "You'll do your best for Parsons, sir?"

"I will do all that I can, I promise you that."

"Thank you, sir."

The Staffelkapitane and Hauptman Promft rose to their feet as von Rinck escorted Mohune from the room.

"Obstinate young fool," said the Senior Officer, "but I like him; he gave me the chance I have been waiting for for years, to get in one at those thrice damned Storm Troopers."

"Do you think that Strumm was drunk?" enquired Promft.

"Of course he wasn't . . . that was what pleased me so much."

"And what will happen to the Englishman now?"

"Ultimately he will die. They will make a strong case against him and that will be the end of him. I gather they have no cause to like your Squadron Leader Peter St. Maur Beverley de L'Epee Mohune, de L'Epee of the Sword," the Staffelkapitane nodded. "He's sharp enough. A pity, a great pity. It's a damned war, Promft."

CHAPTER FOUR

IN WHICH HE MEETS THE SCHULTZSTAFFEL

"Good morning, Mohune."

"Morning, von Rinck."

"Sleep well?"

"Excellently, thanks to you. I did not expect a bed."

"Forget it. We leave in an hour."

"By car?"

"By air. It's dirty weather and I'm not looking forward to it. I'm not a birdman. I only wish we could have
gone by train."

"It takes about twelve days to get to Berlin by train
now, I believe."

"All of that..." The Major broke off suddenly, as
though he had realized that he had said too much. "Of
course..."

"Don't bother to deny it. We know the state of your
railways and I expect you in the Intelligence know it
too, although no doubt the true state of affairs has been
hidden from the forces in general."

Von Rinck made no reply but stood aside for Peter to
leave the room and then followed him to the waiting car
which was to take them to the aerodrome. It was still
raining and the little cluster of buildings which housed
the German Squadron looked gray and dispirited. A
dog, its ribs showing clearly through the staring coat,
snuffled in a gutter. Overhead the sky was gray and

leaden. In silence Peter climbed into the car, followed by the Intelligence Officer, and the journey had commenced.

At the aerodrome Mohune was hustled across the macadam towards the long dark outline of a Junkers 52, a troop carrier, attached to the Squadron for communication purposes. There was a slight pause while the Major was assisted into a parachute; it was noticeable that safeguard of this nature was offered to the Englishman, and while this operation was in progress, airmen going about their various duties stared curiously at the well-groomed and extremely self-possessed figure of the Squadron Leader, noted the spread of his shoulders and his narrow hips, his easy carriage and the smile playing about his lips, the carefree look in his eyes and wondered what fate was in store for him, and conjectured as to how he had fallen into their hands. Certainly he wasn't from that bomber which had flown over yesterday, for had they not been told that that plane had been shot down in flames by their well-directed flak and that all the crew had perished.

Not that you could always believe everything you were told, but this Englishman had certainly come from no burning bomber. His uniform was without a crease and his buttons glistened as though he was going on ceremonial parade. Mohune was now wearing his fore and aft cap, which when flying he always carried stuffed in his belt; his flying helmet he had left with a note presenting it to Promft.

The journey to the Tempelhof aerodrome at Berlin was boring in the extreme. Von Rinck had evidently given up all hope of making Mohune agree to his suggestion that he was a Secret Agent and hardly spoke during the flight, and it was with feelings of relief that Mohune noticed the gradual descent towards the landing ground.

No sooner had the aircraft touched down than a closed van speeded out from the road, a road that Mohune was pleased to notice was liberally pitted with bomb holes and which gave eloquent testimony to the accuracy of the "Bomber Boys." Two hangars at the far end of the aerodrome no longer presented themselves as buildings but as a collection of bent and twisted ironwork; girders, gaunt fingers of destruction, groped at the sky, and a fine array of red flags showed that at least one runway was unserviceable.

"I leave you now," commented von Rinck, as the van drew up alongside; "we may meet again. *Auf wiedersehen.*"

"*Au 'voir.*"

Two members of the Schultzstaffel, the picked men of the Nazi party, jumped from the van, seized Mohune's arms and hustled him into its dark interior. The doors slammed and the van moved forward bumping its way across the uneven surface of Hitler's prize aerodrome. After a journey of about ten minutes the van came to a halt and the doors were flung open and without waiting for the Nazis to lay hands on him Mohune jumped out and found himself in a courtyard surrounded by high stark buildings which might either be a barracks or a very modern hotel. Actually the first guess was the correct one. Mohune had arrived at the barracks of the Schultzstaffel.

There was no formality in the Englishman's reception. In silence Peter was led to a small cell, a hand placed on the center of his back thrust him forward; there was a dull thud on the floor beside him, the steel door clanged to, a key turned, he was alone. A faint light permeated the cell from a grill above the door, and Mohune began an inspection of his domain. A low bed in one corner was the only furniture and light would have been unnecessary to discover it by. Its blankets proclaimed their presence with a penetrating odor. Peter's next discovery was the cause of the thud he had heard when he entered the cell, which was revealed as a small canvas bag, which when opened revealed Mohune's personal possessions taken from him at his interrogation. All were present and despite the rough treatment it had received the wrist watch was still in working order. Parsons' map, however, was missing.

"So this is fame." Mohune chose a spot in the corner of the cell, folded his flying coat as a pillow and sat down with his back to the wall. Hours passed, no one visited him, and at last darkness fell and the corridor was filled with the snores of the other prisoners. Mohune slept.

Some two hours later the cell door opened and a torch was shone on the sleeper's eyes.

"Come."

Mohune rose, blinked at the bright light, stretched himself and sauntered into the corridor.

"*Marsch.*"

Mohune marched. Along the corridor, down a flight of steps, down another corridor, more steps, yet another corridor and to a door before which the party halted.

The leading Nazi knocked, flung open the door and pushed his captive forward into a brilliantly lighted room in which there were already four other members of the Schultzstaffel, who stood in silence watching a man whose only clothing was a pair of civilian trousers. The man was shivering, but as the room was heated to an uncomfortable degree, Mohune realized that the tremors were the outcome of fear. The obvious leader of the party, a man every bit as large as Strumm, shouted an order.

"Touch your toes."

The half-clad victim looked about him, fear, ugly stark fear was in his eyes, and again came the command.

"Don't hit me ... don't hit me ... Oh God, don't hit me."

The Nazis laughed.

"Touch your toes."

With his shoulders hunched the wretch obeyed, looking fearfully from side to side.

Mohune watched the leader of the party step forward, poise himself, then swing his heavy boot back to deliver a brutal kick at the bending man. The victim shot forward as though propelled from a gun, his head cracked against a wall at the far end of the room and he fell with blood streaming from his forehead.

"A good kick, Hans," laughed a trooper, and they all laughed, but their eyes were on Mohune as though awaiting his reactions. Peter's eyes hardened, but the smile remained on his lips and he leant his shoulders nonchalantly against the wall.

"Up! Up! Get up!"

The man made no movement, but lay moaning upon the floor.

"He's foxing you, Hans."

"Is he?" The brute leaped forward. "We shall see who foxes little Hans. Yes, we shall see. Poor little Hans. No one wants to play with him and he's so gentle."

The Troopers howled with laughter and Hans, lifting the man with one fist as though he were a babe, struck him across the face.

"Make a circle, boys," he ordered, and obediently the men ranged round the room waiting for the next move in their game. It came immediately. With a heave Hans threw his prisoner at one of the Troopers who, catching him before he fell, held him up while another Trooper lunged forward and struck the naked shoulder blades with a rubber truncheon. Screaming with fear the wretch was tossed to another of the Schultzstaffel and the treatment was repeated.

Several times during the course of the next few minutes the man fell, only to be kicked and jerked to his feet again.

At last, panting with their exertions, the Nazis tired of their sport and with sweat pouring from their faces, they let their plaything drop to lie unattended on the floor, his back a ghastly pattern of red weals and bruises.

The Troopers turned to Mohune as though they were children expecting approbation from a parent, but if they expected to see any outward sign of fear on the Englishman's face, they were disappointed. He still lounged languidly against the wall; he guessed that his time would come when they had recovered their breath, but he had also a faint suspicion that when that turn did come they would not find their task so easy. The Nazi who had escorted Peter from his cell stood before him, his legs apart, his chin outjutted.

"To them that talk will not that what happened has," he snarled in English and in that language Mohune replied, "Interesting, most interesting. And now?"

"To your cell. *Marsch*."

For the rest of the night Mohune was left alone. In the morning a bowl of tasteless soup and a lump of bread, sour and unpalatable, was thrust into his cell. Later he was taken out for an hour's exercise in a courtyard surrounded by the four wings of the prison buildings. Gaunt, tall buildings, studded with innumerable windows and over whose walls black drain pipes stood out like veins on an old man's hand. It was not until darkness had fallen again that Mohune was taken from his cell.

"Come." Catching up Mohune's flying coat the guard threw it at his prisoner and led him down to the main gates where a car was waiting. Faced by the guard whose pistol did not deviate from a line leading to his heart, Mohune was whisked through the darkened streets to the headquarters of the Gestapo. There he was hurried up a flight of steps through a pair of imposing doors, up a marble staircase, along an expensively carpeted corridor to a large ante-room. There he waited while another Trooper disappeared through the folding doors. Peter still menaced by the pistol looked about him. A typist, her fair hair scraped back into an unattractive bun, hammered at her typewriter. Mohune looked at her curiously; her eyes masked by pebble glasses were intent upon her work and he came to the conclusion that the Gestapo had little or no taste in the feminine line. Then he noticed the white scar on her wrist, a scar which stood out in the horror of a Swastika. Another Nazi jest, he thought, when his attention was drawn by a cough behind him. He swung round to face von Rinck.

"So we do meet again," the German smiled. "I am glad to see you looking so well."

"They haven't beaten me up if that's what you mean . . ."

"Time enough for that. Empty your pockets, please."

"What again?"

"And I would take your coat off. It'll be warm in there. Throw it on that chair there. . . . Ready? Come along then."

Von Rinck pushed open the folding doors and ushered Mohune into the adjoining room.

The first thing that caught Peter's eye was the life-sized picture of Hitler hanging on the wall before him. His gaze dropped and there beneath the portrait of the megalomaniac were seated his inquisitors.

Four men in the uniform of the Gestapo, three of them young, no more than boys, and the fourth who was obviously the President of the tribunal and the cruellest specimen Peter had ever had the misfortune to set eyes on. A long bloodless face, dark hungry eyes and with shoulders which hunched at the extremities, gave the man the appearance of a waiting vulture. When he spoke it was in English, hard and with a marked accent, and the words came through thin lips which hardly moved to allow them egress.

"Peter Mohune, we know you as an agent of the British Secret Service," he began, and then to the guard, "Bring in that typist. Why is she not here? You may then wait outside."

There was a pause while his orders were carried out and until the girl with the scraped back hair had entered and seated herself at the end of the long table. Peter watched her and she examined the point of her pencil, opened her notebook and gave her unattractive hair a few hesitant pats. The swastika scar fascinated him and the President of the tribunal, watching intently, broke in upon his thoughts.

"You have noticed her brand, Herr Major." His voice was cold and without emotion. "That should be a lesson to you. This Freya forgot that she was the property of the Reich and refused a request of a member of the Party. Now she has a permanent reminder. I don't think that she will forget her position again. But to return to your case, Herr Major, we are here this evening to ask you a few questions, and we have with us" (he tapped a bulging file on the table before him) "your dossier. We have your whole history and that of your father before you. Your first attempt at espionage was in Scotland in 1934, your second at Marsden in 1936, your third at Neethley in the same year, and your fourth at Marsden again in 1938. You are in fact an accredited Secret Agent."

"I was perhaps engaged . . ."

"We are not here to discuss that point. That you are M.I.20 has already been established to our satisfaction. The hole in your ear proves that you are the Mohune mentioned in this file, that hole was made by one of my countrymen. It is unwise, Herr Major, to dabble in German affairs."

"Does your information relate that at the time this hole was made my sword went through your agent's heart? It proved that it was unwise for him to meddle in the affairs of the British Empire."

"So you admit everything?"

"I admit that at one time I was instrumental in thwarting the plans of your agents, but since the War I have returned to normal flying."

"Then perhaps you will explain your presence in Nazi-occupied France?"

I forced-landed after an engagement with your fighters."

"A likely story. It is useless to prevaricate, Herr Major. It is well known that your fighters do not fight so far afield and besides our wireless has informed us that the only engagement which took place yesterday was the defeat of twenty of your Spitfires by six of our gallant pilots of the Jadgeschwader."

"You place too much faith in your wireless. As a matter of fact I was in that fight."

"Exactly. You flew over here with the sole intention of landing in France. No Spitfire was engaged by our fighters yesterday over France."

"Your faith in Lord Haw-Haw is most touching."

"We are wasting time, but to prove to you how fallacious are your arguments perhaps you will tell me how this map came into your possession and for what purpose it was intended."

"That map was found by my brother officer in the

car in which he was conveyed to the Kampfstaffel Head-quarters."

"Another stupid lie. You came to France yesterday, you came deliberately, and you came as a spy."

"I was shot down over France yesterday when engaged in normal combat."

"And you brought a German map showing the positions of our aerodromes with you?"

"I have already told you that that map was found by another prisoner."

"A likely story and one that I have no hesitation in declaring a clumsy lie."

"Might I ask you one question. If I had come to this country as a spy, is it likely that I would have come in an English uniform?"

"You are a clever man, Herr Major, but you are not clever enough to pull the wool over the watchful eyes of the Reich. That was a clever trick of yours . . ."

"Do I understand . . ."

"You understand nothing . . ."

"And that is the truest thing you have said so far. I am accused of entering Germany for espionage purposes. If that were so would a wounded officer have accompanied me?"

"You English would do anything. We haven't forgotten the *Athenia* . . ."

"If you believe that rubbish you would believe anything . . ."

"I would of the English and Butcher Churchill."

Mohune shrugged his shoulders. "I have nothing more to say. I have told you how I came to be in France and how that map that you are playing with came into my possession ..."

"And I want the name and address of the Secret Agent who was to receive you, and no doubt would have received you had it not been for our vigilance."

"I have no agent."

One of the other inquisitors leant across and whispered into the President's ear, who listened intently and then nodded.

"There is another solution, Herr Major," he said at last, "and I am of the opinion that it may be the correct one. Perhaps you did not come to Nazi-occupied France yesterday; perhaps you have been there for a long time and that would account for the map being in your possession, and perhaps this other pilot had come to collect you. No doubt you had changed back into your English uniform in anticipation of his arrival."

"And just to draw his attention I flew around in a Spitfire and crashed it. Perhaps you can explain how I obtained the Spitfire, perhaps, you will suggest that Pilot Officer Parsons towed it behind his aircraft like a trailer so that I could fly back in it. Perhaps your soldiers did not see me crash, perhaps I wasn't there at all. In fact, perhaps the whole thing was done by two other men. Why not call Parsons and hear his story."

"We have heard enough lies for one night. We have given you a fair chance, you have had justice ..."

"Fair chance?" Mohune threw back his head and roared with laughter and the typist gazed at him in amazement. "Justice? Ye gods."

"I repeat that you have had justice and you have

spurned it. Very well, you will now be taken back to your cell and there you will be interrogated by Hans Kummer, whom I believe you met last night." A colorless tongue passed across equally colorless lips.

"To-morrow you will answer my questions. Furthermore there are some pamphlets of the type your aircraft have dropped over this country in this wallet of yours. Pamphlets of a most seditious character. You will answer for those to-morrow also. Incidentally your dossier mentions the fact, Herr Major, that you have a certain skill in opening safes, quite the common burglar. Perhaps you will be able to open the door of your cell and make your escape. I do not think that is likely somehow. Hans Kummer will see to that. Call the Guard."

As Mohune walked back to the ante-room he felt the short hairs on the back of his skull rising. Fear was a sensation he hardly knew, but the thought of that brilliantly lighted room and the rubber truncheons rising and falling on to his bare flesh caused a cold finger to run up his spine, but von Rinck, who had watched the proceedings in silence, was amazed that there was a complete absence of perturbation in the Englishman's eyes.

In the ante-room Mohune gathered up his belongings and was about to slip his cigarette case into its normal pocket when he noticed that the case was unfastened and glancing inside he saw that several of the contents were missing and more than that there were faint markings on the matt surface left uncovered by the missing Players. Casually he laid the case under a table light and as he slipped his lighter into his fob pocket, stooped to examine his discovery. Under the brighter illumination the pencil markings resolved themselves into an address, 12 Pestalozzistrasse, the word "friend" and a telephone number. Snapping the slim gold case he slipped it into his pocket. This he decided was probably a trap, he would be searched again later and the incriminating address would be found. Probably it was the address of some inoffensive person the Storm Troopers wanted to remove and who after a mock trial would be placed against a wall and shot for espionage, and Mohune decided to obliterate the markings as soon as an opportunity presented itself.

Peter picked up his flying coat and thrust an arm into its leather sleeve and instantly his fingers contacted a resilient object which caused him to doubt his first opinion of the address.

"Santa Claus is early this year," he said to himself, as he manipulated the rubber truncheon up the sleeve of his jacket. "The situation becomes curiouser and curiouser. It would appear that either I am to be caught with an incriminating address in my possession and a Corporal Dunlop, or else someone really likes me. Let's hope that it's the latter. Party games with Herr Kummer are not to be desired."

The Guard was impatient. He caught Mohune's shoulder and pushed him forward. Down the carpeted corridor they went and then commenced to descend the unlighted marble staircase and it was as they were nearing the bottom that Mohune, who was going down the left-hand side of the staircase with his hand trailing on the wide balustrade, slipped, his left ankle turning under him. He swung round to face the balustrade, his head falling on to his left forearm, his right arm hanging loose before his body.

"Come on, get up you," shouted the Guard in German roughly. He caught Mohune's right shoulder to heave him round but the shoulder came quicker than the Guard had anticipated and with it came a right hand grasping a rubber truncheon travelling like a flail. There was a dull thud as the weapon struck home behind the man's ear. A balled fist caught the Nazi's chin as he fell—an unnecessary blow, for the Guard was already unconscious.

Stooping, Mohune heaved the man on to his shoulder and, running down the remaining steps, dumped the Storm Trooper in the thick blackness behind the staircase, and Peter, with the truncheon swinging from his wrist, walked across the wide hall to the main doors and the safety of the night.

CHAPTER FIVE

IN WHICH HE PAYS A CALL AND DROPS A PAMPHLET

MOHUNE was half-way across the darkened hall when to his annoyance the doorkeeper emerged from the porter's lodge and walked to the main door where he stood with his back to the fugitive, staring out into the wet street. Peter swung his trucheon. To strike or not to strike, that was the question. There was only the porter between him and freedom and the porter was a little man.

Silently, like a cat in the night, Mohune moved towards his prey, with Corporal Dunlop drawn slightly back in readiness to strike the *coup de grace,* but that blow was never delivered, for, to the Englishman's great disgust, the silhouettes of two men arriving at the building showed clearly against the glass panels of the main doors. The porter moved forward to admit the newcomers and Mohune turning on his heel disappeared without apparent haste down the corridor. There he paused, waiting for the men to pass by the end of his bolt hole, but to his increased annoyance they remained in the hall and Peter could hear them laughing as they conversed with the doorkeeper.

The Guard might come to at any moment, seconds were vital, and Mohune retreated further along the corridor hoping to find a window. His fingers trailed lightly along the wall and suddenly slipped off into space, which after a moment's exploration was identified as another staircase. Mohune went on, pleased that another way of retreat had presented itself but still intent on finding a window. At last he reached the end of the corridor and heavy curtains met his outstretched fingers. Gently the hangings were pulled aside and Peter sighed with relief. He had found his window, but at that moment the moon came from behind a cloud and the sigh of relief was changed into a muttered curse—bars, heavy vertical bars, guarded the exit from top to bottom.

Thoughtfully Peter caressed the minute hole in his ear. "Check," he murmured, and glanced at the luminous dial of his wrist watch. Ten P.M. That accounted for the darkness which pervaded the building, the Staff would have gone home. Perhaps an unguarded window might be found on the floor above, but although most of the Staff must have left the building, Mohune realized that the Inquisitors had not yet descended the marble staircase, and furthermore there was still the Guard to be considered, to say nothing of sundry night watchmen who would be patrolling the corridors.

In silence Peter retraced his steps until he reached the staircase he had just passed, and then on his toes as lightly as a dancer, he mounted to the next floor. This corridor was brilliantly lighted and he made for the curtains covering the windows at the far end of the passage, but he had not covered a quarter of the distance when he heard the voices of people ascending the main staircase. To reach his goal was impossible. Without hesitation Mohune flung open a door and leapt into a room, pulling the door shut behind him. He caught his breath, the lights were full on, the room was empty, but the reason that he caught his breath was that he now found himself back in that ante-room which he had vacated only a few minutes before. Miss Ugly Bun's typewriter lay silent under its black cover, the doors leading to the room in which he had been questioned were open and that room was in darkness.

In a flash Mohune crossed to the windows and was about to throw the curtains aside when he remembered the lights. Another leap took him back to the door and the lights snapped out, but instead of returning to the window Peter paused. The voices were coming along the corridor, coming nearer every second.

Suddenly there was a wild shout and the voices were momentarily silent, then they broke out again, all talking at once. It was an easy guess that someone had discovered the Guard. At any moment now a search would be set in motion. Mohune sped across the ante-room, entered the culture's sanctum, pulled the door to behind him and crossed to the window. There with his hand on the curtains he paused again, what was it the President had said? "We have heard of your skill at opening safes . . ." "My friend," grinned Peter, "you've asked for this, and besides I want that plan and my wallet." Peter crossed to the desk and tugged at the drawer in which he had seen the Grand Inquisitor deposit the articles. It was not even locked.

"The conceit of the fools." Plan and wallet disappeared into Mohune's pockets and he was at the window again. The curtain slid back easily. No bars this time, there was another sigh of relief as Mohune pushed the casement open. A twenty foot drop, nasty but not enough to stop him. Gradually Peter lowered himself until he was hanging at the full extent of his arms. A moment later he sprawled on all fours in the concrete yard beneath the window. For a second he rested in that crouched position and then he was up and making for the wooden gates which gave access to a side street and he was about to make his getaway when a party of men, blurred figures in the wan moonlight, ran past the entrance to the yard.

"Waste of time," shouted one, "that damned fool of a porter must have let him go past. Of course he won't admit it. More than his life's worth. The thrice damned Englishman must be miles away by now, and we've got to spend the rest of the night chasing shadows."

The voices and the running feet faded into the distance and Mohune settling his cap firmly on to his dark hair, stepped out into the street and walked off in the opposite direction.

His next task was to find 12 Pestalozzistrasse and that was a riddle which threatened to beat his ingenuity. He had no money, he could not very well ask a policeman, and furthermore he had no idea whatever in which quarter of Berlin the street was to be found. For half an hour Mohune strode along the deserted streets, but no solution of the difficulty presented itself to his mind. He realized that sooner or later he would meet someone who would notice that his uniform was a strange one and then the hue and cry would go up in full blast. The moon, her face cleared of cloud, now shone brilliantly, and Peter found that he was now in a residential area where big houses lay back from the road. Houses standing in their own grounds with imposing porticos and wide sweeping drives, and then dead ahead of him was a blue light and his thoughts switched back to Eng-

land and Police Stations and a Police Station was the
last thing he wanted to encounter. His fears were soon
set at rest when the blue light indicated not a teeming
home of police but an inoffensive telephone kiosk. "And
that would be very useful," he thought, "if only I had
some money, and yet on the other hand, the box is
rather too well lighted and the sight of an English officer
putting through a call might cause a stir."

Mohune walked on, leaving the 'phone kiosk behind
him, but the thought of an English officer nonchalantly
putting a call through persisted in his mind. What
would the passer-by think? Propaganda. The idea was
born. The great dazzling idea which made Peter laugh
happily. So insane, but so terrific, was that idea that
he felt he had to carry it into effect without further
delay. He pushed open the gate leading to one of those
imposing drives, the gravel crunched under his feet,
then with a lithe spring he mounted the wide steps and
rang the bell. Two minutes passed and then a face white
in the moonlight peered round the edge of the door.

"What do you want?" quavered a voice. With an impatient movement Mohune pushed at the door and the
speaker staggered back into the hall, a gloomy cavern
illuminated by a single blue bulb.

"I want to see your master," demanded Peter in fault-
less German.

"Yes, mein Herr, certainly mein Herr. Who shall I
say that it is?"

"You won't say that it is anyone. You'll just take me
straight to him. Lead on, Pansy Face, lead on."

"Yes, mein Herr. This way, mein Herr." At the end
of the hall the old servant stopped before a door.

"In you go," demanded Mohune.

Obediently the servant turned the handle and entered the room.

"What is it, Hans," demanded a quiet voice.

"It's ... it's ... it's a man ..."

"Let me explain." Pushing past the trembling Hans, Peter strode forward to meet the gaze of two pair of eyes. Those of an old man erect and of military bearing who was seated at a table facing an equally old lady with masses of white hair. From the arrangement of the playing cards before them Mohune guessed that he had interrupted a game of piquet.

"As you will see," continued Peter, "I am an Englishman, an English officer to be precise ..."

The old man's eyebrows came together in a puzzled frown while his wife's eyes opened wide in astonishment.

"As you know, we have been dropping pamphlets over most of your cities." The old lady looked at her husband in apprehension. "Exactly," went on Mohune, "I can see that you are aware that it is illegal for your countrymen to read these pamphlets or even to pick them up. This has caused us some distress and we feel that our good work is being wasted. Not only that our bombers are required for work of a more military nature, and so, Service being our motto, we have arranged a house-to-house delivery. Allow me ..." With the gesture of conjurer producing a rabbit from a hat he produced his wallet and, taking a pamphlet from the inside pocket, he gravely handed it to the old lady. They stared as though afraid to touch the flimsy scrap of paper.

"Don't be afraid," smiled Mohune, "only we four

know that you have seen one and we won't tell." He pivoted and faced the servant, all gentility fading from his face, "will we, Pansy Face?"

"No, mein Herr . . . indeed no . . ."

"And you, sir, will you accept one? I thank you. Pansy Face, you will find that you already have one in your left-hand jacket pocket."

The servant's mouth gaped foolishly as he thrust his hand into the indicated pocket and produced a neatly folded pamphlet.

"And now, sir," continued Peter, "you will appreciate that this delivery service costs money. I am sure that it is not asking too much of you to subscribe to such a worthy cause . . ."

"I don't understand, either you are mad or . . ."

"Exactly. Either I am mad or I am an Englist Pilot. Well, that is a question I must leave you to decide for yourself, but time is pressing and I have other calls to make before I return to England. Your subscription?"

"Give him something, Otto," broke in the woman. "Oh, give him something and let him go. It's dangerous him being here. Throw the pamphlets into the stove. Burn them . . . here, give them to me, I'll burn them . . ."

"Steady, my dear, steady. Who this man is I cannot profess to know, but the situation is the most piquant I have savored for many a day. I for one shall enjoy reading them. As for you, sir, you are either a fool or a very brave man. How much do you want?" The speaker produced a wallet which Mohune waved aside.

"My dear sir, nothing so large. Some small change will amply cover the cost of my services . . . I thank you."

Mohune turned to go but paused at the door and with a hand on the door knob faced the old couple. "Needless to say, the essence of our Service is confidence. I do not suppose that you will be tempted to pass on your information to the authorities. It might be a little difficult to explain, and whatever you do I advise you to search your house first for other pamphlets which I may have secreted. The Gestapo would not like to think that you had kept anything from them, would they ... Come on, Pansy Face."

The old couple stared at the door as it closed behind the tall Englishman, stared at it with a mixture of fear and amazement in their eyes and then they both lifted the pamphlets and began to read, while in the hall Mohune was talking earnestly to the servant. He closed his wallet in which he had just written the address of the house. "Brother," he said, "I hate to think what would happen to you should you try to turn this evening to your advantage." He lifted his rubber truncheon and let it fall lightly across the other's neck. Hans let out a squeal and backed away.

"Quite right, brother. It's a rubber truncheon and I wouldn't like to have to use it on your scrawny neck. What's in that cupboard?"

"It's for storing ... hanging coats and hats ..."

"Open it up."

Obediently Hans unlocked the door and having selected the longest mackintosh that he could find and a civilian hat, Mohune pushed the servant into the dark confines of the lobby.

"And there you can stay," remarked Peter as he divested himself of his flying coat and pulled on the

mackintosh in its place. "Not a very good fit," he murmured, "but the adage about beggars must apply. You,
my friend, can stay where you are and meditate. When
you do get out don't forget what I said about searching
the house. Good-night."

Mohune slammed the door and turned the key, then
tiptoeing across the hall, glanced into the room he had
just left. The two old heads were bent over the pamphlets and he heard the woman say, "You know, there's
a lot in all this, whatever the man may have been."
Chuckling to himself, Mohune let himself out of the
front door and threw the key of the lobby into a nearby
bush.

What a jest. Ten minutes of real slapstick comedy
and he had come out of it partially disguised and
with the necessary change to 'phone the house in the
Pestalozzistrasse. He swung off down the street in the
direction of the telephone box and as he reached it he
laughed again at the thought of Pansy Face searching
the house for pamphlets which did not exist.

At first Mohune's efforts to call the house in the Pestalozzistrasse were in vain and he had begun to wonder
whether the whole thing was not a hoax as he had first
imagined when a voice answered in German.

"Yes," just one syllable.

"Friend?" replied Mohune. "The moon is rising."

"Good," announced a man's voice. "I was beginning
to think our plan had failed. Where are you now?"
Mohune repeated the address of the house he had just
left and explained his present position.

"Good. I will send a car for you. The driver will wear
white. It will be a saloon car. You will say the moon is

rising and he will reply that it is a nice night. Good-bye." The line went dead.

Mohune wondered how long it would be before the car arrived and how he should fill in the time until the white-coated driver should appear. He had no wish to meet anyone who might ask awkward questions and so he decided he would go back to the house where he had left the pamphlets and take shelter in the bushes which lined the drive.

It seemed hours before Mohune heard a car coming along the road, although in actual fact it was not more than twenty minutes, but minutes are apt to be magnified out of all proportion to their normal size when one is crouching under a laurel bush and inquisitive drops of moisture are dripping down one's neck with a monotonous regularity. With his flying coat flung across his shoulder, Mohune stepped out into the roadway as the car came to a halt beside the telephone kiosk. The driver was in white.

"The moon is rising," murmured Mohune.

"It is a nice night," came the reply.

The driver flung open the door in the manner of a London taxi-driver. Peter stepped in and the car moved off.

"Have we far to go?" asked Mohune through the glass screen which separated him from the driver.

"In Germany one does not speak unless it is of vital necessity."

"Doesn't one? I will be patient."

"Patience, I am told, is a minor form of despair disguised as a virtue."

"And that crack was vitally necessary, I suppose?"

The rest of the drive was completed in silence and even when the car arrived at its destination the driver had nothing to say. Having watched Mohune alight, he pointed to a house, slammed the door and with a slight screeching of gears made off into the night.

The house was certainly numbered twelve and Mohune could only assume that he was in the Pestalozzi-strasse. The house looked dead and even allowing for the dismal aspect given to everything by the black-out and the pale light of the moon, gloomy and deserted. Pulling the collar of the mackintosh up as high as possible and the brim of the stolen hat down over his eyes, Mohune mounted the steps and pushed a bell button.

Instantly the door swung open. "Trying to advertise yourself," whispered an angry voice. "Hanging about out there as though you had lost something. We've lost a lot of time and there's precious little of it to lose. Come in, come in."

Mohune followed the shadowy form up the ill-lit stairs and into a small room on the top floor. The man was now revealed as a tall slim figure with closely cropped red hair. He had an equally red face across which, running from ear to mouth, was the livid line of a scar which gathered up the lip to give the face a twisted appearance.

"I don't think we've met before . . ." began Mohune.

"You damn well know we haven't," snapped the other. "This is no time for platitudes. I'm Freemantle. We've discovered a vital plot which will strike Fighter Command to its knees. Take that silly smile off your face; you can grin at what the fighter boys did to the blitz in September, 1940, but this new effort will smash them before they have a chance to get going. The details of this plot must be taken to Dettmer at once. It's imperative that the Air Ministry should know what the German Higher Command are about to do. I can't go. I'm known now. In fact, my number's up, they're tracking me down at this very moment. We heard that you had been taken and we did all in our power to organize your escape and you managed to take the chance we offered, though God knows you have taken your time about it."

"Who do you think I am, brother? Quicksilver?"

"Don't talk, listen. These papers here are a detailed account of the whole plot," he pointed to a pile of manuscript on the table. Civilian clothes are on that chair behind you. Get into them right away. As I figure it out there should be a Gestapo raid on this house within the next half-hour. You must be out of here by then. If it comes before you're ready, get out through that window. I'll hold 'em off . . ."

"But you . . ."

"I have told you that my number's up. They have round me out. That's why we have been roped in . . ." While he was talking Freemantle was busy sorting papers. One batch he selected and thrust into an envelope. "There's money in that jacket pocket. You speak German fluently . . ."

"Who told you that?"

"Can't you shut up? We know everyone who has worked for Dettmer. You don't think we got you out of your mess just because you were an Englishman, do you? We've better things to do than that. Get a move on. For God's sake get a move on. I'll have to get rid of your uniform the best way I can. That is, if I'm alive to do it."

'Nerves about to bust,' thought Mohune, as he stripped himself of his outer garments. In silence he watched Freemantle complete his arrangements.

"We had four copies of this report. Two other messengers were to leave this morning. They were liquidated by a firing party before they could collect their documents. I'm giving you one copy, another I hope to get to another agent, but I'm pinning no hopes on that. There is no need for these other copies now..." He broke off and looked at Mohune.

"Good God, aren't you dressed yet? You're not dressing for a ball. Hurry man, hurry..." Freemantle spun round and inclined his ear to the door. "There you are, they're here."

Mohune heard a heavy body crash against the front door, then solid feet pounded up the stairs. Freemantle crossed to the window, pulled back the curtains and flung up the sash.

"Out you go," he ordered. "Take your jacket and trousers with you and finish your toilet on the tiles. Here, catch hold of this and get it to Dettmer." A bulky package was thrust into Mohune's hand and he was hustled towards the open window. There was a click and the light was extinguished. Feeling slightly ridiculous, Mohune dropped on to the leads five feet below. It was the first time he had left a house by the window, carrying his clothes. He grinned and hoped that anyone who saw him might think the worst.

Above him he heard the crash as the door of Freemantle's room was burst open and glancing up he saw a flash of a pistol. Report followed report and then as he dodged behind a chimney a wide shaft of yellow light cut across the leads as someone switched on the lights.

Peter crouched immobile, hoping that Freemantle would call to him and trusting that no other lights would disturb the darkness, and that latter prayer was answered. No doubt Berliners had learned that shooting at night was no concern of theirs. Cursing softly, Mohune pulled on the trousers which, apart from being too small for him, appeared to have tied themselves into Gordian knots about his ankles.

"He's dead enough," announced a voice, and Mohune's hopes faded. It was not the crisp irritable tone of Freemantle. "I wonder why this damned window's open?" The voice was faintly familiar, and when another voice joined in, Mohune's suspicions were confirmed. "Look, Kummer, look. An English uniform."

"*Mein Gott.* So he was here. We have got him now. You go back to Barracks and report. I'll fetch this swine in. He'll be on the roof. I'll settle him." Hans Kummer swung a massive leg over the sill.

"He may be armed, Hans."

"I hope he is. I want to play with that laughing swine."

There was a thud as Kummer dropped down on to the leads and Mohune, keeping well out of the range of the light, dodged behind another chimney stack. How tight those trousers were! Peter began to wish he had remained in his short clothes. Every movement he made was restricted by the tightness of his nether garments. Again he dodged towards another stack, but this time Kummer saw the movement, a pistol jabbed an orange pencil into the night and a bullet splattered on the brickwork where Mohune's head had been a moment before.

"I have you now, my little flying man."

Heavy feet ran along the flat roof towards the stack behind which Mohune was sheltering, then they stopped as though Kummer was debating his next move. Mohune stooped lower and trailed his hand around the floor about him. His fingers touched a piece of loose cement about the size of a squash ball. With an underarm throw he pitched it away towards the next chimney stack. It hit the roof with a smack. The ruse worked. Kummer ran forward but as he passed Mohune's stack, iron fingers grabbed the wrist which held the pistol, his momentum swung him round and his face hit the brickwork with a thud and the gun dropped with a thud.

Kummer leapt back and Mohune sprang after him, a balled fist came up and caught the German under the chin. Kummer shook his head at the force of the blow but with his arm swinging wildly he took the attack to his opponent. Mohune tried to sway away but the trousers spoiled the movement and in desperation he covered up.

Vicious, pile driving blows landed on his biceps, blows which Peter knew would soon weaken his resistance. Suddenly he straightened up, a right drove into the German's stomach, his left countered Hans' vicious swing at Mohune's head. They were apart again, but only for a second. In went Mohune, both hands working in a two-handed attack and another balled fist sank into the German's plexus. Kummer grunted and took a left in the same place, but still he thought that he had the measure of this slightly built Englishman. He brought a knee up to Peter's groin but Mohune, sensing the move, pivoted away, but again the trousers nearly brought disaster and he caught the full force of the knee on his thigh. He overbalanced and fell backwards and then, as the German rushed in, he twisted over on to all fours and scrambled away. With a bound like a released spring Mohune was on his feet again. There was a loud report and Mohune laughed happily. The trousers had split in two. Amazed at this madman who laughed at his punches Kummer paused and took three successive lefts to the jaw for his indecision, took another in the stomach which made him cough, and then letting out a bull-like roar, he rushed forward aiming a swinging left at Mohune's head, but like an eel Peter made a half-turn, caught the wrist with his right hand, caught Kummer's bicep with his left hand, pivoted on his heel bringing Kummer's imprisoned arm over his left shoulder, and heaved.

Hans Kummer, the prize bully of the Schultzstaffel, felt himself sailing through the air. The top of his head struck a chimney stack. He knew no more, for Hans Kummer was very dead.

CHAPTER SIX

IN WHICH HE LEAVES BERLIN

LIGHTLY, ready for the slightest move from Hans Kummer, Mohune advanced towards the recumbent form. The moon had hidden her face behind a veil of cloud and it was difficult for Peter to decide whether Kummer was lying sprawled and inert or whether he was crouching with his muscles bunched in readiness to spring forward in a smashing attack just as soon as Mohune advanced within range, but the Storm Trooper made no movement, and then just as Peter reached the huddled mass, the moon came out again as though she, too, were inquisitive to see what fate had befallen the would-be killer.

Kummer was lying on his stomach but with his large head twisted round in such a fashion as to leave no possible doubt that he was dead. It was very obvious that his neck had snapped like a dry stick when his head with the weight of that massive body behind it had struck the chimney stack.

Breathing deeply, Mohune gazed down at the body. Another Nazi had left the Schultzstaffel; a sadistic bully, but one who had gone out fighting. Then Peter became aware of the cold night air blowing through the gaping seams of his trousers and the delicacy of his own position forced itself upon him. Escape would have been difficult enough without this, but to attempt to cross Germany in a pair of trousers which were nothing more than two legs joined together by a waist band was obviously impossible, and at any moment more Storm Troopers might arrive by way of the window to seek little Hans Kummer. There was only one solution and ten minutes later, Mohune, dressed in the uniform of the Schultz-staffel, stepped away from the body and made his way back to the window of Number 12.

The light was still burning in Freemantle's room and Peter paused for a moment beneath the sill, straining his ears for the sound of movement in the room above him, then with a spring he reached the window ledge. The room was deserted. Freemantle's body had been removed and except for an ominous brown stain on the carpet, there was nothing, nothing whatever to show that any unusual occurrence had taken place in that room so recently occupied by a member of the British Secret Service.

Fingering the hole in his ear, Mohune glanced about him, taking in the furniture, his blue Air Force slacks hanging over the back of a chair, a heaped German greatcoat which had fallen off the table on to the floor, and while he carried out this brief inspection his mind was working on the problem of escape which now lay before him.

The main question which he had to decide was how far he could get in Kummer's ill-fitting uniform, and how long it would be before other Nazis invaded the room and then discovered Kummer's body behind the chimney stack on the leads below.

As soon as that happened, the fact that an Air Force officer was attempting to escape from Germany in the uniform of the Schultzstaffel would be broadcast over the country. Obviously, therefore, the fact that Kummer was dead and that Mohune was wearing his uniform must be kept from the authorities as long as possible.

Peter moved around the room pulling open drawers and searching for anything which might be of value to the people at home, but Freemantle had covered his tracks well, there was nothing to be found, and Peter finished his search no nearer to the solution of his problem than he had been when he had entered the room. He lit a cigarette and perching himself on the edge of table, blew a plume of smoke at the ceiling.

Kummer was invisible from the window, but the shortest search would be sufficient to discover him, and the fact that the corpse was clad in nothing but underwear would bear eloquent testimony as to Mohune's future plans. It was therefore imperative that the Storm Troopers should be kept away from the house as long as possible, or if that could not be arranged, they must at least be prevented from searching the leads.

Mohune crossed to the window, closed it and drew the curtains, then seating himself before Freemantle's portable typewriter, he inserted a sheet of paper and hammered away at the keys. With a jerk the paper was removed and, thrusting his legs out beneath the table, Peter lay back in his chair and examined his magnum opus:

The English swine has escaped. I am going after him. Suggest that a call be broadcast for a man dressed in gray suiting, blue shirt and collar and black tie. No hat.—Hans Kummer.

All right as far as it went, but the trouble was that it

did not go far enough, for if Kummer had re-entered the room to type a message, he would have obviously telephoned to his superior officer to acquaint him of the facts. For a few moments Mohune deliberated the point, then stretching out his hand he reached for the telephone and draped his handkerchief over the mouthpiece.

"I want the Barracks of the Schultzstaffel ... yes ... yes ... the Barracks ... get a move on, you imbecile." Mohune dropped his voice and attempted to imitate the low guttural tones of the late Hans Kummer. "Listen, it's Kummer here ... Hans Kummer. I am speaking from ... all right ... put me through if you must." Another snag, the operator had insisted that the call should be put through to the commandant. "Herr Commandant? Yes, you are very faint, too. It is Kummer here. I am speaking from No. 12 Pestalozzistrasse. No, Herr Commandant, that is what I have telephoned to tell you about. He has escaped ..."

At the other end of the line hell broke loose. "You ignorant clout ... you vainglorious swine spawn, you who sent the others away because you wanted to play with the Englishman ..."

"But Herr Commandant," expostulated the soi-disant Kummer, "I could do nothing. He was away before I could reach him ... Dressed? He is in a light gray suit and still wears the blue shirt of his uniform. No, he has no hat. Yes, Herr Commandant; I have left a message here which they will find ... I cannot speak any louder. Herr Commandant, I am shouting now ... I cannot ... speak any ... louder ... and I can't hear you either, Herr Commandant."

"And if you do not find him, Kummer, you may as well shoot yourself, you will find it easier. Heil Hitler."

"Heil Hitler," murmured Mohune and removing his handkerchief from the microphone, mopped his head thankfully, then rising to his feet he made a final survey of the room, the German greatcoat on the floor caught his eye. The high collar, when turned up, would make adequate covering for the tell-tale hole in his ear.

Ten minutes later Mohune descended to the street; a bold front was now called for. He was a member of the Schultzstaffel, the cream of the earth. With great-coat collar turned up about his ears he swaggered down the steps and on to the footwalk. A loaded pistol in his holster meant that his capture would be no easy task, and Kummer's wallet with identification card and wad of currency notes would simplify his progress. In the inside pocket of the greatcoat reposed Freemantle's let-ter, Parsons' map and his own wallet. Things were look-ing up.

Mohune had decided upon his plan of campaign. The first car that came along would be commandeered, and who would argue with a member of the Schultzstaffel? He would drive that car until the petrol gave out and then he would find another car. Petrol stations, if any were to be found, would have to be avoided, for they are a great source of information to the wrong people.

He had hardly reached the pavement when a car swung round the corner a hundred yards away, making towards him. Without any hesitation Mohune stepped into the roadway and raised his hand. The car came to a halt with brakes screaming and Peter moved out of the subdued beams of the headlights towards the side of the driver to commence his act, but the performance, like many amateur productions, did not proceed according to the producer's wishes. Far from adopting the tone of the bully Mohune found that he was to be bullied instead. A door flew open, a man emerged and a torch blazed into Peter's eyes.

"Kummer?" demanded a voice, "where's Kummer?"

"I don't know," admitted Mohune.

"Who are you? What are you doing here?"

"I . . ." began Peter, his brain working at speed.

"You are not of my troop. Where have you come from?"

The interruption was a godsend. Peter's story was now ready. "I am Otto Hirsch," he announced. "I am from Munich on leave. I . . . well, to be truthful . . ."

"You had better be . . ."

"Exactly, that is what I thought. You see, I was in the next street, the one which backs on to this, you will understand. There is a girl there. I have known her for a long time; we were together in . . . in the dark."

"Naturally, Hirsch, naturally, but what are you doing here?"

"I was coming to that. We were in her bedroom, you will understand, and as I say, it was dark, when suddenly from one of the houses in this street a blinding flash shot out, no curtains, no attempt at shading at all. The full beams shot out across the leads. I crossed to the window of the room I was in and looked out. Then I saw the figure of a man climb out of the lighted window. I took it as my duty to come round and investigate. You will understand that my preparations took a little time, but I dressed by the window and while I was doing so I saw that same figure climb back again and seat himself at a typewriter. By then I was ready. I hurried round, the front door was open, I ran upstairs to find the room empty, but there was a note on the table saying that an Englishman had escaped and that the writer of the note was going after him. The note was signed Hans Kummer."

"Blitzen. Was that all the note said?"

"It said that the Englishman was dressed in a gray suit . . ."

"In that case we had better be off." Mohune heaved a sigh of relief. With any luck he would get away unsuspected, but the man hesitated with his foot on the running board of the car.

"Wait here," he said to the driver. "I will view this room. There may be something that that great ox Kummer overlooked. Hirsch, you come with me."

Pulling his collar close about his ears Mohune followed the German up the stairs and into Freemantle's room.

"The window is closed now and the curtains are drawn."

"They were like that when I arrived," answered Mohune.

In silence the note was read.

"I wonder whether the careless swine thought of reporting this matter to Headquarters. I had better make sure."

Seating himself at the table the Storm Trooper called the Barracks and while he was waiting for the connection to be made he looked across at Mohune.

"So you are from Munich," he remarked casually,

"a marvellous town, the birthplace of our party, Hirsch. That will always be remembered. Must never be forgotten. Munich. I have many friends in Munich. You must have met Fritz Busch?"

Mohune nodded and the other raised his hand for silence. The call was coming through and then at last the instrument was replaced, the German rose to his feet, and Peter hoped that he had forgotten about Fritz Busch.

"It is expected that the Englishman will make for unoccupied France. We are to go to the railway station at once. So you have heard of Busch. What was the last you heard about him?"

"I hardly know. I believe he has been selected for promotion."

"Not Fritz. He's dead. Come we must go."

Relieved that a difficult situation had passed off without mishap, Mohune made for the door, but in the next second his rising spirits were plunged down to zero.

"That's a very badly fitting uniform you have on, Hirsch. I should have thought that you were big enough without having a uniform too large for you. Why, it might have fitted Kummer . . ."

Mohune laughed easily, but the other continued; doubt was entering his mind.

"I suppose you are from Munich?"

"I think the little girl in the house opposite will verify that."

"Your identification card would be a more simple proof. I wonder. Stop a moment . . ."

Mohune faced the speaker. "It is a very strange thing that a member of the Schultzstaffel should not know of the death of Fritz Busch, even if he had never met him he would have heard of his death . . ." The German's hand moved quickly and a pistol was pointed at Mohune's stomach. "Turn down your collar."

Cursing himself heartily for allowing the German to draw his gun, knowing as he did that there were few men alive who could beat him at pistol play, Peter slowly folded the heavy collar of Kummer's greatcoat down on to his shoulders.

"So," leered the other, "we will not have to go to the railway station after all, Herr Secret Agent with the hole in his ear masquerading as a Storm Trooper. They will thank me at Headquarters for bringing you in. Perhaps that fool Pegler will change his opinion of me. You are good at bluffing, Herr Major, but not good enough to bluff me. Turn about . . ."

The pistol jabbed into Mohune's spine.

"March . . . and Pegler, the great Pegler, was convinced that you could speak no German. The fool, the silly conceited fool."

Peter moved slowly and the pistol jabbed him again.

"Hurry," was the order, "and take this word of advice. No little trick, Herr Major, or I shall be unable to take you back to the Barracks. You will be blown into two pieces. Hurry."

But Mohune did not increase his speed, a smile came to his lips, a smile which, had the German seen it, might have given him food for thought. Many years ago Mohune had been taught all the tricks of gun play by a man who staked his life on his knowledge of pistols, their use and abuse, and one of the axioms which he had passed on to Mohune was: 'If ever you have a prisoner

and you want to make him walk, never if you value
your life jab your gun into his back. Jab him with your
left forefinger; he will be unable to feel the difference
between that and the pistol, and keep your gun back by
your right hip. Then, if he turns suddenly you have him
cold, but if your gun is at his back, when he turns
you'll buy a nasty packet.'

And it was even so. Mohune swung around to the left,
his left arm moving like a flail, his left forearm struck
the gun away, causing the German to be swung off his
balance; at the same moment Mohune's right fist followed the direction of his body and a bunch of knuckles
like a granite knob landed under the German's jaw with
all the weight of Peter's powerful body behind it.

The Nazi slumped to the floor and, like a cat, Mohune sprang upon his back. The one thing which surprised him was that the pistol had not gone off. He
knew that in those circumstances it would have been
impossible for the German to shoot him, but he had
expected the Nazi to fire as the weapon was struck away.

"You're not very good at your job, brother," he
murmured; "you may be supreme at beating Jews, but
I'm beginning to believe that real strong arm stuff is a
little beyond you." He flicked out his handkerchief and,
having twirled it into a miniature rope, forced it into
the German's mouth. "Not one of you," he went on,
"would have lasted a day in Chicago in Capone's time.
To stick a gun in a man's back is foolish enough, but
to forget to ease off the safety catch is simply asking for
trouble. I hope you're not ticklish," he concluded, as he
deftly removed the German's belt and braces.

Five minutes later Peter rose to his feet and dusted

himself down; the Nazi lay neatly trussed and gagged at his feet.

"Pleasant dreams, brother, pleasant dreams."

Humming *Waltzing Matilda,* Mohune ran down the stairs and out to the waiting car. Without any hesitation he opened the door and climbed in. "He's staying behind," he announced to the driver; "he's found some papers. He 'phoned to the Barracks. We're to go on to the station."

"Which station?"

"Search me. He didn't say. All he said was that the Englishman would be making for Holland."

"Where he's making for makes little difference; what makes the difference is what station is in working order; they've all been bombed by these blasted English and it's the devil's own job to know where trains will be running from. If you want to go to the North you generally find that the trains go from the station which usually takes you to the South and even if you get a train it's no good to you. Do you know that it took a friend of mine twelve solid days to get to Cologne ..."

"Pretty bad in Munich, too ..."

"Hirsch, you can report me if you like, I'm fed up. We were supposed to be in London a year ago last September, and where are we? Just where we were before the war started. Our gallant Air Force ... I've got a brother, he told me that he reckons that we've lost six thousand planes. I'm sick of it, but mark you, Hirsch, if you do report me I'll say that it was you who tried to spread disaffection, not me."

"All right. Don't you worry."

The station which the driver had selected was like an

ant heap; soldiers and storm troopers hurried in all directions. Trucks stacked high with baggage clattered to and fro. Orders and counter orders were shouted into the darkness, the harsh sibilant of escaping steam filled the air.

Mohune and the driver left the car and thrust their way through the crowded booking hall and on to a platform where a train so full of troops that it appeared to be overflowing was obviously awaiting the signal for departure.

"That's the train he'll catch, if he can," commented the driver, shouting to make himself heard. "They are few and far between and if he misses that one he'll be here for the night—yes, that's the one he will try to catch."

"He certainly will," agreed Mohune.

"Look," put in the driver again, "there's Pegler himself. He's obviously come down to direct operations. I'd better go and report to him." He moved away and casually Mohune watched him approaching a uniformed figure who was standing under the only arc light.

The man turned and Peter's eyes narrowed. So that was Pegler. Peter shook his head; the soubriquet of Vulture suited him better. The Grand Inquisitor. Then turning on his heel, Mohune allowed himself to be caught up in the swirling stream of humanity, until, when he was safely away from the man he wished to avoid, in the same manner as a twig floating in a stream becomes detached from the main current, Peter slipped behind a stationary truck piled high with officers' baggage.

Passers-by regarded the figure of the Storm Trooper

incuriously as he stopped to study the various labels
while he thought out his next move.

A sudden flood of memory swept Mohune back to
Victoria Station. How often had he seen similar piles of
valises waiting to be thrown to the van to accompany
their military owners to their destination. He picked
out a label and read it casually—"Hauptman Freidl
Brandt." He was about to turn the label over to discover more about this unknown Captain when a hand
clapped him on the shoulder.

"Come," said the voice of the driver of the car, "come
on, you won't find the Englishman hiding in a suitcase.
Pegler has held up the departure of the train for five
minutes. We are to make a search . . . come on."

Obediently Mohune followed the Nazi towards the
train where a party of the Schultzstaffel were gathered
about one of the doors. "Hurry," demanded a voice,
and a hand shoved at Mohune's shoulders. Peter pressed
forward eagerly, he knew that voice and the owner of
the hand and he had no wish to meet the Grand Inquisitor face to face. Along the corridors they went,
invading every compartment, disturbing everybody.
Officer or common soldier it made no difference, all had
to make way for the Schultzstaffel, but at last Mohune's
party who had entered the rear of the train, met a party
who had entered from the front.

"Well, he's not on that train," muttered a Trooper,
dropping out on to the platform, and Mohune, who was
now in a queue of Nazis waiting to disembark, grinned
happily.

"I'm not going to wait all night for these swagbellies

to get out," he muttered to the man behind him; "I'm going to look for another exit."

Holding himself in he squeezed past the man he had just spoken to and strode off down the corridor. At any moment now the train would be off and Mohune had every intention of being one of its passengers. With this end in view he turned the handle of a lavatory door and slipped inside and bolted the door behind him.

Pulling out his cigarette case he selected a Player and flicked his lighter into action. His fingers were without tremor and his eyes as he watched the smoke drifting out of the window, held a carefree smile of contentment.

Outside on the platform a whistle blew, the train shuddered and moved forward.

CHAPTER SEVEN

IN WHICH HE TRAVELS BY TRAIN

THE train roared onward into the night, bearing men to the invasion ports, a serving hatch to the dining room of the god of war, carrying men to face destruction, death or mutilation in an endeavor to safeguard a system which they themselves had come to realize was corrupt and bestial.

Leaving the sanctuary of the lavatory, Mohune made his way along the swaying corridor. At first it had seemed to him that the way of escape lay open before him and all that he had to do was to wait until the train reached its ultimate destination, and then chance his luck to get out of the country. But ten minutes' reflection had sufficed to show the dangers and pitfalls of this plan. Sooner or later the Nazi in Freemantle's room would either escape or be discovered and then the driver of the car which had taken him to the station would tell his story. Telegraph keys would tap furiously and a select committee of reception would await him at a station somewhere along the line. It was therefore essential that Mohune should leave the train at the earliest possible moment.

A railway official turned sideways to pass him but Peter stretched out a detaining hand.

"Where is the first stop?"

"Arnhalt by rights, but in these days we stop at every

known place and most of the unknown. The train should split at Arnhalt; we've been told that owing to the bad weather the English bombers have not been over recently and that the track is repaired. They hope to get six troop trains through before morning."

The man proceeded on his way. In an hour and a half his characterization of a member of the Schultzstaffel must end. Mohune leant on the window rail and stared out into the night. Long glistening fingers of rain were streaking diagonally across the glass, but neither their parallel lines nor the rhythmic beat of the wheels over the shining metals beneath him brought Peter any solution. His mind became a blank and only the noises of the train held any significance.

Rat-at-tat-tat ... ratat-tat-tat went the wheels, impinging their monotonous beat upon Mohune's brain until subconsciously he began to fit words to the rhythm. One, two, three, four ... knock at the door ... one, two, three, four, knock at the door ... rat-at-tat-tat ... rata-tattat ... rat-atat Freidl Brandt ... ratattatat Freidl Brandt ... Freidl Brandt ... Freidal Brandt ... Freidl Brandt ... Hauptman Brandt ... rat-at-tat Freidl Brandt ... FREIDL BRANDT.

Impatiently Mohune pushed himself away from the rail with the words Freidl Brandt singing in his ears. At least he knew the name of someone on the train. Freidl Brandt whose luggage he had inspected on the Station.

If Freidl Brandt was on the train there was an avenue of escape to be explored. Peter thrust open the door of the compartment opposite.

"Is Hauptman Brandt here?" he demanded.

Eight Officers looked up at him. "Never heard of him," said one. Mohune backed out and moved on to the next compartment and as soon as he had closed the door conversation broke out.

"Saw a bunch of those swine get on the train before it left," announced the one who had disclaimed knowledge of Freidl Brandt, "but I thought they had all got off before we pulled out."

"Oberst-leutnant, it is never wise to refer to members of the Schultzstaffel as swine, whatever your private opinions may be."

"But Herr Major, we are going to England. We shall be free of them there."

"Do not delude yourself, my young friend. Even in England men will be spied upon and those who are thought to be enemies of the Reich . . . well, they are apt to disappear. You have an example to hand, you surely do not imagine that that man who has just left us was looking for this Brandt to ask him about his taste in beer. No, Hauptman has trouble spelt with the largest size in capital letters awaiting him. As for you, you have been indiscreet. It is my duty to report you. I will consider the matter . . ."

Mohune continued his search. Compartment after compartment was entered without success and all the while the wheels maintained their incessant chant of Freidl Brandt . . . rat-at-tatat . . . Freidl Brandt.

At last only one coach remained unexplored and Peter was beginning to believe that his time had been wasted and that he would have to think of some other way of liquidating his impersonation of a member of the Schultzstaffel. He crossed the swinging gangway

which led to the last coach and pushed open the door
of the first compartment. The narrow space was crowded
with officers. Four of them immediately inside the door
were playing cards on an open edition of the *Volkischer
Beobachter*, two others lay asleep against the cushions,
and another glared at the intruder angrily.

"Shut that damned door" he demanded, "there's
enough damned draught in this damned train without . . ." He broke off suddenly, staring foolishly as he
realized who it was that stood in the narrow doorway.

"Is Hauptman Brandt here?" demanded Mohune,
and a man in the corner seat replied, "That is my
name."

Peter's heart leapt. "Come with me," he ordered, and
backed out into the corridor where he was joined a
minute later by the Captain.

"You call yourself Freidl Brandt," began Mohune in
a harsh voice, looking the Hauptman up and down. The
two men were of equal height and there was little apparent difference in their ages. Brandt was tall and
carried himself well, had a well-formed jaw and his
eyes, before one of which was a monocle, met Mohune's
proudly.

"I have told you that that is my name."

During his journey along the length of the train
Mohune had noticed that in one of the luggage vans
there was an empty space between high walls of baggage
and to this retreat he led his captive.

"You say that you are Hauptman Freidl Brandt?
Have you any means of proving that?"

"I have my papers."

"Hand them over."

"Why should I?"

"I cannot advise you to take that tone with me, Herr Hauptman. Your papers."

For a second the German tried to stare Mohune out of countenance, then with an impatient movement he pulled open the buttons of his great coat and, having delved into an inside pocket, produced a wallet which he thrust into Mohune's hand.

"There you are. You will find they are all in order. I shall of course report this matter to my Commanding Officer and demand an apology from you."

"That attitude is useless. It is of no use bluffing or trying to bluff me . . ."

"I am leaving the train at Arnhalt . . ."

"You most certainly are. We return to Berlin together."

Brandt's jaw dropped. "But I tell you . . ."

"You can keep your explanations for Herr Pegler . . ."

"Pegler? Gestapo? But . . . but . . . but what am I accused of?"

"I am not here to answer your questions, but I want answers to mine. You say that you are Freidl Brandt?"

"I have told you twice that that is my name . . ."

"Your regiment?"

"17 Bavarian."

"You say that you are leaving the train at Arnhalt. Why?"

"I join a train for Kaiserlautern there."

"You are returning from leave?"

"You are trying to put words into my mouth. I have been on a Course, a special duties Course. I am joining this regiment for the first time."

"The name of your Commanding Officer?"

"I do not know. I tell you that I am joining this regiment for the first time."

"Is there anyone on this train who can verify your statements?"

"There is not. I know nobody in this regiment."

"But there must be others who are going to Kaiser-lautern?"

"Maybe, but I tell you that I have been on a Course. Selected officers have been posted to various regiments which are taking part in the forthcoming invasion. One officer to each of a group of regiments."

"Yours is not a very convincing story, Herr Haupt-man. You do not know the name of your Commanding Officer and you can produce no one to verify your story."

"I have told you that I am leaving the train at Arn-halt and that until this morning I had no idea that I was to go to the 17 Bavarians. I had never heard of the regiment before then."

"A Jew would have thought of a better lie than that. Anyhow your game is up..."

"Game? What game? What have I done? What am I accused of?"

"Herr Pegler will no doubt be only too pleased to answer your questions if you ask him nicely. Now get over into that corner and keep quiet."

Mohune turned his back on the bewildered officer and allowed his face to relax into a smile. So far so good, better even than he had dared to hope. An irate Commanding Officer standing up for his fledgling would have been a difficult complication, but this Brandt alone and unknown was just the necessary piece required for the next move in the game, although on that next move Mohune had not yet decided. Fate seemed to be playing a strong hand and for the moment he was quite prepared to leave the lead to her.

At last the chattering wheels changed their note, the troop train was approaching Arnhalt. Mohune turned to the German.

"Come."

The coaches shuddered as they came to a halt and then as Peter opened the door and forced Brandt out on to the station, the massive engine which had drawn them from Berlin let out a powerful gust of steam as though it was breathing a sigh of relief at having successfully completed the first stage of its journey. In silence the two men walked to the shelter of a wall and Mohune noticed that Brandt's head was still proudly erect and that his shoulders were squared to meet the world.

"My baggage?"

"You said that you were getting out here. No doubt it will be removed for you."

"But my personal kit in my compartment?"

Mohune shrugged his shoulders. "I have no time to worry about that," he snapped, "and anyhow I don't expect that you'll need any of your baggage again."

A porter emerged from the wall of darkness.

"The next train back to Berlin?" demanded Peter arrogantly.

"In two hours, if we are lucky, mein Herr."

"What is that on the far platform?"

"An empty . . . should be leaving for Berlin in the

morning, but what with the bombers and the state of
the track, you never can tell. Maybe it won't be until
to-morrow night, maybe it won't go at all. It's a sickening life being on the railways in wartime. Poor food,
bad pay—it's a dog life, that's what it is, a dog's life.
It's all very well for you soldiers going to England,
you're pampered, but our clothes don't even keep the
cold out. It's a dog's life."

The porter disappeared and in the safety of the darkness Mohune grinned; another lucky break, he had
been taken for a soldier, so much was obvious. No one
would have dared to express sentiments of that nature
to a member of the Schultzstaffel. His thoughts turned
to the empty train on the far side of the station and
another idea was born. Once again Fate was weaving her
threads into the lattice work of life.

"Losing your grip, are you not?" suggested Brandt
with a sneer, "I thought that the Schultzstaffel sent men
to the concentration camps for expressing doubts as to
the quality of their clothes, or is it that there is a spark
of humanity in some of you. Ah well, so we have to wait
two hours for our train."

"When is the train for Kaiserlautern due here?"

"In an hour, I was told."

"Perhaps we won't bother about the train for Berlin.
March."

Mohune hurried the German across the rails to the
empty train. "Where are we going?" demanded Brandt,
but Peter made no reply, and the hint that he might
never need his baggage again flashed through the
Hauptman's mind. "What are you going to do? I demand to know. What are you going to do with me? You

are not going to ..." The man's voice rose to a higher pitch; his control was slipping.

"Yes, that's it," he went on. "I see it all now. You're going to shoot me. Shoot me in cold blood. That's what you do, isn't it? I've heard of officers disappearing and being found dead months afterwards. But why me? I've done nothing. Take me back, take me back to Berlin. Take me before the Gestapo if you must, but give me a chance ... don't shoot me out of hand ... it's ... it's criminal ... it's insane. For God's sake say something ... listen to me ... listen to me ..." He clutched at Mohune's arm imploringly, but was shaken off

"Don't kill me now. Give me a chance to explain. Let me go to my regiment. I'll get myself killed there. I will, I swear it. My God, think of my father, the disgrace ... it will kill him too. Let me go to my regiment. You can't deny me that ... I'll get killed ... Oh God, and I said that you had a spark of humanity in you ..." Brandt laughed harshly.

"Shut up." With a jerk Mohune pulled open a carriage door. "Get in." His hand snapped down to his pistol butt. "Get in, I said." They entered a compartment and Peter, having seen that the blinds were drawn, snapped on the lights and Brandt, calmer now, turned to face him. With an effort the German squared his shoulders.

"Well," he said quietly, "get your dirty work over. I feel ashamed that I should have pleaded with you. To think that I, Brandt, pleaded with scum like you for his life. Everything I said I take back. Do you hear? Everything. I am now glad to die, more pleased to die at your hands than I would be while fighting the British, for death found during the invasion would serve no useful purpose. The British are not the enemies of my country. Did you hear me say—my country? I say it again. My country. Scum like you have no country. The British are fighting for the same thing that every decent man in Germany would like to fight for—the overthrow of your regime. Of spying, robbery, torture, all the filthiness that you have built up in a stinking wall about our beloved Fuehrer. To die like this is to die for a cause, for an ideal, and every body of a murdered man that is found binds true Germans closer together. That is why I am ashamed I pleaded with you." Brandt's chin jutted defiantly. "I am ready."

"Your trouble is you talk too much. Get undressed."

"What . . . ?"

"Get undressed or I"ll smack you across the eyes with my gun, ideals or no ideals."

"I don't understand . . ." began the other fumbling at the buttons of his greatcoat.

"I said you talked too much. Hurry."

Two minutes later Brandt was stripped to his short clothes. "Now lie down on the seat."

"I won't . . ."

Mohune's open hand shot out in a cutting motion, the teak hard edge of his palm caught Brandt under the angle of his jaw and the German slumped on to the seat.

"A little trick taught me by Lieutenant Okuda of the Japanese Navy," murmured Mohune in English, "and if he tells me true, which I must say he always has done in the past, you'll sleep for at least five minutes."

A train whistle from the other side of the station de-

noted that the train which had brought them from
Berlin was proceeding on its way. Without any semblance of hurry Peter set about the task of pinioning
Freidl Brandt; wrists were tied together tightly with
Mohune's braces, Kummer's military belt served to strap
the officer's ankles and then those ankles were forced
over to meet the middle of the Hauptman's back and
a handkerchief was used to lash them to the tethered
wrists. Gently Mohune forced his thumbs into Brandt's
cheeks, forcing the mouth open, and another handkerchief was inserted between the white teeth and knotted
at the back of the head. Then Peter stepped back and
reviewed his handiwork and quickly began to change
into the German's uniform, and as he screwed the monocle into his eye, Brandt opened his eyes.

"Sorry, youngster," smiled Mohune, busily employed
in removing the tobacco from a cigarette, "but you see
I am not a member of your friends the Schultzstaffel.
I'm just a humble English Squadron Leader attempting
to make good my escape." The body on the seat writhed
impotently, and shaking the remaining shreds of tobacco
from the paper, Peter thrust it into his mouth. Then in
amazement Brandt watched Mohune bite a thumb until
he fetched blood, then having removed the chewed
paper from his mouth, he kneaded it against the wound
until it was faintly pink.

"Unfortunately," went on the Englishman, "I have a
slight blemish to an otherwise perfect appearance. Some
years ago I had a fight with one of your countrymen
who seemed anxious to let the light of sense into my
mind by a hole drilled in my body with a sword. Actually he only succeeded in drilling a hole in my ear.

That hole, as you may have noticed, has never completely closed again. Nevertheless it is a well-known hole ..." Mohune forced some of the paper into the aperture in question and stood up to survey the result in the glass above the seat on which Brandt was lying.

"Not so bad," he went on, "I think you will agree that you would have to look twice before you realized that there was a hole there now. Now to continue ..." Mohune lifted Kummer's greatcoat from the floor and spread it over Brandt's body; "you'll be cold, probably damned cold," he continued, "Before anyone finds you, and you may be hungry, but you will appreciate that there is little that I can do about it. I think you will agree that were our positions reversed, you would do the same as I have done, although I must admit that I sincerely hope that you won't be discovered for some little time as my life has been somewhat lurid during the past forty-eight hours and I don't want to be forced to adopt another disguise until I have had something to eat. And now one word of advice. Don't try to make a noise by rolling off that seat, because I don't expect anyone will hear you and if you do you might easily break an arm or leg. *Auf wiedersehen.*"

Flicking off the lights, Mohune passed out into the corridor, pulled the door to behind him and climbed down into the night.

Quickly he crossed the lines again, as far as he could tell his actions had been unobserved, but as he approached the crowd about the main Waiting Room, he halted and caught his breath as the sound of running feet came to his ears.

"The train from Berlin?" demanded an angry voice

from a party of men who were surrounding a bewildered porter, "when is it due to arrive?"

"Arrive, mein Herr? It's been and gone."

"Then why the thunder wasn't it stopped? You received an order from Berlin to stop it."

"I, mein Herr? I have received no order. I am only a porter ..."

"The Station Master. Where is the fool? We will teach him to disregard our orders. Where is the Station Master?"

"I am here, Excellence ..."

"Where have you been hiding, you dog? Why was the train from Berlin not stopped? How comes it that the orders were disobeyed?"

"I had no orders. Our communications are very bad now and even if I had received such an order I doubt that I could have put it into execution. It was a troop train and couldn't be delayed. Besides, there are other trains following it."

"Would you argue with me? Did a member of the Schultzstaffel get off the train?"

"I saw no one, Excellence ..."

"There were but two who got off that train ..." put in the porter. "One was an officer, his baggage is here on the platform."

"Baggage. Fool. The man we want carries no baggage. He is an enemy of the Reich who is escaping. Where does that train make its next stop?"

"Who can tell?" the Station Master shrugged his shoulders expressively. "It should go to Hanover without a stop, but in these days ..."

"Hanover. *Gross Gott*. We shall be driving for the rest

of the night and on into the morning. Station Master, should we hear that that message reached you, and that you failed to carry out its instructions, you will be lucky to escape a concentration camp."

The party of Storm Troopers hurried away and at that moment a train fussed its way into the station. A swarm of figures which included Mohune clambered aboard. It was too early to be the train for Kaiserlautern, but any train traveling west suited his purpose. He walked along the ill-lit corridor and found an empty compartment, but he was not allowed any privacy that night, for as the train moved away from Arnhalt, the door opened again and three young officers, all talking at once, crowded in upon him.

"What a jest. What a side-splitting jest . . ." laughed one.

"Tell us about it. Don't keep it to yourself," demanded another, and the first speaker continued.

"Well, you saw me talking to the driver of that car. At first I thought it was Liselotee come to see me off, but he was Gestapo. Oh God, what a jest . . ."

"If you don't stop cackling to yourself I'll murder you . . ."

"All right. All right. Give me a chance to get my breath," pleaded the other, and having glanced at Mohune who was sitting in a corner with his hat pulled down over his eyes, he continued: "It appears that an English pilot was shot down yesterday, captured and taken to Berlin for interrogation by the Gestapo."

"By the Gestapo?" put in the third member of the party incredulously, "why that's a job for Army Intelligence."

"I know that, but they took him just the same. Apparently he had some secret plans in his possession or something, and evidently this warrior not only escaped when he was on the way to the Schultzstaffel Barracks, but he killed a fellow called Kummer."

"Hans Kummer. I've heard of that swine. He was once of Killinger's killers in Austria. A giant of a man. The rubber truncheon king of the Barracks . . . strong as an ox . . ."

"Well, this Englishman killed him with his bare hands."

"I should have put on gloves before I touched a man like that."

"Don't try to be funny, Fritz . . . it doesn't pay nowadays."

CHAPTER EIGHT

IN WHICH HE REACHES PARIS

MOHUNE dozed in his corner, the wide peak of his cap
pulled well down to conceal his face. The train clattered
on through the unresisting night, and to Peter sheltering behind the German headgear with the world cut off
from him, it might have been an English train in which
he was riding. After the express had been travelling for
nearly a quarter of an hour, the door of the compartment opened and a man whose heavy breathing announced that he was not in the prime of condition,
forced his way in among the junior officers. The lower
part of an army greatcoat passed before the narrow
limits of Mohune's vision, but he made no movement
and the newcomer stepping over the Englishman's outstretched legs, sank into a seat at the far corner of the
compartment, and it was immediately obvious from the
hush which settled on the company that the man was of
high rank. The prattle ceased as though a tap had been
turned off, and then as though a chill had fallen upon
them the youngsters rose and left to find more congenial
accommodation elsewhere. Peter remained motionless.

It was not very long before a rumble of sound announced that the late arrival had fallen asleep, and
then it was that Peter turned slightly and surveyed his
travelling companion. A close-cropped head showed
plainly through a bristle-like growth, a heavily-lipped

mouth gaped foolishly in sleep and a uniform stretched tight across a protuberant stomach proclaimed its owner to be a General. Mohune smiled happily and settling his broad shoulders into a more comfortable position went to sleep.

It was daylight when Peter awoke, a cold dismal morning with gray clouds lying as a billowing blanket across the upstretched fingers of the trees. The coldness had entered his compartment and the Englishman was stiff and uncomfortable. He eased his long legs, flexed his arms and then settled back with his cap down over his nose again to await the awakening of his opposite number, who snored belligerently in his corner.

The train was traveling very fast now as though the daylight urged that Paris must be reached without delay, the wheels rattled and the carriages rocked, and as they swept around a wide bend the General's hat dropped from the rack and smote its owner sharply on the bridge of his prominent nose. The sleeper grunted and awoke and having glared angrily at Mohune, turned his attention to his haversack from which he produced a large sausage and some hunks of bread. Mohune decided it was high time for him to wake up, at least a portion of that sausage must find its way to his side of the carriage.

His resuscitation was a skilled piece of acting. His cap slipped forward and dropped into his lap, his eyes opened owlishly and he stared blankly round the compartment; suddenly it seemed that the scene before him had been conveyed to his bemused brain, he scrambled to his feet, clicked his heels and bowed stiffly.

"Hauptman Brandt," he announced, "17th Bavarian.

I ... I ... er—I had no idea that you were in this compartment, Herr General. When I went to sleep there were youngsters here ... I hope my presence has not inconvenienced you, sir."

"I should have kicked you if it had." The General waved a large red hand. "Be seated. You have slept very soundly. Where are you making for? Paris?"

"Walls have ears, Herr General."

"We are safe enough here. Paris?"

"And beyond," Mohune added an unspoken "I hope."

"Channel Ports?"

"Yes."

"Lucky man, so am I. Boulogne. The big show you know ... the day we've all waited for."

"I'm for Le Havre. Intelligence."

"Intelligence in the Bavarians. That's good, very good." The General laughed loudly. "What use will you be in England? Eh? tell me that?"

"I've only just left there, sir."

"What's that? What do you mean?"

"I was in that country of pipe-smoking nitwits when the war broke out. I only managed to reach Germany a month ago."

"How did you manage it?"

"It's a long story. By way of Ireland and South America."

"You know England well?"

"Very well."

"The part called Sussex?"

"Intimately."

"The town of Chichester?"

"Very well indeed."

"That's to be my Headquarters for the first week. Not that I shall have any of the amenities of a Headquarters that I expect. No food except stuff brought from here, and that bad enough. Our commissariat is hopeless these days. I've just come back from Russia. Scorched earth; frozen earth I call it. Bad food, no wine, no women, and now we are going to a starving country. Before long I shall be thin enough to dance in the ballet." The General gave vent to another burst of laughter.

"You'll get all the food you want there, sir."

"They're starving ..."

"Don't you believe it."

"It has been officially announced, and for an officer to contradict an official announcement is an offence against the State."

"I am aware of that, Herr General, but the fact remains that I was in that country a short while ago and I know they're not starving. If our men think they are going to be up against a half-fed rabble, they're going to get the shock of their lives."

"Poof. Their army!" The General threw back his head and this time Mohune thought that the raucous laughter would never cease, the very carriage seemed to shake with its reverberations. "Army," he gasped, when the paroxysm had died down. "Look at it at Dunkirk. The flower of the British army unarmed and untrained rabble, and the Home Guard, old men too old to work who are going to face the cream of our Panzer Divisions. It'll be a picnic, that's what it will be, a picnic."

"I hope I'm there to see your picnic," smiled Mohune, "I like that kind of picnic."

"You do, eh? Got an eye on my sausage, I suppose. Here, help yourself. You're a droll dog, Brandt, and I like droll dogs, even though I suspect this sausage was made out of one."

Too easy. Mohune sliced a generous chunk from the proffered food and munched in silence.

"So you know Chichester, eh?" continued the General, "you'd be useful to me, but there you are, postings can always be depended upon to put the right man in the wrong place. Le Havre . . . that means Hampshire, and I'll wager you know nothing of Hampshire. I'd like to have you on my Staff, Brandt. As I say, you'd be useful to me. I'll arrange a transfer when we get to Paris . . ."

"But I must go on to Le Havre . . ."

"And I say that you'll stay in Paris and that's an order . . ."

"But my Commanding Officer . . ."

"To the devil with him. Your Corps Commander of invasion troops will be there. The Fuehrer himself is to address us. I expect that you know many private houses near Chichester where they still have cellars full of wine?"

"Most assuredly, though I have done my best to lower their stock."

"Excellent. I think that I shall like my picnic."

"When is the move to commence, sir?"

"The Fuehrer will announce that to-morrow. It depends on two things. The stars and the Luftwaffe. They have had a hammering lately. Take some more sausage."

Mohune accepted the offer gratefully. The strain of events in Berlin was beginning to tell even upon his constitution, and the lack of food was beginning to make itself unpleasantly evident.

"When we get to Paris we will go direct to General Headquarters and put a call through . . . that is if the lines are going. Between you and me, Brandt, this Air Force of theirs is playing havoc with our communications. You will stay at my hotel . . . you will at least be sure of a meal there. If I get a chance I will introduce you to the Fuehrer himself. He will be interested in your story. By to-morrow evening you will be on my Staff and furthermore we will attend that conference together. It'll be a big show, all the Leaders will be there . . ."

"What a chance for the bomber boys," thought Mohune, "all in Paris and we won't be there to bomb them."

"You're silent," continued the General, "your amazing good fortune stuns you and well it may. It is not often a junior officer gets such a chance. You'll find that I am easy to work with provided that you do your work. Work hard and play hard, that's my motto, and I've no time for anyone who can't do both. With your knowledge of Chichester we should have plenty of amusement. I'll sweep their defences away in twenty-four hours and then we'll have a few days while the armies consolidate. You'll know plenty of pretty girls I'll be bound, eh, you dog? Not that I like English girls, mark you. Too stiff, too thin, too cold, too damned bored, but we'll soften them and maybe fatten them, you and I." The General leaned forward and smote Peter on the knee. "Brandt," he announced, "I'm looking forward to this."

Mohune returned the leer with a knowing smile and changed the conversation.

"They don't seem to have done much damage to this line with their bombs," he suggested.

"Much damage? Not here. Maybe it's too near Paris. They still think that the French are on their side, but way back they've blasted it to hell and the Luftwaffe has done nothing to stop them, despite Goering's boastings that not a single English bomber would cross German territory. Every time a new track has been laid it has been blown higher than the Eiffel Tower. That hasn't appeared in the press of course, but it's happened right enough, but to-day the track is clear, for to-morrow the Fuehrer travels to Paris; thousands, literally thousands of Poles and Czechs have been drafted to this railway during the past week. The Fuehrer's train must not be delayed. If there's a raid to-night someone will lose his job and quite probably his head."

The General ranted on. He was a garrulous old man very full of his own importance. He had been in one of the recent raids on Cologne and hadn't liked it a bit. The British had used some of their new bombs and he felt sore, mentally and physically. He was furious with the Royal Air Force and even more furious with the Luftwaffe for allowing it.

Paris was drawing rapidly nearer. Many subjects had been discussed, the campaigns of Poland, France, Greece and Russia, the mad fighting of the Australians, the stubborn resistance of the English Guards, the stamina of the British, the bombing of London, which the General was inclined to think had been over-exaggerated, for he reasoned he had seen the effect on the morale of the Berliners, and what happened to them must have happened to any other people; and then back to the coming invasions.

It appeared that the General was to be met at the station by a Senior Intelligence Officer who was flying from Berlin, a man whose name the General had temporarily forgotten, but a man who despite his comparatively low rank was a master of his job and who would be of great assistance in effecting Mohune's transfer to the General's Staff.

The train rumbled into Paris and Mohune, so used to the din and clatter of a French terminus, was amazed at the change. The large station was quiet, strangely quiet. German uniforms were in the preponderance, but the noisy throng of porters was hushed. The General rose to his feet and struggled into his greatcoat and then stood waiting for the train to stop. No sooner had the engine breathed its final snort of satisfaction than the German flung open the door and stepped out, calling to Mohune to follow and to bring his, the General's, haversack with him.

Mohune moved forward, but the haversack hanging freely in his hand became entangled in the doorknob so that it was a full half-minute before he left the train, and by then the General was already some way ahead striding along and brushing all and sundry aside in his passage towards the barrier. As Mohune hurried after his traveling companion he saw an officer step forward and salute. His gaze focused sharply; there was something familiar, unpleasantly familiar, about the set of that particular officer's shoulders. Without undue hurry, Peter moved behind a pillar as though sheltering from the wind while he lit a cigarette, and from the other side of his hiding place he looked again. How fortunate that the haversack had caused that slight delay. There was no shadow of doubt that the officer who was at the moment staring along the platform was his old friend von Rinck.

"Not so good," murmured Mohune, "not at all so good." He drew heavily at his cigarette and sent twin plumes of smoke downwards through his nostrils. "It would appear that after all I am not cast as Procurator Mark One for His Excellency's little play in Chichester." He glanced around, seeking another exit, but barriers and impenetrable walls of sandbags faced him on three sides, and to make matters worse the General and von Rinck were striding towards him along the platform.

Ring-a-ring of roses around the pillar apart from drawing attention to himself could only end in ultimate capture, and Mohune with a chill feeling creeping down his spine visualized the Gestapo Barracks. How pleased they would be to see him again. How their palms would itch to flay him with those pliable steel rods, how amused they would be at his fruitless endeavors to squirm away from their blows, and how satisfied they would be when with his kidneys crushed he lay before them dead, a mangled shapeless mass at their feet; a dismal prospect but one which seemed to be inevitable unless an avenue of escape presented itself within the next few seconds. He shrugged his shoulders and decided that he would have to try and bluff his way out. Another shrug. Bluff von Rinck . . . that was the height of impossibility.

Mohune took half a step backwards and a truck piled

high with luggage smote him sharply on the shoulder. The small aged Frenchman pushing it swore vehemently as only small and aged Frenchmen can, and then realizing he was swearing at a German officer, was struck dumb and almost as vehemently began to apologize, but Mohune with a casual gesture waved him off. The truck proceeded on its way, forming a screen between Peter and the two Germans who were searching for him, and parallel with the truck walked Peter St. Maur Beverley de L'Epee Mohune. It was a slender chance, for if either the General or von Rinck should look back Peter was bound to be discovered, but he walked nonchalantly forward as though he had not a care in the world and as though time was his servant.

He reached the barrier undiscovered. A military policeman saluted and gave him passage, and then he heard the one thing he had dreaded, the General's voice calling "Brandt" behind him. Even then Mohune barely increased his speed, for he was working on the assumption that the General would be too dignified to run and that von Rinck, whose suspicions should not have been aroused, would be thinking that this Hauptman Brandt who the General thought so much of would be sure to wait for his benefactor in the entrance to the station, but when a line of waiting cars came into view he broke into a sprint and leapt for the nearest car, a long gray tourer. With a lithe spring he vaulted into the seat beside the astonished driver. "Follow that car," he demanded pointing impartially at the moving vehicles ahead.

"I'm Colonel Zimmerman's driver," began the soldier in protest.

"I don't care who the hell you are," snapped Mohune, "there is an English agent in that car and if you let him get away you'll pay for it with your life."

"The car shot forward almost before the sentence was completed. "Which car, Herr Hauptman?"

Mohune selected one a long way ahead and the tourer leapt forward in pursuit.

"Full tank?"

"Yes, Herr Hauptman."

"Excellent. It may be a long chase, I fancy. He has friends some way out along the Boulogne road. I don't want to catch him or let him know that he's being followed too soon. After that it will be too late. Understand?"

"I understand, Herr Hauptman."

"I hope you do," thought Mohune, "because I'm damned if I do."

The pursuit continued with Mohune's car maintaining a discreet distance. At first it was a straight chase and then the car ahead began to twist and turn, doubling down side turnings and taking corners when it seemed that the driver had decided to pass them.

"He has guessed that we're after him," suggested the driver.

"So it would appear," agreed Mohune, and smiled into the upturned collar of his greatcoat. What a jest! No doubt some harmless person in the car ahead had formed the opinion that some undesirable agency, probably the Gestapo, was after him.

"Keep your eyes open, man," shouted Mohune suddenly, "he's turned left."

"Right, sir."

"Left, you thrice damned fool. That wasn't our car. Ours turned left, I tell you."

"But Herr Hauptman ..."

"Keep your ugly mouth shut and turn left when you reach the turning."

In sullen silence the man obeyed. They swung to the left and found themselves in a road which bore sharply to the left a hundred yards ahead. The engine roared and the car accelerated again. They sped on, mile following mile, but with never a sight of the car that they were supposed to be chasing and which Peter knew perfectly well had turned right even as the driver had said.

"All right. Pull up, you fool," demanded Mohune at last, "you've lost him. Of all the idiots I could have chosen. My God, you'll pay for this. I'll see that Himmler himself hears about your stupidity. I believe that you were in league with him. That would account for your unwillingness to start the chase ..."

"No, no, Herr Hauptman. I didn't ..."

"Shut your mouth and make for the Boulogne road. We may be lucky, and if I were you I'd pray that we are."

The man was frightened, too frightened to protest. Too well he knew what a report to the Gestapo might imply. The car was turned and in silence they headed for the coastal road and in less than twenty minutes they had reached the open country. The driver was getting more nervous with every mile they left behind them and no car presented itself as a hare. From time to time he cast startled glances at the uncompromising contour of Mohune's upturned collar.

"All right, stop here, it's no use going any further. We'll wait here for an hour. Get out and stretch your legs."

The car was pulled into the side of the road and both men got out. Then: "Driver, come here. I don't like the look of this tire. It won't take us much further."

Obediently, the soldier walked round the back of the car.

"Looks all right to me, sir," he announced.

"I said you were a fool, are you blind as well? Look."

Mohune pointed to an imaginary blemish on the lower half of the wheel. Suspecting nothing, the German bent forward and the edge of Mohune's palm chopped down at the exposed neck.

"Yet another point to Lieutenant Okuda," murmured Peter, and stooping, lifted the man easily and dropped him into a ditch.

"You'll have a very stiff neck when you wake up, comrade, but perhaps you will remember that I might have killed you."

A minute later Mohune was at the wheel of the tourer and Dieppe and not Boulogne was his objective.

CHAPTER NINE

IN WHICH HE REACHES AN INVASION PORT

So far so good, but driving a stolen car through a country under martial law presents difficulties which are hard to surmount. Mohune knew only too well that it could not be more than a few hours before the hounds would be hot on his trail. Indeed, he was pleasantly surprised Freidl Brandt had not been discovered before he reached Paris, but when the driver of the tourer who now lay in the ditch on the Boulogne road was discovered, the roads would seethe with Storm Troopers and Gestapo agents on the lookout for the escaping Englishman.

It was late afternoon and already long shadows were being thrown across the fields on either side of the road which stretched out ahead in an unbroken and dusty ribbon.

Anxious as he was to reach Dieppe, Mohune had no desire to arrive at that small port in daylight or in a stolen car and yet there seemed to be no alternative, for Dieppe was only fifty miles away, but he decided it would be madness to proceed any further in that gray tourer, for even if the driver had not already been discovered, the owner, Colonel Zimmerman, would be raising the wind and no doubt von Rinck would be putting two and two together, so when one of the very infrequent side turnings presented itself, Mohune turned down it, pulled in under some trees and waited for darkness to catch up with him.

When at last the time came for him to continue his journey, Mohune's plan of action was already formulated. He would travel this road for another thirty miles and then the car which had served him so well would have to be abandoned in the most lonely spot that presented itself at the time and then he would walk through the night to Dieppe. But it all depended on that thirty miles. Mohune put his foot down and the car shot forward.

For all he saw, Peter might have been alone in France. Twenty miles had been thrown behind; in another fifteen minutes he would have to seek a hiding-place for his millstone.

The road bore to the right, brakes screeched; ahead, dead ahead, was a barrier. The road was completely closed. There was no possibility of turning, no chance of retreat. The fields presented the only avenue of escape. With a little movement, Mohune left the driving seat.

"Halt, who goes there?"

"Friend."

A light, a bright dazzling light, smote through Peter's eyes into his brain and behind it he heard footsteps approaching.

"Your papers."

"Who are you?"

"Gestapo. Your papers."

"I'm . . ."

"I don't care who the hell you are. Your papers."

"I'm on urgent duty, you're delaying me."

"You are delaying yourself. Your papers."

Mohune handed over Brandt's wallet. . . . "You'll find them in that."

The light was lowered and for once Mohune's temper boiled over.

"It's insufferable," he declared.

"What's insufferable?"

"The airs and graces you thugs give yourselves. Here am I on urgent duty hampered and hindered at every twist and turn by ignorant, stuck-up, swollen-headed little perverts.

"Careful, Herr Hauptman."

"Careful, be blistered."

"Quiet. Heil Hitler."

"Hail the seat of your pants."

"You are now under arrest."

"Try and arrest me. Just try it."

The Nazi felt for his pistol.

"I'm sorry, I spoke without thinking. I've had a trying day."

"Your troubles are only just starting. You stiffnecked soldiers are all the same. You rant and swagger and think you own the earth. You think that orders are for you to ride roughshod over. Orders which are issued to ensure the safety of the Third Reich. You, Hauptman Brandt, think that you can enter the fortified zone without showing your credentials, and to cap everything you insult the Fuehrer. You will be taken to Headquarters, where you will be dealt with as you deserve."

Mohune heaved a sigh of relief. It was only a routine challenge. The real Freidl Brandt was still undiscovered. Nonchalantly, he stooped to pick up the wallet which the Nazi had dropped when he had reached for his gun. The German's pistol followed his movement with the muzzle pointed at his chest, then the quiet tempo of the proceedings broke into double time. Mohune's left hand caught the German's wrist, his right slammed against the pistol, turning the barrel towards the face of its owner. There was a short pencil of orange flame, a bullet tore into the German's body, he stiffened, crumpled at the knees and fell forward, and Mohune, with the pistol now in his right hand, went forward to the barrier expecting to meet with further opposition and feeling perfectly ready to deal with it when it presented itself. But all was quiet and the barrier itself offered no greater obstacle than a farm cart drawn across the road between two large concrete blocks, and against one of these rested a motorcycle.

Thoughtfully, Peter returned to the dead Nazi, and carrying him to the car lowered the body into the front seat. Then slipping into the driving seat, he put the tourer into reverse and went back some fifty yards along the road.

"Now for it." The car shot forward at the solid ramparts of the barrier, there was a shattering crash and the shock of the impact stove in the radiator so that a cloud of steam mingled with the night air. Then Peter was out on the road again.

"Sorry, Fritz, but this has to be done." The small flame of a cigarette-lighter flickered in the night breeze and then steadied as it licked a disconnected joint. Mohune jumped away, sprinted through the barrier, leapt on the motorcycle and was away on the road to

Dieppe, while behind him flames from the blazing car shot skywards.

Dieppe. Mohune had chosen Dieppe on account of his knowledge of its environs. In happier days he had fenced there in the Annual Internationale against such masters of the sword as Buchard, Hostalier and the Comte Paul Oziol de Pignol, and even now as he hurried along that silent road he found it hard to realize that the days had not slipped back and that he was returning from a day in Paris to fight in the Casino on the following morning. Had it not been for the darkness Mohune's dreams of those days of peace would have been stifled in their nascent stages. Darkness, which throughout the history of the world has covered rapine, lust and pillage, now laid its softening mantle over the armed might of Nazi Germany as it sprawled like a satiated beast across the Channel Ports of that fair land of France. On either side of the Paris road German infantrymen, shock troopers, were quartered in low camouflaged huts, in the homes of the French people, or in small bivouac tents sheltering under the protection of the hedges.

Two miles from the town Mohune discarded the motorcycle. It had served its purpose and now at last the real business of making his escape began. Up to now he frankly admitted Lady Luck had been his partner and she had dealt him a hand stacked with aces and court cards, and now, provided that she gave him one more correct lead, he had a good chance of finding an old friend.

Pressing the stud at the top of the Luger's butt, Mohune released the magazine and then he rubbed the clip's sharpest edge against the rear tire of the motor cycle until he had incised a long gash, and in another minute there was a rush of air as the inner tube was punctured, and hoping that it would appear to the finder of the cycle that its rightful owner had abandoned it on account of a most obvious burst tire, Peter went forward into the darkness towards Dieppe.

The Hotel Brighton was Mohune's objective, and it was here that Lady Luck must play the master trump, for if the hotel was empty Mohune's chances would be in jeopardy. He quickened his pace and his footsteps echoed over the quiet cobbled streets. He turned a corner and sighed with relief. There ahead, bathed in the moonlight, was the Brighton and apparently open.

With Brandt's greatcoat collar pulled up about his ears, the peak of his cap down over his eyes, Mohune pushed open the swing door, no longer panelled with glass but with coarse unplaned boarding, and strode into the little bar.

A small group of officers hid the counter from view, but they turned as he approached and made room for him, and there at the far end of the bar with her back to him was a girl serving drinks. Lady Luck had led her ace.

Patiently Mohune waited to be served, his gaze downwards at his boots.

"Monsieur?" the girl was addressing him in French and in that language, marred by a rasping German accent, Peter answered her as he ordered his drink.

"It is time, Fraulein," he continued, "that you learnt the language of the Fatherland. It is an insult to the

Fuehrer that we should have to speak the tongue of
a beaten country."

"I am sorry, mein Herr. I am not clever enough." The
girl's voice was listless and her every movement proclaimed the dejection of her spirit. She pushed the glass
across the bar and Mohune's hand moved out to reach
it. The glass rocked and fell, sending a stream of golden
liquid across the polished surface.

"Little fool," snarled Peter, "little imbecile. Look at
my sleeve." He shook the moisture from his cuff, then
folded it back and dabbed his right wrist with a handkerchief.

"I'm sorry, Monsieur."

"Don't use that word to me, Fraulein, and don't stand
there doing nothing. Can't you mop the mess up or
are you trying deliberately to insult me. I warn you,
Fraulein, that we have our methods for people who
do that."

"I assure you, mein Herr . . ."

"I don't want your assurances. Mop the mess up."

Obediently the girl reached for a rag and commenced
to sponge away the liquid, and at that moment Peter's
right hand, with the forearm still bare, shot out and
pounced, catching her above the wrist and turning it
so that her hand was palm uppermost on the bar while
his bare arm rested on her finger tips.

"Little Fraulein," Mohune's voice had softened into
a smooth unctuous tone, "I didn't mean to frighten you,
little Fraulein." The fingers of his left hand moved
across the wet counter. "Women are not for war, they
are for love. Not for the sword, but for the moonlight.
The moon and the sword."

From beneath the shelter of his peak and collar Mohune watched her glance at the pattern so idly drawn on the damp surface of the bar. A crescent moon pierced by a sword. He felt her stiffen in his grasp and then the fingers began to play very gently on the surface of his arm. She suddenly began to tremble and kept her eyes on the hand which was imprisoning hers.

"That's right, little Fraulein, the moon and the sword. I think you understand. I will come back when there isn't such a crowd about. Oh, you may be sure that I shall come back. And now you are disregarding your other customers. Don't be sorry about me. I will see you later."

With a sudden jerk the girl pulled her hand away, and with a scarlet face she turned her attention to the laughing crowd who had been enjoying the scene from the far end of the bar.

Mohune clicked his heels and saluted the back of her head. The officers laughed again and with a grin which conveyed that he knew the technique of affairs such as these, he strutted out into the night.

At any moment now the Military Police should be closing the bars and tap-rooms but until that happened Mohune knew only too well that the Brighton was a dangerous area, and in consequence he strode off on a tour of inspection, but apart from a solitary challenge from a picket whom he satisfied, Mohune was left in peace. One hour later he turned to the Brighton by a succession of narrow back streets and slipping into an alley which led to the kitchen entrance, he knocked with three short taps and a long one, the V sign, on the hotel's back entrance. Immediately the door was opened. Peter edged his way into the narrow passage and closed the door behind.

"Madeline," he whispered.

Arms went about his neck, soft curls rested against his coat. "Petar, Petar, Petar de L'Epee. Oh, Petar." She held him tightly, almost fiercely, for a full minute and then suddenly she backed away. "Not here," she whispered, "not here. We cannot talk here. She caught him by the hand and led him in silence up the twisting staircase to her room on the topmost floor of the building, then having closed the door, she put her hands on his shoulders and stared upwards into his eyes.

"Oh, Petar, my dear, is it really you? How you frightened me. I was cold, oh, so cold, that I was sick with fear, and then I felt that scar on your arm. That was clever of you, Petar, to think of that and of the sword and the moon." She looked at him bravely, her eyes dancing. "Peter St. Maur Beverley de L'Epee Mohune ... see, I do not forget."

Mohune caught her wrists and shook her gently. "Little witch," he murmured, and then pulling off his cap sank on to the bed, pulling her down beside him. "I had to get in touch with you. Everything was just a little involved. Then I thought of that scar and guessed you would remember that."

"Remember it," there were tears in her eyes now, "I remember it as though it was yesterday. It was the Internationale Championship. Your opponent's sword broke and pierced your arm. It bled, oh, how it bled, and you had to miss your next fight and the judges disqualified you from fighting the rest of your matches, and how angry I was with you because you said that the French were not sportsmen . . ."

"And how well you bandaged me up." One hand slipped about her waist and the other ruffled her curls.

"But you were right, Petar, so very right. Oh, how ashamed I am of my country. No backbone. No what you would call . . . what is it? Guts." She broke off for a moment, then went on again. "Do you remember when I first met you? How angry you were, furious with rage. You had come to Dieppe to fence and there was no room for you at either of the big hotels and so you had to come here. Beverley de L'Epee Mohune was not amused. The great milor was much put out."

"Little Goose."

"Oh, but you were. The Brighton was no place for you, and yet within two days you were down in the kitchen learning to make omelettes from our own Pierre."

"How is Pierre?"

"Dead. They shot him. But what are you doing here now? Why are you dressed in that hateful uniform? Obviously, quite obviously, you're in trouble."

"A large packet of it, my dear. I'm riding a frisky horse in a crooked race."

"Petar, you joke at me as you always do. What have I got to do?"

"Madeline, I'm starving. Can you? I mean I know it's difficult, but I could eat anything."

"Silly." Madeline sprang to her feet and crossed to a small table beneath the window. "*Voilà!*" With the gesture of a conjuror, she whisked away a cloth to disclose a pile of sandwiches and three hard-boiled eggs. "And here..." from beneath the table was produced a golden-necked bottle.

"My child, you are an angel."

Twenty minutes later the last sandwich had disappeared and the girl was in possession of Mohune's story. "And so all that I want now," declared Mohune, as he eased the cork from the bottle and filled two glasses, "is a trusty ship to take me back to England." He raised his glass and regarded her through the foaming cascade. "Can that be done? Can I get a fishing boat?"

"A fishing boat. No." Madeline accepted her glass and stood facing Peter. "No, there are no fishing boats now, but to-morrow I will see what can be done. Jules, my cousin, Jules Laffitte, may know of something. Oh, Petar, it is so good, so very good to see you again."

"Happy days, Madeline."

"Happy days, Petar. Now we must go to bed. You turn and face that wall while we undress, and I will face this one."

"But you can't..."

"Silly boy, I can and I will. Where else do you think I can go? If I sleep in another room someone will be sure to ask the reason and most assuredly in these days walls have ears. And if you slept in another room they would be sure to find you, and if anyone does come, well they'll think that at last I have a *bon ami* and then they will think no more."

"But, Madeline..."

A small hand was placed across his mouth. "Enough.

Never has anyone shared this room with me. Never, you must believe that. Perhaps it is because I have waited to find someone like Peter de L'Epee, and now I have him." She laughed ruefully, "and it's all make believe."

CHAPTER TEN

IN WHICH HE MEETS THE BLITZ AGAIN

MOHUNE did not undress that night. He was still in every sense a fugitive, but for the first time since he landed in France he experienced a measure of security. The tenseness left his muscles and he slept like a log. It was not until a small hand rested on his shoulder that he awoke.

"Wake up, sleepy head."

Peter turned over on to his back and opened his eyes to find Madeline fully dressed standing by the bedside.

"See," she announced, "I have your hot water and a razor. Your face is very much like a wire brush. I know because it scratched me in the night. And what is much more to the point, I have seen Jules."

Mohune sat up with a jerk and swung his long legs off the bed. "Already?"

"It is nearly mid-day, Monsieur."

"And Jules?"

Madeline shook her head. "He is not very hopeful, I'm afraid. The boats are all carefully guarded by day and by night doubly so, but he will keep his eyes open and he will see what he can do." She wrinkled her nose and laughed at him. "I know that it will be all right."

"Nice work. Anybody been inquisitive?"

"No, Petar. I think that you are safe so far, but you must remain hidden for all of to-day and then to-night

146

you will meet Jules. I will bring you something to eat as soon as I can, although I fear it will not be an English breakfast." She dropped him a curtsey and Mohune, rising to his feet, bowed low.

"And now to work," she declared, blowing him a kiss, and he, catching her fingers, kissed them gently.

"You are very good to me," he smiled.

"It must be because of your eyes. It is a shame that eyes like that should be given to a man. You know they are beautiful."

"Be off with you, baggage, before I start making love to you."

"Oh! Oh! Oh! as if that were possible. Monsieur de L'Epee is very charming, like a lazy tiger, but he has no heart. *Au 'voir.*"

The door closed and she was gone. Mohune set about the task of cleaning himself up.

The day passed slowly. Much of it was spent in sleep and Peter realized only too well that the next phase of his progress towards England would be the most arduous stage of the journey and would call upon the utmost limits of his strength and test his powers of endurance to the limit.

At ten o'clock that night came news from Jules Laffitte. He had made an extensive search, there were no free boats to be had, no craft at all that were not under the immediate eye of the military, but there was a boat, a launch, moored by a rope to the mole of the main quay. This was the same quay from which the Newhaven Channel steamers left in the days before the war, but there was not the remotest chance of making a getaway that night for the troops were going to carry out an embarkation practice and the piers and streets would be thronged with soldiers moving towards the flat-bottomed, prime-moving barges in the harbor. But to-morrow night it would be worth trying, always provided that the launch was still there.

"Petrol?"

"Jules did not know. He had no means of finding out and obviously did not wish to draw attention to himself."

"Quite. Civilian clothes?"

"No." Madeline shook her head. "Jules did not advise civilian clothes. Civilians round the quay were objects of suspicion, whereas an officer might get through un-questioned."

"A man of perception, Jules," said Mohune, blowing a smoke ring towards the ceiling. "Yes, there is certainly something in that, as the monkey said. Is Jules coming here?"

Again that toss of the dark curls. "Jules doesn't want to come into this house. He thinks he will be of greater assistance if he keeps at a distance, but of course he will report to me should anything untoward occur."

"That suits me. So we go to-morrow night. I wonder when we'll meet again, Little Goose." He smiled at her and then as he saw the tears welling in her eyes he stretched out an arm, curved his fingers behind her neck and gently pulled her head forward so that her face was close to his.

"Come away with me?"

"That . . . that sounds like . . . like an invitation to a naughty week-end." She was being very brave and Mo-hune kissed her lightly on the forehead. Her arms slipped round his neck. "Petar, oh Petar, don't go and leave me. I can't bear it any more. Life has been one long hellish nightmare since the Boche arrived. Spying on your every movement, leering at you when you are serving, pawing you at every possible moment. Once it was horrible. They forced their way into my room and made me undress. Said that I was suspected of carrying information to enemy agents in my underwear. They stood and laughed when I cursed them. They aren't men, they're beasts." Her control dissolved and she sobbed on Peter's shoulder. Minutes passed and then at last when she was a little calmer Mohune picked her up and placed her on the bed.

"Poor kid," he murmured, and pulling a handkerchief from his sleeve wiped her eyes gently. Then holding it over her nose said, "Now blow."

"You are right, Petar. You always are right. I am a little goose, but . . ."

"Now, no more of that. By this time to-morrow we'll be in England."

Madeline sat up with a jerk. "No," she declared adamantly.

"What do you mean, no?"

"My place is here. I might be able to help someone else to escape, and besides there is your victory campaign. Someone must organize that. We had an organizer, but one day we had a meeting in a cellar. I wasn't there, but the Gestapo had been warned and they just killed everybody. Mowed them down with machine-guns . . ."

"But . . ."

"No, Monsieur de L'Epee, my mind is made up. I am

going to stay here and not even you with your violet eyes can persuade me to run away. I was a little fool just now, but no one has been kind to me for such a long time, I couldn't hold out any longer. And do you know what I think? I think that lazy tiger has a heart after all."

"Listen, child," pleaded Mohune, placing an arm round her slim shoulders. "Change your mind and come with me. You've done your job of work. You'll be safe in England . . ."

"Safe!" There was a note of derision in her voice as she answered. "Safe! I don't want to be safe. Petar, do you think I want your brave English people to point at me and say 'there is another Frenchman who has run away'? Do you think I could eat the food that other people need and do nothing in return? No, I shall stay here and then when France wakes up again and regains her backbone we will meet again. I won't talk about it any more. Have you met any of de Gaulle's men in England?"

"Just a few. They're a good crowd. They come from all parts of the world and by every manner of means. Some have rowed across the Channel, some have stolen aircraft and flown across. That great army of unconquered men from conquered lands are making a brave show. The Poles, the Czechs, the Belgians. 'Death to the Hun' is their war cry. Their English is very funny, just like yours used to be when I first met you."

"Like your French."

"Hush your mouth, baggage."

"All right. Go on, tell me about them. What do they say?"

"Oh, all sorts of funny things. I controlled a Polish Squadron for a long time. One thing that they could never get right was when they called up on the radio. They would never say 'Are you receiving me?' but 'Am I receiving you?'...and 'O.K.' is a general answer to everything." Mohune was trying hard to take her mind away from Dieppe and was succeeding. Madeline had snuggled up against him and was smiling.

They talked far into the night and twice Mohune tried by every persuasive method he knew to make the girl change her mind, but each time he met with the same uncompromising refusal, and so it was on the next day Madeline declined to discuss the suggestion that she should accompany Peter to England.

Night again. A clear night with the heavens wearing the full galaxy of stars and decorations. A fine wide night with the moon casting her cold light over the buildings of the old town. Mohune was standing by the bed examining his pistol.

"You're going now, Petar?"

Mohune slammed the clip of ammunition into the butt of his Luger, jerked back the slide to force a round into the breech, and eased on the safety catch.

"Yes, Little Goose, I'm going now."

"Take care of yourself, Monsieur de L'Epee."

"I will, and for the last time..."

"No." She forced a smile. "You'll think of me sometimes? Yes?"

"Yes, very often. The bravest soldier of France." He slipped the pistol into the pocket of his greatcoat and took her hand. *"Au 'voir,* Little Goose."

"Kiss me, Petar." She lifted her head and he kissed her gently. "Now GO."

At the door he turned and saluted her gravely as she stood with her hands at her side, her fingers gripping the edge of the dressing table. Her eyes were clear and very bright.

Silently, like the lazy tiger he had been compared with, Mohune descended the stairs and let himself out into the night, while in the room above Madeline threw herself on the bed and abandoned herself to despair.

There was a marked difference to be observed abroad in Dieppe that night from the scene on Mohune's arrival in the town. Then the streets were deserted, but now columns of troops were marching over the cobbles, motorcycles spluttered and roared and large touring cars edged their majestic way through the throng. Dieppe was awake and full to repletion. A dense but orderly mass was surging towards the harbor. This was not what Mohune had been led to expect, and his fingers strayed to that small hole in his ear. According to Jules, the embarkation practice should have taken place on the previous night and the streets should now have been deserted instead of presenting as they did a crowd scene from one of Korda's more ambitious films. He had grave doubts as to whether he would be able to attempt an escape that night after all, but with the idea of making a personal reconnaissance he went forward towards the harbor, crossed the little square, passed the wreckage of a small café where he had often refreshed himself after strenuous matches, and finally reached the entrance to the quay.

Here chaos seemed to reign unchecked, and he made

his way to the mole unmolested. Hoarse voices barked orders. Men swarmed everywhere. On the quay itself, down ladders, across gangplanks and into large barges moored side by side which completely filled the basin. Elbowing his way forwards, Peter gained the extremity of the seething mass and passed the outermost barge. No troops had intruded upon this area, and apart from two other men, dim shadows in the shelter of a hut, Mohune had the mole to himself. He walked to the edge and looked down upon the oily surface of the water. Twenty-five yards further on, even as Jules had said, was his boat swaying lazily at its mooring, which was a heavy iron ring set in the wall of the mole. Escape beckoned him on. He moved nonchalantly and then suddenly became aware of the fact that the two men had disengaged themselves from the shadows and were following him. He heard a voice say in French, "There he is," but Peter went on as though he had heard nothing, but behind him he sensed that the men had quickened their pace.

"So we meet again, Mohune."

Peter turned on his heel to face the two men, one in civilian clothes and the other in the uniform of the German Army. An eyebrow was raised at the pistol in the German's hand.

"I am ..." began the Englishman.

"You are Squadron Leader Peter St. Maur Beverley de L'Epee Mohune, M.B.E., D.F.C., A.F.C., a man with more lives than the proverbial cat. We thought that you had eluded us, but our friend Jules Laffitte brought us back on your trail."

Peter laughed. "All right, von Rinck. You win. As for

Jules," he shrugged his shoulders, "he should be at Vichy. They would appreciate his sterling qualities there."

An aircraft flew overhead at no great height and the Frenchman looked up apprehensively. "Don't worry, comrade," concluded Mohune, "that is just one of your kind German friends on its way to bomb another London hospital." He turned his back on Jules. "And now?" he demanded of von Rinck.

"You wouldn't like to give me your parole?"

"Have you read *Pygmalion?*"

" 'Not bloody likely'!"

"Exactly. You were quick off the mark, von Rinck."

"Partly luck, of which incidentally I think you have had more than your fair share, and partly through your own mistake. I had no idea that you had got away from Berlin, and certainly never dreamed that you were in Paris, and even when I was looking for Brandt at the station I didn't expect that anything was amiss until I found the stub of a Player's cigarette on the platform. That was luck. I dropped my glove and on stooping to pick it up I saw the vital clue. Good Germans, Mohune, don't smoke Players, and this one had been recently discarded."

"Quick," nodded Mohune, "quite quick."

The aircraft droned overhead and the German continued.

"The next move was simple deduction. The General was going to Boulogne. Brandt was going to Le Havre. That ruled those two ports out as being your destination, and even when we found the driver in the ditch I was not put out. I had made up my mind that you would try Dieppe. But that trick of crashing the car into the barrier nearly had me foxed. I did think that you were dead then. It was a neat trick and it was quite by chance that I decided to come on to Dieppe, but then when I heard that there was an Englishman attempting to make a getaway, hope revived."

"Full marks, Nazi, and two for neatness. And what's the next move?"

"We wait here until the exercise is over. I'm not going to trust you in that crowd."

"Wise man, but do me a favor. Just ask your stool pigeon, the beautiful Jules, to stay at a decent distance. I don't want to make a pun on his name Laffitte, but he does stink you know."

The Frenchman's tongue slipped back into his teeth, his hand flashed to his belt and a knife glimmered in the moonlight. At that moment three aircraft tore across the heavens, tore across with that peculiar high-pitched whistle of English aircraft, and as they passed another whine was added to the silence of the night, a whine high-pitched and menacing that travelled downwards from the sky. Mohune's balled fist shot out as the first bomb exploded three hundred yards away, and Laffitte, taking the full force of the blow, staggered backwards. Mohune followed up and another punch took the Frenchman under the heart, but, catching him before he fell, Peter held him as a screen between himself and the menace of von Rinck's pistol.

Bombs were dropping fast now, a stick straddled the landward end of the basin, ear-shattering explosions rent the night, while the screams of men in mortal agony added to the turmoil as a salvo of two hundred and fifty pounders crashed among the tightly-packed barges. A tongue of flame leapt upwards from a line of buildings on the wharf as though to lick the aircraft droning overhead. Then yet another stick screamed down while Mohune continued to hammer blows on to the Frenchman's body.

"That's enough, Mohune. Stop it or I'll drill you." Von Rinck had jumped to one side and stood a dark silhouette against the orange background of flaming buildings. Mohune's answer was to send the Frenchman staggering against the German. Von Rinck's pistol was levelled and then a hail of debris splashed into the water behind them, a hot blast of dragon's breath picked up the three men and flung them across the wharf. Another shower of lethal debris filled the air, a brick caught Mohune's shoulder as he tried to rise and slammed him back to earth. Flak of all kinds tore upwards at the sky, tracers, orange balls of fire followed each other with such rapidity that they appeared as brightly-colored necklaces. A cone of searchlights ringed the town, struggling against the heavy pall of acrid smoke that hung over the quayside. In the dark water which the flames played upon, soldiers shouted for help and climbed upon the shoulders of their drowning brothers, while heaps of masonry splashed down beside them to the harsh staccato laughter of the light automatic guns, and amid that modern version of hell, Mohune still gave his attention to escape. He rose to his feet in time to see a huddle of men bunched like frightened sheep mown down by an unseen scythe.

Von Rinck, too, was attempting to regain his footing, and then captor and captive faced each other, swaying drunkenly. Slowly the German raised his pistol, steadying his arm against a bollard. A shot, a small sound in that devil's babel, spat into the night and von Rinck pitched forward. Mohune had fired first.

"Sorry, Nazi," grinned Mohune, and then as another batch of screaming fiends came down towards their target he flung himself at full length. The blast surged across him, dragging at his clothes; more and even more bombers were arriving. Bomber Command was having a night out. A thousand-pound bomb caught the mole near the railway and tossed it into the air as a child will toss a handful of sand. Minutes later beams, pieces of barges and shattered men were still falling upon Dieppe. And then it was over with that suddenness with which a raid always ends, the bombers going home leaving Dieppe without an invasion port and Germany without fifteen hundred of her picked troops.

Mohune raised himself on one elbow and saw Jules crouching a few feet away. He drew his toes up and sprang, landing plumb on the Frenchman's back. "Well, my little rat!" Strong fingers gripped Laffitte's neck forcing his nose down on to the cobbles. "There is one thing that I want to learn from you! Was it you in your brave patriotism that informed upon that gallant band of true men who were helping France in Dieppe? And have you informed on Madeline and what she had done for me?" Jules squirmed but made no reply. "Answer me, rat!" The nose went harder against the cobbles.

"Yes, I told on them."

"And on Madeline? Have you mentioned her name? Have you? Answer me. Have you?"

"No. No, not yet ..."

"Not yet? But you will, is that it?"

"They paid me. I have to live."

"Why?" Mohune's tone was gentle.

"I won't tell. I won't tell. Before God, I won't tell."

"Before God is right, Jules Laffitte. You are a traitor to your country and to the people who love you. You should be tried as a traitor and shot. There is no time or opportunity to take you before a Court, but ask yourself what would be the verdict of those gallant men you condemned by your treachery to be shot like dogs. Would they not find you guilty? Would they not sentence you to death? Are you not guilty? Answer. Guilty or not guilty."

"I did it, yes, I did it. Let me get up and I'll make reparation. I'll do all I can. All I can. I swear before God . . ."

"Jules Laffitte, I am your judge. I find that you are guilty of treason and you know what the sentence must be. You may make your defence to your fellow countrymen before God." The fingers tightened.

Little groups of men dazed and bemused staggered among the flaming ruins of Hitler's invasion fleet as Mohune rose to his feet and walked slowly across the remaining portion of the wharf and lowered himself into the launch which by a miracle appeared to be unscathed. The engine answered readily to the starter, and casting off the rope, Mohune headed for the open sea with the prow bumping against the human flotsam as it surged with the ebbing tide.

CHAPTER ELEVEN

IN WHICH HE IS BEATEN UP AT SEA

In the "Hole"—the name given to the Group Operations Room—the Group Controller sat in his glass cage and studied the large map of the Group Area on the "floor" below him; he turned to his Operations Officer.

"Get me Westmere. I want their Controller."

The call was through within five seconds and a voice speaking from the Sector Operations Room answered.

"Hallower? Controller Westmere."

"That you, David?" demanded Group.

"Yes; what can I do for you?"

"What do you think of raid 146?"

"To tell you the truth, old boy, I haven't even considered it. What do you think of it?"

"It seems to be making up its mind to be coming our way."

"But not into my Sector . . ."

"No, but it's coming in low; I thought your boys might go and have a look at it. It's behaving like a body snatcher on the search."

"There's been nothing on the board this morning, so I should hardly think it could be a body snatcher."

"True enough . . . There you are—have you got that last plot? I'm certain that he's looking for something; he's circling around one particular spot. Put a section up to have a look-see. I'll pass you the necessary order."

"O.K., you old devil. No peace for the wicked!"

The Sector Controller replaced the Group 'phone and called to his Operations Officer.

"One section of 1616 Squadron take off. Course One-two-Zero. Get 'em going!"

"Very good, sir."

In three minutes Red Section of 1616 Squadron were airborne and gaining height.

"Hello, Pitpat Red One, Red One; Bellboy calling you. Understand you're airborne. Over to Red One, over."

"Hello, Control; Pitpat Red One answering. Yes, I am airborne. Have you any instructions for me? Over."

"Hello, Red One." David's voice was languid. "One Bandit at about Angels three ahead of you on your present course. You should see him in seven and a half minutes. Over."

"O.K., Bellboy. Listening out."

The minutes passed and raid 146 continued to circle that spot in mid-channel and the plots of Red Section grew steadily nearer to their objective.

"Hello, Pitpat Red One, Red One; Port Five. You're getting close to him now. Bellboy over to Pitpat Red One. Over."

"O.K., Bellboy; message received and understood. I can't see that blighter yet. Listening out."

Another full minute went by and the Controller consulted his stop watch thoughtfully. Seven minutes had passed.

"Hello, Bellboy. I can see him now. He's beating up a motor launch. I'm going into the attack now. Over."

"Well done, Red One. Slap him down. Listening out."

"Hello, Red Two; Red One calling. Attack Line Astern. Line Astern; go!"

The formation broke and Red One peeling off, dived, Blue noted, to the attack.

At Westmere, David lay back in his chair—a languid devil, but a master of his trade, and whose split second interceptions were famous throughout Fighter Command—and now that the fighters were engaged there was nothing for him to do but await results; he was far, far too experienced in the art of control to bother the pilots while they were engaged in a fight, with unnecessary "nattering" . . . and then at last came another call from the leader of Red Section.

"Hello, Bellboy; Pitpat Red One calling. He's crashed all right. What shall I do about the boat? There seems to be a body in it; looks very dead. Is this understood? Over."

"Hello, Red One; Bellboy answering. If you can't bring the boat back with you, you'd better circle present position and I'll get the launch to deal with it."

"O.K., Bellboy. Not being a Walrus and/or tug, I shall carry out the last part of your message. Listening out."

The Operations Officer at Westmere had watched David while he was speaking to Red One and as the Controller replaced the hand-set, he looked at him interrogatively. David nodded and leant back in his chair while the Operations Officer put a call through to Group.

"Hello, Group? Westmere Ops. here. Raid 146 is

caput. What? Yes; a Heinkel 60, I expect. They were beating up a motor boat. The Controller is arranging Air Sea Rescue now."

Within ten minutes a fast-moving motor launch was throwing the sea aside as it made for the derelict boat, and David, having informed Red Section that the "bell-bottomed boys" were on their way, 'phoned the Meteorological Officer to discuss the probabilities of duck shooting that evening.

With naval efficiency the R.A.F. launch swung alongside the Heinkel's target, which bore obvious testimony to the accuracy of the German's shooting. The port side was riddled like a colander, and the floorboards were awash in a green flood, a flood iridescent with patches of floating petrol; face downwards across the controls sprawled the inanimate figure of a man.

A boathook sought for a grip; an airman with his sea-boots folded back to his knees, sprang into the battered craft and inspected the body.

"It's a ruddy Hun," he announced, with obvious disappointment, "and a dead ruddy Hun at that. 'Struth, to think I've lost me ruddy afternoon off to come and rescue a ruddy Hun who's too ruddy dead to be even worth rescuing. Wouldn't be so ruddy bad if he'd been alive and kicking, but a ruddy dead 'un—I ask you!"

"Are you sure he's dead?" a quiet voice demanded from the prow of the rescue launch.

"Well, sir, he ain't moving, and there's a tidy bucket of gore about. Not that it seems to come from him."

The airman examined the body more closely.

"No, I can't say as how he is ruddy well punctured, but he certainly ain't moving."

A hand was slipped inside the German's tunic.

"Blimey, sir, you're right. His ticker's going sure enough. What shall I do with him?"

"Bring him aboard. Harris, lend a hand."

"Aye, aye, sir."

Gently the limp form was transferred to the rescue craft and taken below. The officer with the quiet voice—an Interrogation Officer from Westmere, who, incidentally, was a pianist of international repute in the far-off days before the war—forced brandy between the man's lips. The broad shoulders stirred, eyelids fell back reluctantly, and a pair of very deep blue eyes looked up at the swaying figure above them, closed again quickly as though the light had hurt them and then reopened to stare at the Interrogation Officer.

"Feeling better, Herr Hauptman?" demanded the man from Westmere.

"Hauptman be sugared! I'm . . ."

"You're Hauptman Brandt. Freidl Brandt. I have your wallet here; it fell out of your pocket as you were brought aboard."

"That be damned for a tale! Name's Mohune—Squadron Leader, stationed at Marsden."

"And these papers?"

"Stole them to make my getaway. Damn nearly didn't. Got away from Dieppe in that sieve during the Bomber Boys' visit last night. Petrol gave out; probably holed by a bomb splinter. Heinkel 60 came out to finish the job off. I must have collected a ricochet. They nearly succeeded in their little party."

"Not a very convincing story, is it?"

"Convincing! Stiffen the crows! What do you think I

am—a second Hess? Here have I been spending the last few days trying to convince the Jerries that I'm Freidl Brandt and now it seems that I have got to spend a week convincing my own people that I'm English. Must be a better actor than I thought I was. My own wallet is inside my tunic, together with important documents for Whitehall. Touch those at your peril! I'm getting browned off with this. Any more brandy?"

The Interrogation Officer laughed.

"This is a bit deep for me," he admitted, pouring a liberal tot of spirit into a collapsible cup and holding it to Peter's lips.

"That wasn't very deep, anyhow," complained Mohune.

The cup was replenished, while the airman who had brought Mohune on to the launch licked his lips reflectively.

"I'll make some enquiries as soon as I get back; you see . . ."

"Oh, I know, I know. Give me a cigarette, *mon vieux*. You know Dettmer?"

"I know the name," admitted the Interrogation Officer, offering his cigarette case.

"Of course you do. He's your boss. Jamake. Well, this is what is going to happen: just as soon as we land, you are going to take me to London in your car and we're going straight to him."

"But . . ."

"But me no buts. That envelope I mentioned is for him and it contains information that he must have without delay. You may sit beside me with a loaded gun if it pleases you, but I must see Dettmer and I must see him to-night. Group Intelligence and the whole of Fighter Command can go to the devil, and furthermore, you're to keep your mouth shut. I don't want anyone to know that I'm in England. Let the Hun think he's scuppered me. Understand?"

"It's very irregular..."

"Blazes, the whole war is irregular. I know as much about the Chain of Command as you do—I know all about Combat Reports, Intelligence Summaries and forms in triplicate—but for once you're going to forget the Chain of Command." Mohune forced himself into a sitting position.

"Be a good fellow and get some of this muck out of my eyes; I feel as stiff as a board."

"I'm still not convinced..."

"All right, be cautious; it's your job. Ask me questions. Ask me anything you like. Quite candidly, without wishing to appear conceited, I thought you might have heard of me."

"Oh, I've heard of Mohune well enough."

"Well, then..."

"But how do I know that you're Mohune? What are your other names?"

"Peter St. Maur Beverley de L'Epee."

"So far, so good, but there's one thing wrong."

Peter's eyebrow quirked up; "And that is?"

"Squadron Leader Mohune has a hole in his left ear."

"Very true. You'll find it stuffed up with a temporary filling."

"How did he get it?"

"How did I get it? A little bother with a German

agent. He pushed a sword through it in Scotland in 1935."

"He was instrumental in discovering a sabotage plot; where?"

"At Port Richboro' in 1938; following a masterly performance as a defending Officer in the Court Martial of a man by the name Binacle."

"His father is?"

"Sir Robert St. Maur Beverley de L'Epee Mohune, of Townley Court, Townley, Hants, who chastised me regularly with a cane when I was young. That I cannot prove as the marks have faded with the passage of years."

"His friend is?"

"Legion."

"A particular friend?"

"The Women's Auxiliary Air Force."

"A Flight Commander in his Squadron?"

"Flight Lieutenant Salter, D.F.C., known as Batchy, and he's all of that." Mohune's voice changed to Batchy's drawl: "Fan me. Question—do I know Peter Mohune? Answer—verily I do so."

The Interrogation Officer laughed.

"Hobbies?" he persisted.

"Opening safes; preferably other people's."

"O.K., sir. I'm convinced. I'll take you to Dettmer."

"Thanks, but let me remind you that closed lips, ears and eyes are the order of the day. And . . ."

"Yes, sir?"

"Is there any more brandy?"

The flask changed hands.

"Is David still Senior Controller at Westmere?"

"He certainly is. He did the interception on your Heinkel."

"Good old David. I'll give you support by letting him clinch my identity, and what is more, we'll go in his Bentley to London Town."

And so it was.

CHAPTER TWELVE

IN WHICH HE SEES DETTMER

In the seclusion of the Controller's Rest Room at West-mere David had dispelled all doubts from the I.O.'s mind and in consequence Peter, with a Service mackintosh covering his German uniform, had set off at once in David's Bentley for London. It was dusk when the long black car approached the Metropolis; long diaphanous veils of mist had trailed themselves across the sky and the sun hanging low in the west appearing strangely distorted, glowed like a Chinese lantern as Mohune crossed Putney Bridge.

Peter smiled happily. That long stretch of dark green water had, years ago, provided him with his daily exercise, that was when he had served at the Air Ministry, whose hive of cell-like offices had claimed him by day, but where in the evenings he had rowed with the giants of the London Rowing Club, whose tall flagstaff still stood in front of the Club House, topping all others, an emblem of the Club's superiority.

On through Chelsea, where an occasional bald spot brought memories of the night blitz, and then the calm of Regent's Park.

The car was brought to rest before a large white house, and discarding his mackintosh Peter stepped out on to the pavement. Two pedestrians glanced at him casually, attracted by his size and uniform.

"One of the Free French, m'dear," murmured one with the voice of authority. *"Bong soir, monsieur."*

Mohune smiled, waved a hand in airy salute and mounted the short flight of broad steps to the front door; his thoughts were of the shock that the butler was going to receive in a minute's time—even his pomposity would wilt at the sight of a German officer on the doorstep. He pressed the bell and almost instantly the door was opened.

"Good evening, sir." The butler, urbane and pompous, his face devoid of expression, unless perhaps there was just a slight pursing of the lips and infinitesimal signal of disapproval at the sight of a German uniform. "The Air Commodore is in the library, sir."

Mohune swallowed. "You know me?"

"We are not likely to forget Wing Commander Mohune."

"Well I'm damned. At least you have made one error; I'm still a Squadron Leader."

"May we be allowed to correct you, sir. The news of your promotion and the award of the Distinguished Service Order was conveyed to us at the same time as that of your untimely demise. May we say that we are glad that the latter statement was an exaggeration?"

"You may, Parkes, you may. I may say that I share your relief. Lead on MacDuff, I am on urgent business."

There was now a suspicion of humor in the butler's rather bovine eyes. "May we," he ventured with a slight bow, "remark that we have remonstrated on the inaccuracy of that quotation. 'Lay on, MacDuff,' sir, is what the Bard wrote."

"I know, but I prefer my own version. Parkes, you're

a placid old humbug. I really thought that I would puncture your complacency to-night."

"Had you done, sir, we should have been delighted to have eaten umble pie."

"Do I detect a fallen aspirate?"

"No, sir. The expression is correct. Umble pie is a concoction made from the entrails of deer. It bears no relation to the word 'humble' meaning 'unpretending,' 'modest' or 'meek.' Your hat, sir?"

The butler's hand, which moved forward as though to take the German cap, was checked and his eyes followed the cap as it described a parabola towards an oak chest on the far side of the hall. Then with incredible dignity the portly figure led the way across the tessellated hall towards a white door upon which he knocked, conveying with the action all the dignity of a high officer of the Court of St. James. A muffled voice said, "Come." History was repeating itself and Mohune's thoughts sped back to that night in 1938 when he had first been summoned to Dettmer's sanctum.

The oak-paneled library was in darkness save where a reading lamp sent a vivid splash of light across the pink blotting paper on the large desk.

"Lights."

The butler made a short but stately journey to a switch panel and two standard lamps sent wide areas of illumination across the thick carpet.

Air Commodore Dettmer, short, gray-haired and dapper, removed a pair of tinted spectacles and glanced at the German officer on the other side of the desk.

"Why, Peter! Going to a fancy dress ball?"

"Stiffen the crows, this is too much. Here am I back

from the dead and no one takes the slightest interest. Parkes, the 'King of Pomposity,' " . . . the butler, about to leave the room, paused and bowed slightly before making his exit, "merely corrects my rendering of Shakespeare, and you, sir, ask me whether I'm going to dance a light fandango. Upon my Sam, it's a little too much!"

Dettmer laughed. "Take a pew and tell me your story. Where are you from? What have you been up to now? I heard that you had been killed in action. I suppose you've picked up something of interest?"

"I believe so, sir. I have a letter for you from Freemantle."

"Freemantle!" A pencil clattered on to the desk. "How did you meet him? No, tell me the whole story from beginning to end. It will save questions later. Cigarette?"

Mohune lay back in his chair and related the facts of his trip through Germany and France.

"That's about the lot, sir," concluded Peter. "By the way, I have to congratulate you."

"Huh! Going to say I'm lucky to have you back, I suppose." Mohune laughed.

"Hardly that. I was going to congratulate you on your promotion. The last time I saw you you were a retired Colonel, and now . . ."

"Nothing to it, I assure you. More income tax to pay; same work to do; same fools to look after, to educate and worry about. I do worry about you all, you know. Just a bit now and then when I'm not getting hot under the collar through your nonsensical behavior. Now there's just one point: Have you any idea who it was that helped you to escape from Pegler's clutches?"

"No, unless it was von Rinck."

"Hardly likely when he took all that trouble to catch you again afterwards. It's a small point, anyway. Freemantle's report?"

"Here it is." The bulky envelope changed hands. Complete and utter silence invaded the room while Dettmer read the first page of the secret agent's letter. As he was about to turn the page the Air Commodore glanced across at the Wing Commander. "You've read this?"

"No time."

Dettmer nodded and bent his head over the papers, then: "This is no time for joking, Peter."

"Joking, sir! I assure you that I haven't read the report."

"Didn't say you had. Where's the rest of it?"

"The rest of it?" enquired Peter blankly.

"That's what I said. This is but one page of a long report with several carbon copies of that page attached."

Mohune stared. "That's all I had when I was with Freemantle. He was sorting the stuff out. He was flustered . . ."

"So it would appear." Dettmer lay back in his chair and stared at the ceiling. Suddenly he had become tired and old. "This is a blow to me, Peter, a bitter blow. I'll outline the position to you as I see it. Germany has taken a hard crack on the Russian front. The Russians are dealing out punishment with both hands and it's hurting Hitler and hurting him badly, but it's not Russia that he's worrying about. Russia can't fight without weapons, and this little island is supplying a great quantity of them. Our tanks, our guns, our fighter planes are doing the damage, and he can't stop it. Can you imagine the frenzy that that must produce? There at arm's length is our arsenal that is providing munitions to all his enemies. He knows that to win this war that arsenal has got to be scuppered. He tried it in September '40, make no mistake about that. The Battle of Britain was the prelude to invasion; it was necessary then and it is a hundred times more necessary now. Hitler's one objective must be the stoppage of England's factories and he's got to try and win the trick soon. Now our job is to find out how he will do it. He learnt a bitter lesson in the Battle of Britain and he must know that unless he can find another trump card in his hand the Luftwaffe will meet the same fate as before.

"He knows he's got to beat down our Fighter Force, he knows that dive bombers, Ju 87 and troop carriers, be they Junkers 52, 89, 89b or the old 90, cannot be used until our Fighter Squadrons are grounded, beaten out of the air, defeated.

"He's on the move again; that sudden raid on Marsden the other day, *in which you were killed,* the first large-scale raid since October, 1940, was a try-out. What he hoped to prove we cannot tell, but that trump card must have been dealt to him.

"Yes, we believe that he thinks he's found that trump card, and even now we can only guess at what it is. Gas? Perhaps; anyhow, that's what I sent Freemantle to Berlin to find out, and the galling thing is that he did find out and then with a messenger ready to bring the dope back to England, makes the biggest blunder of his life. All he says in this damned first page is that Fifth Columnists are active in England, that he believes that their H.Q. is somewhere near Brag, in the New Forest, that invasion is coming and that full details are given on the succeeding pages; and those pages are in Berlin—useful, so damned useful."

"We could put the Security people on to Brag. I've passed through it; it's not a large place. It should be easy enough to check up on the local inhabitants. A man who is organizing a scheme of this magnitude must be a fellow with some intelligence. That would rule out quite a large percentage."

Dettmer sighed: "My dear boy, the New Forest is the stamping ground of wild ponies and retired professional men in equal proportions. Our man might be a doctor, General, or the local J. P. One hint to the quarry and he's off like a fox, twisting and turning over the breadth of England. No, for the moment we must keep this to ourselves."

The Air Commodore jerked upright in his chair.

"Richard's himself again," murmured Peter.

"Exactly, and to cap your quotation—'Hark, the shrill trumpet sounds; to horse; away!'—but it ain't Richard who rides; it's you, my boy; I've a job for you."

"Want me to go back to Berlin to collect the rest of the report?"

"Don't be a fool—though I believe you'd do it. No, you go to Brag."

"My Squadron, sir."

"They think you're dead; let them continue to think. in fact, I will see that you remain dead. Clothes? You'll need clothes. Can't have you swashbuckling about England as a Prussian officer."

"Seventeenth Bavarian, sir."

"All right, Bavarian, but the point remains that you still need clothes. I suppose everything's at Marsden. You say you know Brag?"

"Yes, there's an emergency landing ground there. Forced-landed there once after a scrap over Pompey."

"All right, you can do it again. You'll need uniform and a suit of mufti. You can be flown down from Hendon. They're used to peculiar people taking off from there. Once in Brag you must choose your own line, but remember Peter Mohune is dead. Call yourself what you like, but Peter Mohune remains deceased. I'll have the Security Officer there to meet you on arrival—understand?"

"Perfectly."

"Good. How will you get your clothes?"

"Suggest you get in touch with Batchy Salter. Spin him a yarn. He knows you. Tell him that you think I had some papers sewn in the lining of my clothes, or something like that. Impress upon him that he must bring the stuff up to-night. In the meantime..."

"In the meantime you can wear Jack's stuff. I've... er... I've still got some of them left."

"Thank you, sir," replied Mohune quietly.

Jack Dettmer had been one of those gallant Pilot Officers who did not live long enough for His Majesty to pin the diagonal-striped Distinguished Flying Cross upon his chest.

The Air Commodore coughed and went on:—

"I'll do that, Peter, but I don't want Batchy Salter to come to this house, damned if I do. You can meet at the Orwell Court Hotel. That's still on our books, and as you know it is a place of many exits. Parkes will

book Room 13; you remember it, in Batchy's name. Go
along and get changed now."

"Jamake"—Peter rose to his feet and made for the
door.

"A minute."

Mohune pivoted on his heel, his hand on the door
knob.

"You make a good Hun, Peter," continued Dettmer,
"and you've done a good job of work—a damned good
job of work—but one word of warning. Don't take this
job lightly; from now on it's a heavy fight. The affair
of the pamphlets was amusing, but damned dangerous.
That's all, except that I'm damned glad you got back
safely."

As Peter left the library, Parkes entered and approached the Air Commodore; both men watched the
door close behind the Wing Commander.

"Would to God there were more like him, Parkes.
Giving with both hands, with no thought of what he'll
get in return."

"The Bard put it nicely, sir—

" 'How well in thee appears the constant service of
        the antique world,
    When service sweat for duty not for meed.
    Thou art not for the fashion of these times
    Where none will sweat but for promotion.' "

"How damned true."

An hour later Mohune set out to meet Batchy Salter;
he had at least two hours to spare and with his hat set
at a characteristic angle, he made no haste as he walked
through the night towards Baker Street Station.

He became a piece of the human flotsam that surged along in the congested stream towards the escalator which was to transport him into the warren of the Bakerloo. A girl brushed against him, moved on hurriedly, stumbled and fell forward; instinctively Peter's hand shot out, caught her arm and steadied her, then she was gone, whirled onward in the swirling stream. In that brief second, Mohune had only caught the slightest glimpse of her face—or rather her profile—in that instant it seemed to him that she had deliberately turned her face away. He shrugged his shoulders.

The tube train came in with a rattling roar of defiance as though it wanted to get through the station as quickly as possible and then, as it realized that its endeavor was to be thwarted, it gave vent to a loud sibilant sigh of exasperation as it came to rest and threw open its doors to admit the crowd which had awaited it.

The mass surged forward, crowding about the central doors. Women tall and women thin, women in furs, women in threadbare coats, joined in the fight, forgetting for the minute the gentleness of their sex as they elbowed and jostled for a seat within.

Mohune squeezed in behind the throng, felt the doors slide to behind him, a slight jar as the monster moved forward again, and then, as an ape in the jungle, Peter was hanging to a strap and swinging with the movement of the train. Casually he looked about, quietly interested in the diversity of types that go to make a big city. The monster gave an impatient swerve and he swayed forward; his glance fell downwards to investigate his resting place should he fall. The passenger before him was the girl who had stumbled. She was regarding her neat shoes; in consequence Peter was able to study unashamedly the picture before him. His gaze followed hers down to make an interception on the neat bows of her shoes and his brain registered instant approval. Small, tiny feet crowned by slim ankles. Perfection in hosiery disappeared beneath the soft edge of her fur coat. Her lips were slightly parted and gave a fleeting glimpse of perfect teeth. Her cheek, delicately colored, was caressed by the long dark lashes that fell with her lowered gaze.

Perfect, quite perfect, decided Mohune and watched the play of her hands as she pulled back the edge of her glove to study the minute watch upon her wrist. Suddenly his eyes narrowed and his attention, which had been casual, intensified; beneath that watch and stretching along the back of her hand was a scar, and no ordinary scar; in its white brutality it stood out against the tender skin as the symbol of Nazi Germany. A scar identical to the one he had observed on the wrist of that plain little typist in the Gestapo Headquarters in Berlin. But how different the owners of the scars; the first with her hair scraped back into an ugly bun, with shiny nose and nondescript clothes, was the complete antithesis of this beautiful damsel before him. But two scars, two swastika scars; Mohune forced the thought from him and tried to catch another glimpse of the one before him, but the glove had fallen back into its correct position and he decided that he must have been mistaken; he was getting too fanciful. Swastika scars forsooth; he was tired and was imagining things. He turned his attention to the advertisements as the train rumbled through Regent's Park, a contented roar as it eluded one of its obstacles; the monster plunged into the tunnel again and subconsciously Peter noted that fingers were playing with that glove again, noted that the glove was coming off this time; then his eyes were scanning that wrist again.

Mohune's shoulders gave a slight shrug of resignation; it was a swastika scar and the other fact which presented itself for consideration was that something ought to be done about it. The scar in Berlin was probably in no way connected with the scar in the Bakerloo tube, but it was a swastika and that was enough.

The monster rushed into Piccadilly Station, stopped with an angry jerk and flung its doors open with a malevolent hiss. Miss Swastika rose to her feet and passed out on to the platform, followed at a discreet distance by Wing Commander Peter St. Maur Mohune.

At the first escalator he nearly lost her, but by the time they reached the top of the second flight of moving stairs the chase was on again. Mohune's height made it possible for him to keep the girl in sight as she threaded her way round the circular gallery and then up the steps leading to the north side of Upper Regent Street.

Blackness, thick deep blackness, awaited hunted and hunter, and Mohune lessened the distance lest he should be left behind. Luck was with him, for Miss Swastika produced a torch and its small circle of light on the pavement made an adequate homing beacon, as the Wing Commander, oblivious to all eyes, followed in pursuit.

For fifteen minutes the chase continued, until Mohune began to wonder if the girl ahead of him really knew where she was making for. First to right, then to the left, then left again, then right, but the speed of her pace did not alter, it went on at a purposefully brisk pace; then suddenly it stopped, stopped so suddenly that Mohune was on top of her before he realized what had happened, and with realization came the knowledge that there was yet another figure before him. A small hand caught his sleeve, a low-pitched and quite delightful voice spoke, but the words were not addressed to Peter.

"I want to make a charge against this man, officer. He has been following me."

"Oh, really; he has, has he?" said the newcomer, and a light flashed into Mohune's face. "And what have you got to say for yourself?"

"What, me?" This was a little too much. "Me?" he repeated. "Is it suggested that I followed this young lady?"

"You know perfectly well that that's what you've been doing; as soon as I left Regent Street I heard your footsteps behind me."

"It has not occurred to you that your way might conceivably be my way..."

"All right; where are you going to?"

"I—er—" Mohune laughed. "Well, now you ask me..."

"There you are, Constable, I told you so; is that enough for you?"

"Just a minute," interjected Mohune quietly; he was

beginning to enjoy himself. "How long do you suggest that I have been following you?"

"For fully twenty minutes."

"There have been plenty of people that you could have appealed to, have there not?"

"You know perfectly well that we haven't seen a soul until this officer appeared so providentially."

"Exactly. So that if I had wanted to accost you, if I had been a black-out pest, I would have had ample opportunity during the past fifteen minutes. That is my case, Constable; I think you will agree that all that remains for me to do is to apologize to this lady for her imagined interference and to fade into the night."

"But . . ." began the girl.

"Just a moment, just a moment," put in the arm of the law. "It may be just as you say, sir, on the other hand it may not; there are a good deal of these black-out pests about and, for all I know, you may be one of them . . ."

"That is a slanderous statement, officer," murmured Mohune.

"I'm not saying you are, sir, I'm only saying, for all I know, you may be. If this young lady will accept your statement, well and good. I'll just take your name and address from your identity card and I'll say no more about it. If, of course, the young lady insists on making a charge . . ."

"No, I won't insist on that, as long as you can ensure that this man does not continue to follow me."

"I think I can guarantee that. You go along now and this gentleman will stay with me until you're well on your way. Good-night, miss."

"Good-night, officer."

"But dammit, aren't you going to take her name and address?" expostulated Mohune, who saw that his quarry was about to elude him.

"I don't think that's necessary, sir, because if I did, I should have to put a report in and we don't want that, do we?"

"I'm not so sure; now that I've satisfied you that I had no intention of making an unprovoked assault on this lady, I think that we should both come clean, as the Yanks so aptly put it, and provide you with proof of our identity."

"I . . ." began the constable, when a small hand found the small of his back and pushed him forward on to Mohune and both men, temporarily unbalanced, fell against the wall; when they regained their balance, the soft patter of footsteps fading away into the distance mocked their masculinity.

"And that's that," grinned Mohune, with quiet admiration at Miss Swastika's ingenuity. "I'll bid you good-night, officer."

"Just a minute, sir. I haven't got your name and address."

"Oh, of course, I'm Wing Com——" Peter bit the word off short; he was no longer Wing Commander Peter St. Maur Mohune, for Peter St. Maur Mohune was dead; the fact that he was nobody struck him very forcibly.

"My name's . . . er . . . Salter."

"Salter."

"That's right."

"Of what address?"

"Well, as a matter of fact, I haven't an address; that is to say, not in London, you see . . ."

"I'm afraid I don't, sir; can I see your identity card?"

"I'm afraid I haven't got it with me."

"And your name is Salter?"

"That's right."

"Doesn't look right to me, sir. No address, no identity card. Might I ask where you were going to stay to-night?"

"Oh, some hotel."

"Just some hotel. You'll have some luggage, I suppose?"

"Of course; it's at the Orwell Court Hotel."

"Orwell Court Hotel. Well, that's something we can check up on; we'll just go along to the Station and we can 'phone up from there."

"Am I correct in assuming that you are arresting me?"

"No, sir, you are not. We are just going along to the Station in order that I can check up your statements."

Mohune shrugged his shoulders in the darkness.

"Check," he muttered.

"You're not offering me a bribe, sir? That is a serious offence."

"Bribe, my good man—nothing was further from my mind. I said 'check.' It's a term used in a game called chess, a game of many pieces, which move about the board in various directions."

"I am aware of the pastime."

"I would hardly call it a pastime, but letting that pass, you will no doubt appreciate the similarity. The Queen has moved off at speed, leaving the knight in jeopardy."

"Funny night altogether, if you ask me. We turn left here."

The journey to the Police Station was a short one and the brightly-lighted charge room came as a welcome change from the heavy blackness of London's raid precautions.

Mohune greeted the Station Sergeant with a slight bow and an upward and quizzical twitch of the left eyebrow.

"Good evening."

The Station Sergeant ignored the greeting and gave his attention to Mohune's companion.

"Well?" he demanded.

"I was on my beat in Berners Street at about, well it would be about fifteen minutes ago now, when I was accosted by a young lady who claimed that this gentleman had accosted her . . ."

"Sounds like a new game, doesn't it? I accost, you accost, we all accost, and that'll cost you fourpence."

"Be quiet."

"As I was saying, Sergeant, this young lady . . ."

"Yes, we all know about that. Who was she? One of the regulars?"

"Oh, no, Sergeant; I said a young lady."

"Name?"

"I—I don't know . . ."

"There you are," put in Mohune, "I warned you."

"I didn't think it necessary, Sergeant, because you see, as it turned out, this gentleman hadn't accosted her at all. He explained what had happened and she—well, she accepted his explanation and went on her way."

"Admirably put, Constable, admirably put; apart from

a few trifling inaccuracies such as the fact that she did not accuse me of accosting her, but merely of following, you have summed up the proceedings fairly accurately."

"Well?"

"Well, Sergeant, you see it was like this; this gentleman had no identification card with him and he could give me no permanent address, so I asked him to come along here to—well, just check up, as it were."

"But he did not bring the young lady along as well," suggested Peter.

"We'll come to that later," supplied the Sergeant. "In the meantime, just tell me where you are living."

"Orwell Court Hotel. Name of Salter."

"Do you know the 'phone number?"

" 'Fraid not. It'll be in the directory."

The Sergeant pulled a directory towards him and turned over the pages . . .

"Hello, hello . . . Orwell Court Hotel? Blenheim Street Police Station here. Yes, that's right—Police . . . Have you a Mr. Salter staying with you? Salter . . . S for sugar, A for apple, L for—L for . . ."

"Try Hell for Leather," murmured Mohune.

"L for leather, T for tommy, E for Edward, R for Robert. Salter; Salter—no, no, not Edward Robert Salter, just plain Salter . . ."

"Not so much of the plain, comrade. I have my public."

"Yes, that's right, Salter. You have . . . no, no, that's all, thank you"; the sergeant was about to remove the earpiece from his ear and Mohune had already sighed with relief at the thought that his adventures for the day were nearly over, when the unseen speaker at the Orwell Court Hotel caught the sergeant's attention.

"What's that you say?" He glared sharply at Peter across the desk. "What's that? Oh, he is, is he? No, thank you. Oh, no thank you. Good-bye."

The handset went down on to its cradle with a crash.

"And so you're Mr. Salter of the Orwell Court Hotel? That's what you said, isn't it?"

"Correct, perfectly correct."

"Well, it may interest you to know, Mr. Salter, that Mr. Salter is already at the Orwell Court Hotel and is now busy unpacking."

"Of course he is," murmured Mohune, and producing a slim gold cigarette case, offered the contents to the Station Sergeant. The offer was impatiently declined.

"What do you mean, of course he is? You said you were Salter, didn't you?"

"I did and I am," Mohune was completely unflurried; with elaborate deliberation he selected a cigarette, placed it between his lips, replaced his case, produced his lighter, flicked it into action and inhaled deeply, then as he watched the plume of smoke mounting towards the ceiling, "but, remember I claim no copyright."

"What are you getting at? It seems very odd to me."

"Maybe, but that is probably because it has never struck you that there is more than one man living in this world of ours to-day who proudly bears the name of Salter. It is my brother who is unpacking; if only you had been a little less anxious to jump your fences

I could have told you that when you were on the 'phone a minute ago; as it is, another call appears to be indicated."

"I've a damned good mind to put you in for the night."

"Think again, comrade. You might have a little difficulty in framing the charge."

"Ever heard of Section 18b?"

"Ah, ha, consorting with the enemy. You'll be saying that the lady I was with ... the lady who ... what was it the constable said? Oh, yes, I have it—went on her way, was in fact a beautiful and dangerous spy branded with the dread mark of the swastika. Now, then, let's put an end to this nonsense; just put that call through and then I can go and have a stoop of ale in—er—happier surroundings."

"Your brother's Christian name?" demanded the Sergeant as the dialing disc whirled beneath his blunt finger tip.

"Oh, just ask for Batchy. And my name's Peter, Peter St. Maur."

"Batchy—if you ask me, the whole family of Salter could answer to that."

"Agreed, *mon vieux*, agreed."

... "Mr. Salter?" There was a pause, then Batchy's voice blared into the Sergeant's ear and the words cut across the silence of the Charge Room. "What ho, what ho, Salter here."

"Er, Mr. ... er ... Batchy Salter ..."

"Question Batchy Salter? Answer Batchy Salter; and who might you be, Angelface?"

There was a suppressed chuckle from Mohune's

friend, the constable, and the Sergeant continued with forced dignity.

"This is the Blenheim Street Police Station. There is a man here who claims to be your brother, gives his name as Peter Seamore..."

"Don't you believe him, Pansyface; I have no brother..."

"Thank you, sir, that's all I wanted to know..."

"Here, here, I say. I mean, fan me; did you say Peter, Peter St. Maur? My gosh, poor old Peter; yes, he's all right; I'll come along; I mean to say, you know, blood is thicker than what not..."

"But you've just told me that you have no brother..."

"Nothing of the sort, dear old flatfoot. Fan me; absolutely not. I started to tell you that I had no brother who would get himself into the calaboose, but you were too quick, Angelface, positively snapped at me. Of course, I've brothers, hundreds of 'em. Poor old Peter St. Maur, hold on to him. I'll come and collect him, as fast as petrol evaporates. Fan me."

During the ensuing minutes the members of the Metropolitan Constabulary took little or no interest in Mohune—or to be more correct, they studiously avoided him; he was for the time being beyond their reach, but the look in the Station Sergeant's eye was unmistakable— it was there for all to read: "If this man is not Peter St. Maur Salter, let him beware. That's all, let him beware."

Peter had crossed to a large board liberally adorned with handcuffs, which he was leisurely examining, when the door leading to the street burst open and Batchy catapulted himself into the small room. It was as though a typhoon had hit Blenheim Street. His tall lanky form dominated the assembly.

"What ho, what ho, what ho, I mean, what. Question, is it brother Peter I see before me? Answer, it is brother Peter. Stap me, Peter, but you're for it. I mean to say, Sergeant, I ask you. Here is my respected brother, beloved of the whole family of Salters and who is believed to be visiting his Aunt Fanny, and is he there? Question, is he there? Answer, he is not; oh, most decidedly not. He is incarcerated, in durance vile, in clink, in the veritable calaboose and dungeon and what will you. Think of the scandal, I mean to say, I ask you. Will the stately chins of the Salters ever regain their proud tilt? Will they? Answer, they will not. Peter St. Maur, I'm mortified, I'm injured, and what will your Aunt Fanny say, I boggle to think. Come, we will away, and endeavor to scrub this stain from our escutcheon. Sergeant, I bid you good-night. Come, Peter."

"This is your brother, then?"

"Answer, this is my brother; have I not said, have I not expounded . . ."

"All right, sir, all right. But take more care of him in future."

"I'll leave his Aunt Fanny to do that."

The incessant flow of inanity was still in full flow as the two officers reached the pavement and made for Batchy's Alvis, and it continued in force until the car had snaked its way out into the traffic of Regent Street. Suddenly it stopped.

"Let me look at you, Peter," declared Batchy, bringing the car to rest and shining a torch on to Mohune's face. "I knew that something was up when I received instructions to take your kit to the Orwell, but that I'd see you again, I was past hoping for. You're dead, man; you were shot down. God, it's good to see you again. What happened? Fan me, this calls for a drink and a large one at that. Where have you been? How did you get here?"

Mohune laughed joyously.

"All in good time; that can wait until we're at the Orwell Court. How's the Squadron?"

"Grand. That's the only reason I'm sorry that you've turned up again. I've been leading them in your absence and I'm far better at it than you are. Are you all back?"

"No, Batchy, we're not. Parsons is P.W. and the rest are ... Done any work while I've been away?"

"Answer, most definitely no. I took 'em out yesterday morning; Old Dusty was controlling, he's damned good. False alarm; up we went and down we came; you know, flip, flap."

Batchy's long arm swung out of the car in graphic description and a driver close behind swerved for safety.

"Peter, Peter, Peter; fan me, but I'm glad to see you. I'm not the demonstrative type. Quiet and silent, that's your Uncle Batchy, but fan me, by the Five Jumping Demons of Bangor, I'm glad to see you."

CHAPTER THIRTEEN

IN WHICH HE HAS AN UPSET AND MEETS MISS SWASTIKA

MOHUNE and Salter had talked late into the night, but while the sun was just commencing its daily fight with the gray skies, they had arrived at Hendon.

Mohune in uniform, a jacket upon which Phillpot, Peter's batman, whose blind faith in his master had been unshaken by his failure to return from patrol, had altered the lace on the sleeves to the three wide bands of a Wing Commander and had rearranged the medal ribbons, so that they now commenced with the maroon and blue of the Distinguished Service Order.

None of these alterations, however, were visible, for over his uniform the Wing Commander was wearing a full flying suit and had also donned helmet, oxygen mask and goggles, not that there would be facilities for R/T or oxygen in the plane he was about to fly, but as an added disguise against prying eyes or talkative friends.

Batchy Salter had attended to all the preliminaries, had visited the duty pilot, had signed the authorization of flight book, and had obtained a route forecast.

The engine was ticking over and Batchy, standing on the port wing, was having a few final words with Peter.

"Weather's O.K. as far as Basingstoke, cloud nine-tenths at twelve thousand, visibility five miles, and the wind is north-east at fifteen miles an hour, so that won't worry you. I mean to say, even you, Old Commandant, couldn't get lost in those conditions. After that it gets worse and the clouds creep down towards the ground and the birds are surely walking, but according to the Met. there's nothing below four thousand west of Swampton. That's about all; keep clear of artillery zones and 'ware balloon barrages..."

"Heck, you nurse me as though I were a bog rat on his first cross-country..."

"Not a bit, not a bit, but you know, well if you think I want to spend the next few days searching the countryside for you and finally find you with your head stuck into a hillside with your tail quivering like a dart, I don't. There's one other thing though; can I tell the boys that you're safe?"

"No, Batchy, to all intents and purposes, I'm defunct..."

"But, fan me, they'll debag me when they find out that I knew that you got back and that I didn't tell them. I mean, think of my prestige, think of my position, I mean, fan me..."

"I'm only thinking of you running about the mess in your short clothes and the prospect pleases me..."

"But, Peter, there's another aspect to it all; those blighters at Oldkirk are running us pretty close with the numbers of Jerries to their credit, and your bag the other day will give us a clear lead; I mean to say..."

"All that will have to wait. So long, Batchy. My bag in the back?"

"Trust your Uncle Batchy."

"I don't. Bye."

"Cheer ho. Wish I was in on this with you."

"That's a lie if there ever was one. You go back and lead MY Squadron for me and mind you lead 'em well or I'll have your pants off."

Batchy laughed and having bestowed a hearty slap of farewell on Peter's shoulder, he jumped to the ground. Mohune gave a quick look round, opened the throttle and taxied into wind. A final scrutiny to satisfy himself that the ground and sky was clear, then his gloved hand moved forward; the engine note reached a purposeful roar and the Magister moved forward across the green surface of the aerodrome, a short run and up into the peach-colored sky of the dawn. A gentle take-off; no thrills, nothing spectacular to catch the eyes of casual observers. Twice he circled the aerodrome, that historic field where Grahame White used to navigate his flimsy craft, where the heroes of the past had come to demonstrate their prowess in those far-off days before the last war, where Aerial Derbies had taken place, where the miracles of 1912 had been flown round colored pylons and where in later years the Royal Air Force Air Display had been an annual event, an event which had drawn fabulous crowds; crowds that had filled the vast space and had overflowed on to the hills beyond; gay crowds with fashionably-dressed women, for it must be admitted that the Air Display had been the social gathering of the Air Force, and while husbands had cricked their necks to watch the evolutions of their friends and had studied the new types, wives had studied with equal attention the trim lines of the other wives and had studied the fashionable array about them.

The sky was clear, as clear as it had been when Mohune had set off on that ill-fated patrol. The railway stretched its snake-like length out below, a black snake leading off to the mass of buildings of Greater London; with a gentle turn he turned the Magister towards the south-west and settled himself more comfortably in the cockpit. The Squadron, in fact, the whole of the Royal Air Force, were left behind; there was no wireless in the Magister and so there was no possibility of Authority changing its mind and recalling him; from now on, he was alone; the thought that it might be a long time before he led the Pimpernels into action again was a depressing one, but there was a distinct possibility that the job in hand would not prove boring, and furthermore it was a job that he was experienced in and liked. He let his mind travel back over the other cases that fate had led him into; his first affair, which had nearly ended in his death and from which he had counted extremely lucky to escape from with no further injury than a sword thrust through the ear, and then after numerous adventures, the amazing affair at Port Richboro', when he had met Euryale, the delightful spy who had eventually fallen in love with him and saved his life. Peter laughed happily; he had enjoyed that little business, and the thought that, with any luck, his present mission might prove to be equally exciting, did much to banish his disappointment at having to leave his Squadron in Batchy's hands.

Over Guildford a Hurricane swept up alongside and made a wide circle around him. Mohune answered the pilot's cheery wave and then the Hurricane was away and again Mohune was alone. As the Magister approached the coast, Peter agreed that Salter's warning was not ill-founded; the clouds were certainly lower, casting great areas of grayness over the fields beneath; he passed over an aerodrome and saw a section of Spitfires taking off and climbing like rockets into the heaped cloud formation, saw other aircraft circling the 'drome and executing circuits and bumps, then they, too, were left behind his tail plane. The end of his journey was approaching; he turned a few degrees to the north to give Southampton a wide berth, cleaved his way through a particularly low mass of cloud and shot again into the welcome sunshine, and there it was, no more than two hundred yards ahead, a thousand feet below and traveling on the same course, was a Jerry.

The Magister is no fighter plane, it is unarmed and unarmored; but even had Mohune been flying the latest make of Spitfire he would have known that for once his duty was to evade combat. In a "Spitty" that would have been easy, but the Magister is incapable of showing a clean pair of heels to any Dornier.

Mohune eased on bank and rudder and for a moment it seemed that he would go into the shelter of the cloud unobserved, in fact, in three seconds it would have given sanctuary to the little craft, but a stream of bullets spat out from the E/A's rear gunner, bullets which slashed their way through the flimsy covering of the Magister's fuselage, and one—skidding off the engine cowling—shattered Mohune's windscreen, sending a million fragments about his flying helmet. Then he was enveloped in the friendly cloud.

Half a minute later the Magister re-emerged into the sunshine and Peter, looking about in all directions, heaved a sigh of relief, for there was no sign of the Dornier; the widespread masses of cloud to the north had swallowed it up. Peter turned back on to his course.

Then suddenly a shadow passed between Peter and the sun; he jerked his head up apprehensively, then grinned as the section of Spitfires he had seen take off skimmed over his aircraft. He flew on; he was on the edge of the New Forest now; only a few more miles, but all was by no means well with his aircraft; a disheartening cough had afflicted the engine, a cough which increased with intensity and Mohune began to realize that it was going to be no easy matter landing this damaged plane. He had no means of telling whether the undercarriage had been damaged, but if it had and however slight it was, a damaged undercart is not a thing to be taken lightly even on a good runway made of solid concrete, and at Brag no carefully-levelled ground awaited him. He debated the question of baling out, but came to the conclusion that a landing must be attempted; a wrecked aircraft and a pilot descending by parachute would attract a crowd of rubbernecks, and to Mohune at this moment a small urchin would constitute a crowd.

The engine's malady became steadily worse and as though a deliberate hazard had been placed in his way, the cloud before him swept down until it appeared likely that only a short way ahead it would caress the forest itself. To turn north and seek the edge of the blanket would be useless, for the pilot knew by the sound of his engine that its disease was fatal; a few more minutes and it would expire.

He was in cloud again, thick wet masses of it that closed his visibility to precisely nothing. He glanced at his altimeter; the needle was steady, very steady, and

pointed forebodingly at zero. Peter grinned as he remembered how a certain well-known pilot when flying as
a passenger and the engine fell out of the aircraft at
forty feet, was heard to remark quite casually, "This is
where I takes off me hat and says 'Good morning,
God!' "

That man, like Mohune, had no nerves, and the smile
was still present behind Peter's oxygen mask when the
Magister's engine gave its final cough and expired. Mohune had no intention of flying headlong into any hill
that might rear its ugly head in his course; he had no
intention of, as Batchy had so aptly put it, being found
with his head stuck into a hillside with his tail quivering like a dart. He was too low, far too low to bale out;
quite casually he applied bank and eased his plane into
a side slip; better, far better that the expanse of wing,
slender though it was, should take the force of the impact, than that he should hit nose on and the defunct
engine come on back to his chest.

The Magister had been slipped to port and Mohune
leant over to the starboard side of the cockpit. A second
passed as the plane fell through the air, then it struck.
Mohune had a fleeting impression that the shock had
not been so sudden as he expected or so fierce, then something struck him on the nape of the neck. Stars hot,
pointed, burned into his brain; he slumped forward,
limp and motionless.

Mohune opened his eyes. The tangled remains of the
Magister, from which a wisp of smoke curled upwards
in the still air, were some twenty-five yards from him.

Immediately beyond the wreck visibility dropped to zero.

"How do you feel, sir?"

Peter turned his head and red-hot daggers stabbed at his back and shoulders.

"Pretty much as though a steam-roller had flattened me out. I refuse to say 'Where am I.' "

"I'll tell you that, sir. You have arrived at Brag."

"Goody goody."

Gentle hands lifted Mohune on to a stretcher and within a minute he was in an ambulance making for Brag's sick quarters.

"I'm Davis, the Security Officer, sir."

"Pleased to meet you."

"I've been expecting you. Heard that you had left Hendon and wondered how the devil you would get in."

"Bit of a bump, what?"

"Hardly the perfect landing, sir. Don't know how you found the place at all."

"Luck, sheer luck."

"I can't believe that, sir."

"Truth. Anyone see the debacle?"

"No, sir. The murk shrouds everything from the road."

The ambulance came to a halt and Mohune was carried into the sick quarters where, for the next fifteen minutes, he was examined by the M.O. while the Security Officer hovered in the background.

"Nothing broken. Maybe slight concussion. I'll be able to tell after I've had you under observation for a couple of days."

"Couple of days my foot! I've got a job of work to do . . ."

"But . . ."

"But me no buts. This is vital and if you say there's nothing broken I'll get cracking."

"There may be internal injuries."

"I'll risk that. Can you give me a massage? Just to stop the stiffness."

"I can do that if you insist that you won't lay up."

"Can't be done. Let me have a hot bath and Davis can tell me the story now trembling on his lips while I have my bath."

Then, while Peter lay in the steaming water, Davis narrated the information which he had gleaned from the countryside.

"Not much to tell you, sir. There are very few residents apart from the villagers. There are a few big houses. I've marked them on this map."

The map was unfolded, spread out on the sponge rack, and Mohune raised himself to a sitting position.

"This house here is called 'Taverners,'" continued Davis. "Major Truscott, ex-Indian Army, writes a lot and drinks a lot more."

"This is 'The Furze,' Mrs. Wilberforce—old, very old. Three daughters, known to the countryside as Huntin', Shootin' and Fishin'. The old woman breeds dogs, mostly bitches. Very county, so hoity-toity."

"Here's 'The Towers.' Author lives there. Fearnley Davigore. Pornographic stuff I'm told. Haven't read any."

The Security Officer's finger moved on.

"This is 'The Trundle,' Professor Hammerstein's

place, Austrian brain specialist. And here's 'The
Haven.' Dr. Bellew. Has one topic of conversation—how
he ran the west coast of Africa on castor oil and potas-
sium permanganate. Over this ridge in the valley here
is Captain Dudley's place. He's blind, very sad. Had a
boy in the R.A.F."

"Ralph Dudley?"

"That's the name."

"Knew him during the blitz. He shuffled off early.
He was a good lad. Damn fine pilot, too. Any more?"

"One, sir. An artist at 'The Outlook,' name of Tipler.
Don't know much about him. Keeps very much to himself. That's about all I can tell you, I'm afraid."

"Plenty to go on with. Any recent arrivals in the
village?"

"Strange that you should ask that. Very few people
come to Brag, but there is a newcomer at the 'Dolphin'
—a pretty piece. Had an accident or something, got
her wrist bandaged up."

Mohune's head, which had been lowered over the
map, jerked upwards.

"Bandaged wrist. I wonder. It's a slim chance but
I think I'll investigate the 'Dolphin' this evening. Did
they salvage my kit from the crash?"

"Yes, undamaged."

"Good show. I'll have this massage, then I'll sleep for
a bit, then this evening, in gent's natty suiting, I'll start
with the 'Dolphin.' Where can I get in touch with you
if I should want you?"

"I've a cottage down here called 'Tintagel.' Telephone Brag 107. Incidentally, there is a troop of youngsters who have formed themselves into a pony club.

They patrol the forest and report any breaks in the Army telephone lines. As a matter of fact, they are doing a damn good job of work, and if at any time you wanted to get a message to me they might come in handy."

"A little risky, isn't it? Anyhow, I'll bear it in mind, though I have a marked aversion to using people under age. When I was in France in the early days we had a heap of trouble with broken 'phone lines, not accidental breaks but deliberate sabotage; we set traps for the Fifth Column but at first we had no luck at all. Then one day the Army made a capture. I saw them coming in; it was a most amusing sight; three hefty Guardsmen and in between them two very small and very dirty urchins. I thought at first it must have been a childish prank, a love of destruction, but was it blazes! They both had wire cutters—German wire cutters—which they said had been given to them together with 5 francs apiece, and promises of further largesse if they succeeded in cutting any telephone wires. More than that they would not tell.

"They became as dumb as the Trojan Horse. We took them into the mess and crammed them with ice cream, but even then they would not say who had given them the cutters. We let the little blighters go, couldn't do anything else, and the trouble went on. We got more kids, but never the agent; then we came to the conclusion that he had left the area. Then one morning at about dawn a Jerry went over and from it dropped a parachutist. The pilot must have been out in his calculations for the dropper hadn't a hope. We sent a party out to rope him in and they had a couple of hand grenades thrown at them for their trouble. One or two were knocked out, others opened up with their rifles and bowled their target over but they had another shock awaiting them. They removed the flying helmet, and instead of a close-cropped Prussian head a wealth of golden hair which had been imprisoned by the close-fitting helmet fell down over the girl's shoulders. She was young, very young. Certainly not more than sixteen, and under her drap flying suit she was wearing a pretty print frock. She had a haversack with wire cutters and money. She was dying, but as she died she spat in the face of the man who was holding her up and said 'Heil Hitler.' "

"Terrible!"

"Yes, Davis, it was terrible. Terrible to think that a man can use children in his plans for world domination, and even more terrible to know that such blind un-reasoning faith, such a damnable canker, can be infused into children's minds, that they are willing to die for such bestial, pestilential swine."

It was a lovely evening when Mohune, in civilian clothes, set out for the "Dolphin"; the heavy clouds had drifted away and the land seemed calm and contented; the narrow country lane leading to the village was deserted save for a small herd of Jersey cows heavy with milk, sleek fat beasts plodding a docile way towards their farm.

Mohune had no plan of action; it was his experience that in these individual affairs, coincidence and the vagaries of human nature played such large parts, that a script was generally of little value. He had one rule, however, which whenever possible he adhered to, and that was Personal Reconnaissance, knowledge of the ground, the configuration of obstacles were studied in detail, and on this occasion Mohune had little intention of doing anything but spy out the land and to check his hunch that the girl with the bandaged hand was in fact Miss Swastika.

The "Dolphin," a Georgian building, with a white-pillared portico and situated in the main street of the little village of Brag, was reached without incident, but even as he approached the hotel, a girl emerged, turned in the opposite direction from which Peter had arrived and walked off down the main street towards the railway station.

The height was right, the coat was right, the hat was even right; without the shadow of doubt it was Miss Swastika; without hesitation Mohune entered the hotel and approached the reception desk.

"I want a room, please."

A bored-looking girl glanced up from her book, saw that the newcomer was more than presentable and deigned to give him her attention.

"For how long?"

"A week maybe. My baggage will probably arrive to-night. There seems to be some delay on the railways."

"What name is it?"

"Marjoram. Paul Marjoram. Shall I sign the register?"

"Please. I'll have all the forms ready for you when you've seen your room. It's a lot of nonsense, all this form business. Just as though we are likely to get spies in a place like Brag. What'd they come here for? What does anyone want to come to Brag for, I'd like to know. It beats me."

"I expect it does," agreed Mohune, with a smile, pulling the register towards him. "Many people here?" he added.

"Only one, and she's just gone out. Miss O'Regan. She's expecting her brother—or she says it's her brother. You're not him, I suppose, and forgotten that you ought to call yourself O'Regan?"

"Phyllis, I'm surprised at you. No, my name is Marjoram, and I know of no one named O'Regan."

Peter scrawled the signature of the mythical Paul Marjoram, a name he had chosen because it coincided with the initials of his own on underwear and cigarette case. It was an old pseudonym and one for which he possessed the complete collection of identification cards and ration books. Before pushing the book away across the narrow counter, he noted that Miss O'Regan was occupying room seventeen.

"Your room is number nineteen, sir. Shall you want anyone to show you up? Seeing that you have no luggage and the porter is off as usual . . ."

"That's all right; I guess I'll find my way. Key?"

The receptionist languidly turned her head and shoulders and selected a key from the rack behind her.

"First floor," she announced. "Turn left at the top of the stairs."

"I thank you."

Mohune mounted the wide Georgian staircase and obediently turned left at the top, but it was there that —to use an expression of Batchy Salter's—"Error crept in," for it was not at the door of number nineteen that the Wing Commander stopped, but at a door bearing the figures 17. Gently the knob was turned and the door swept back to reveal Miss O'Regan's room.

"Foolish, Miss Swastika, foolish. Turn of the hand and your secrets—if any—would have been secure."

Very quietly Mohune closed the door behind him; then for a full half-minute he stood in the middle of the room studying it minutely.

The suitcase on the bed, unlatched, with a foam of silk and lace projecting from one corner, the dressing table with the customary array of bottles and jars, the neat line of even neater shoes, a pale green frock thrown negligently over a chair. All very commonplace and very unsuspicious. Mohune moved forward and began his search, commencing with the suitcase upon the bed. . . .

Soft, delicate garments moved through Peter's hands. Every article was carefully scrutinized.

> "An expensive young woman, Miss Swastika,
>   Who may be quite fast if not quicker,
>   But it's not with young Mohune
>   That she's going to spoon,
>   Who's purer than Brag's local vicar."

The suitcase revealed nothing to Peter as a secret agent, however revealing it might have been as a bachelor, so having satisfied himself that the bag contained no false bottom or double lining, he replaced the contents exactly as he had found them, even to the foam of lace protruding from the corner and turned his attention to the drawers of the dressing table, but there again, although he found enough to turn ninety-nine girls out of a hundred green with envy, he discovered

nothing which would increase Air Commodore Dettmer's pulse beat by one throb per minute.

Mohune pushed his hat back and then fingered the
hole in his ear; he was baffled. There was simply nothing in that bedroom to connect Miss Swastika with the
beast of Berlin.

One avenue alone remained to be explored and that
was a door behind the dressing table, which on investigation gave access to a deep closet. Mohune stepped
inside and the door swung to behind him. There was
plenty in that cupboard to claim his attention; another
suitcase and a hatbox were opened and their contents carefully scrutinized, but as he decided that there was nothing else to interest him in that closet, the bedrom door
opened and he stiffened into immobility. If the newcomer did not come to the cupboard, Mohune knew
that he was safe; there was nothing to betray him in
the room; everything was as he had found it, even to
the foam of lace protruding from the corner of the
suitcase on the bed.

"I thought you would come by train," announced a
girl's voice.

"Train! Is it loikely that Oi'd buy a ticket for Brag?
No, Oi came by car. Use your brain, sister, and furthermore, whoile we're talking of sisters indeed how about
a little kiss for this big handsome brother of yours?"
The man's voice was deep and heavily impregnated with
the Southern Irish accent.

"That's quite enough of that, Mike."

"And is it so, indeed? Whell, me little Freya . . ."

"Well, me little Mike, you can just forget that name
of Freya; while I'm in this country, which I trust will

not be for long, my name is Florence or Flo O'Regan."

"Sure, sure, but we can have that little kiss whatever you may be after calling yourself."

"Listen, Mike; I'm over here on duty and not for a petting party. If you think I've come all these miles just to play games, you're barking up the wrong tree. I need you, I admit that, and I also need the cover this brother and sister act will provide, but you can keep your hands and your mouth to yourself. Remember that and we will get along fairly well. Forget it and I'll . . . I'll bite you."

The Irishman laughed.

"And sure, that would be noice too, but listen here now, don't go getting any fancy ideas into that pretty head of yours. Oi'll provide the cover, sure Oi will, but for just as long as you play my game. It's not often that Oi meet pretty girls like you, and you were sweet enough to me in Berlin . . ."

"I was not. I never . . ."

"Well, well! Shall we say you would have been if we had had an opportunity, but cheat me now, sister moine, and well, Oi guess that one word to the cops would put paid to you. They hang people like you in this be-noighted country. A secret trial they give them and then no one hears a solitary word at all until there are a few short lines in the papers, which say that the beautiful spoiy, having eaten a hearty breakfast, walked with a firm step to the scaffold. Oi've seen people after they've been hanged and sure, it's not a pleasant sight at that. Now, little sister, do Oi get that kiss?"

"You do not. Sit yourself down while I finish my packing and then we'll be off."

"Sit meself down, is it. Oi'll be after thinking that you've collected some funny ideas . . ."

"Oh, shut up, Mike. You'll have the whole village talking if you start a scene here. Now, just relax and we'll talk the whole thing over when we get to our . . . our destination."

The girl crossed to the window and tugged at the heavy black-out curtains and Mohune could hear the rattle of rings on the pelmet pole. One of the rings seemed to have stuck, for Miss Swastika continued to tug impatiently at the thick material. Heavy feet moved across the floor in the direction of the window.

"Faith, me dear, Oi don't think that Oi am prepared to wait all that long for me little kisslets. Have one now; just as a token of good faith, you'll understand."

"You seem to be in difficulties with that curtain. Can I be of any assistance?"

Two heads flicked round as one, two pairs of eyes stared with amazement at the man standing behind the dressing table. Mohune's left eyebrow rose, he bowed ironically.

"Good evening, Fraulein," he murmured.

There was no reply; Miss Swastika seemed to be paralyzed, and although Peter was watching the redheaded Irishman, prepared for Mike's first move, he could not help admiring the picture the girl presented. With her back to the heavy curtains, Freya had one hand above her head, still clutching the recalcitrant fold; the other hand lay against the whiteness of her throat, as though to hold back a pulse which threatened to choke her. Her red lips were parted, her eyes were wide.

"You," she murmured.

"Even so, Fraulein. It's a long way from Berlin to Hampshire, is it not?"

"Cops, eh?" growled Mike O'Regan, speaking for the first time. "At first Oi thought maybe it was a lover that you had picked up while you were waiting for me, which would have accounted for your shyness. But a cop, a lousy cop!"

O'Regan spat and rubbed his palms together.

"All right, sister, don't you be after worrying. Oi'll just alter the beautiful face of our little pansy here. Then we'll be on our way. Get on with your packing. It won't take me a minute."

"I think ..." began Mohune.

"I'm not caring at all what you may be thinking," interrupted O'Regan. "You won't be thinking at all when Oi've done with ye."

"No, Mike. You can't ..."

"Hush your pretty mouth. It's a pleasure, Oi'm telling you."

The Irishman's hand moved across the front of his jacket and when it went forward again it held a razor between finger and thumb.

"Don't squawk now, copper. You'll get yours before anyone can reach this room. Oi don't loike Englishmen and Oi loike their coppers less. Faith, and it's your nose Oi'm going to shave off your face."

Mohune smiled; he knew perfectly well that he could end the matter whenever he liked. The pistol swinging freely at his hip would put an effective full stop to the proceedings at any time he liked to apply the closure, but—and there was a but—he had no desire to start gun-play and thereby focus the attention of the inhabitants of Brag on to Room Seventeen, and so his eyes narrowed slightly as he smiled and murmured, "What a pity, what a shame."

Mike moved forward on his toes.

"Now, you yellow bast . . ."

With no preliminary backward movement, Mohune's right foot shot out. There was a crack as his toe-cap met the Irishman's shin; his right hand flashed across, caught the Irishman's right wrist, pulling it downwards, and as the man's body passed in front of him, Mohune struck downwards at the nape of the unprotected neck. Mike O'Regan was out!

Mohune's grip on the imprisoned right wrist softened the bump as the body met the floor.

"And now, Fraulein," began Mohune, slipping the thug's razor into his pocket and turning to the girl, "we can have our little talk. Your handsome boy friend will be in no condition to disturb us for a while."

"You fool; you utter, utter fool!"

The girl advanced on him with her hands clenched.

"And they told me that you were smart! Smart! Save the word . . ."

"I beg your pardon?" Mohune smiled.

"Oh, take that silly grin off your face. You've ruined everything. Everything. Can you understand?"

"I didn't think that I had progressed that far, but I have certainly made a start."

"Made a start! I'll say you have made a start, and you have come to the end of the course at the same time."

"At least I've got you."

"Got me? What on earth are you talking about?"

"Well, shall I say that I heard enough to have you arrested as a spy?"

"Arrested as a spy!"

It was the girl's turn to laugh, but there was no humor in the sound.

"Mother mine; did I say that they told me you were clever? They must have been mad."

The girl's anger, which had been temporarily liquidated by astonishment, returned in full force, and Mohune thought her more attractive than ever.

"A spy?" she laughed again. "So you think that I'm a spy?"

"Surely you are not going to deny that you were the shorthand writer at my so-called trial before Pegler?"

"Of course I'm not. Didn't I give you Freemantle's address? Didn't I put a rubber truncheon in your flying coat? And a nice mess you and Freemantle made of it between you."

"Well, well, well! So that was your work. I didn't think you would have had time. Pegler sent for you almost as soon as I had left your office."

He moved towards her and caught her gently by the arm.

"Come and sit on the bed. I can't stand about looking at you; it takes my mind off the job in hand. I suppose you have been told you are beautiful?"

"I have."

The girl was still angry.

"Yes, I didn't think I was being original. So you gave me my leave ticket. That was very sweet of you."

"Sweet of me!" she snorted. "Don't be silly. You

don't think I did it because of your beautiful eyes, do you?"

"Didn't you?"

"Do you think you mean anything to me? Why should you?"

Mohune nodded agreement.

"If I had thought that you would have helped the show more by dying, I should have let them kill you. I am beginning to be sorry that I didn't."

"Thank you."

Mohune took her chin in a cupped hand and turned her head so that her eyes met his.

"Didn't your mother tell you not to tell fibs? But never mind that; if not because you felt sorry for me, why did you do it?"

"Because I had seen the signal saying that you had been taken prisoner, because I had heard of you from Freemantle. I saw the dossier that Pegler had had prepared for him about you. I knew that Freemantle's days were numbered. He was cracking; his nerve had gone and they were after him. They got him that night, also the man that drove his car. I thought that Freemantle could use you. That's why I gave you that address and slipped a truncheon into your sleeve. After you had left, I managed to get word through to Freemantle to say that you might be coming along."

"Clever! And after that?"

"I heard that Freemantle had been liquidated by the Gestapo and that you had been killed in trying to escape. I thought I could help more by coming to England."

"How did you manage that? The bus route?"

"Of course."

"Wish I could have made use of it, but I didn't know the times of departure."

"Of course you didn't. Freemantle didn't know them either. He refused to accept the information towards the end, but still, you did quite well considering."

"Thanks."

"I'm sorry." Freya's anger melted with a smile. "I'm afraid that I have been rather a beast to you, but you have rather mucked things, you know."

"We'll talk about that later. Why did you put the police on to me in London?"

The girl laughed, but this time it was a happy laugh which Mohune thought was entirely delightful.

"That was funny, wasn't it? I had no idea that it was you until the Bobby showed his light on your face. I had the shock of my life. I had thought until then that you were an enemy agent. When you started demanding my address I thought that it was time to go. I hoped that the Bobby would move off and I could have explained everything to you; you would have been so much help. Where did you first pick me up?"

"In the Bakerloo. Your scar gave you away. Did you go to Dettmer?"

"No, he's not my branch, but I did hear that the stuff you had brought was useless and the pity of it is that my information isn't much better. That's why I'm down here."

"Complete with brother..."

"That thug! Do you know who he is?"

"Can't say I do. He doesn't appeal to my finer senses."

"Slug O'Regan."

"Slug just about fits him."

"He's an I.R.A. boss. I met him at a conference in Berlin. I knew he was in the Fifth Column over here and connected with the present plan, but that's all I knew. I contacted him in London; he runs a big garage. I bluffed him that I had special instructions for the Big Noise and that he was to take me there and verify my credentials. He believes that I'm one of Himmler's advance agents, and to-night he was going to take me to this house in Brag."

Her voice fell to a despondent note. "And now, as I said before, you have mucked everything."

"Remains to be seen, as the mortuary keeper said, but just before I set about the task of awakening our sleeping beauty, who exactly are you? I know that your name is Freya, but that's about all I do know."

"It's rather a long story; he may wake up."

Mohune bent over the recumbent Irishman and lifted an eyelid.

"I don't think it's likely, and if your story is really interesting, I can put him to sleep again."

"My name is not Freya at all; it's Schnoodel, Schnoodel Holech. My father is a Czech, or was . . ." she paused and then hurried on, "My mother was English; she died in 1936. My father was shot by the Nazis when they moved into Prague. I had a brother Toni; he got away, or at least I think he did. There were ten of them and seven bodies were brought back to Prague, having been shot by the frontier guards. They took me away and tried to make me tell where Toni was. I didn't know; even if I had, I shouldn't have told them. They branded me with this as a warning to others who would not talk and then I went to a concentration camp."

She looked down at her scarred wrist.

"I could stand that, but there were other things. I could have got off more lightly perhaps if I had agreed . . ."

She looked up at Mohune and smiled, "Well, agreed to the fate that is known as worse than death, but I have always been fastidious."

Gently Mohune took possession of her wrist and raised that swastika to his lips.

"Why did you do that?" she demanded.

"I don't quite know," he admitted. "But tell me, how did you get to Gestapo Headquarters?"

"There was a minor purge in the officers of the concentration camp and one who had always been a little more human than the rest took over the command. In time I proved that I was a good Nazi." There was a metallic timbre in her voice. "My every waking minute is devoted to their destruction; they're worse than savages; they're perverts and sadists. And there's one man I'm going to kill if ever I get a chance; that's a man called Kummer, Hans Kummer."

"You didn't hear?"

"Hear what?"

"I killed him that night in Berlin. Look out, the Slug is coming to; now just leave everything to me and follow my lead."

Mohune gave the girl's fingers a steady squeeze of comfort and then with scant ceremony, caught O'Regan by the hair and lifted his head.

"Snap out of it!"

O'Regan opened his eyes, but he made no attempt to rise from the floor.

Mohune's fingers cracked across his face.

"I said snap out of it!"

O'Regan struggled into a sitting position and a pair of baleful eyes stared up at Mohune.

"Slug O'Regan, eh? Local Big Shot, eh? Well, perhaps by now you have realized that it is unwise to forget your manners before an officer of Nazi Germany. Get up ... Get UP ..."

The Irishman made no attempt to make any further movement and again Mohune's fingers slashed at his cheek.

"Now will you get up or shall I kick you in the guts?"

Obediently Mike struggled to his feet.

"I've got one or two things to say to you, Slug. The first is that if you don't show more respect to me, I shall bash your face in."

"Huh! You caught me with a trick."

"Listen, Irishman, and listen carefully. My name is Brandt, and just to impress it upon you I will add that I am on General von Killinger's staff. Does that convey anything to you? Ah, I see that it does; there are glimmerings of intelligence in that red head of yours after all. I am here to select the General's headquarters. He himself will arrive on the second day of the invasion. The reports on people and conditions which I shall make to him will carry a lot of weight. So walk carefully, Irishman, walk carefully."

"Sure, sure, but how was I to know?"

"You heard me say to the Fraulein who now poses as your sister that it was a long way from Berlin to

Hampshire; that should have been sufficient guidance for you. Our little Freya and I are old friends, are we not, Fraulein?"

"Yes, indeed, mein Herr," stammered Schnoodel.

"It was I who gave her a birthday present; not one of your tawdry baubles, Slug, but one that she can never lose."

Mohune grasped the girl's wrist and displayed the sprawling scar.

"Incidentally, Fraulein, you were told to keep that bandaged in England. Why have you not done so?"

"I did until this afternoon. I . . ."

"Don't forget orders, little Freya, or we shall give you cause to keep both wrists bandaged, even if you have proved yourself useful to the Reich."

Mohune swung round to face Mike.

"As for you, O'Regan, I am prepared to overlook this incident, but next time, Slug, I'll smash your jaw and see that it stays smashed. You may be a big shot in this effete country, but by Thor, I'll soon teach you that you're just scum to us. Heil Hitler!"

There was a deadly silence.

"I said Heil Hitler!" Mohune's balled fist drew back.

"Heil Hitler," mumbled O'Regan.

"That's better, much better. Now let's go; where's your car?"

"In the park, round the corner . . ."

A sly look seeped into the Irishman's eyes.

"O'Regan, I feel that you are a sick man. Something tells me that it won't be long now before we are ordering you a nice bunch of flowers. Your trouble, Slug, is mental. You can't see the brick wall that you are banging your pate against. You have heard of von Killinger?"

"Sure, sure."

"And you have heard of the Erhardt Brigade, our brigade of steel? Do you know, Irishman, that we wear a star for every liquidation or execution that we take part in. One day I'll tell you about my stars, but now just to impress your memory, I'll tell four little stories about von Killinger.

"There was a woman who, for some reason or another, refused him a certain request. Killinger stripped her, flung her on the floor and ordered a man to flog her. This was done while the Shadow—that's what we call Killinger—the Shadow stood and watched, interjecting 'More, more,' from time to time, until her back was covered with blood and she lost her senses. He had her branded with a swastika; now she's a loyal member of the party.

"A man once joined issue with the Shadow, Mike, rather as you have done this evening with me, but his offence was less than yours, for he only argued. I seized his arms and the Shadow said, 'One more word from you and you won't speak for a fortnight.' That was enough for me; I smashed his jaw there and then with a hand grenade.

"I started with von Killinger in 1929; there was a threat of a general strike in the air and we heard of a factory where a Socialist newspaper was being printed. He was quite excited that day. 'Good,' he said, rubbing his hands together, 'that helps. We will smash that press. Never mind the people. Knock 'em down.'

"We did; we knocked them down all right. We drove our lorries through the mass of them. They screamed as we bumped over their bodies. We got the press, by Thor, we did.

"A woman spat at me once; a punch in the mouth taught her better manners; by the time I had finished with her, she had learnt her lesson. She will never spit at a member of the Erhardt Brigade again. How the Shadow laughed when I told him that she'd have to lie on her tummy for a week.

"No. O'Regan, it doesn't pay to double-cross me. Furthermore, the Shadow is a member of the People's Court, the tribunal which sends men and women to the ax and from which there is no appeal. Before the war he helped to organize your I.R.A. activities for you in this country. It was, of course, in that respect that you visited Berlin. There is a good mark star against your name in the Shadow's files at the moment, Mike, but one word from me and that star changes to a black cross.

"You remember that in 1920 he ran guns into Ireland for you? You know his school where his agents and tourists are trained? Before long he will be here himself. He told me that you and your men would be responsible to him for my safety until his arrival. So watch out, Slug, watch out."

O'Regan had wilted visibly during Mohune's discourse. The braggart balloon had been punctured. Mohune moved forward and stood close to him, thrusting an open palm under the Irishman's nose.

"I have you there, Mike."

A long finger stroked the center of the open hand, the fingers of which curled slowly inwards.

"In a very short while the Swastika will fly over Buckingham Palace; our troops will march in triumph along Whitehall; you have the choice—you can march with them or you march with your enemies to Tower Hill. Now go and get the car. Be at the front door within five minutes."

Peter pivoted on one heel.

"Fraulein, finish your packing."

"But I was told to take the Fraulein to the house before midnight," expostulated Mike.

Mohune swung round like a striking panther. A balled fist rocked O'Regan back on his heels; the edge of a palm moving upwards from waist level caught him under the nose and threw him back against the wall.

"I, Freidl Brandt, give orders here by virtue of the authority vested in me by General von Killinger. Get out."

"Sure, sure."

"And remember, be back in five minutes."

"Sure, sure."

Heavy footsteps clattered down the stairs and were lost in the silence of the hotel. Peter turned and caught Schnoodel by the shoulders.

"How am I doing, Ugly Bun?" he demanded, glancing at her quizzically.

"Marvelously. Wherever did you get the local color?"

"Local color, Little Goose? I read it in a book. It's all true, every word of it. Killinger wrote it himself. Putsch Life . . . Stories Grave and Gay . . ."

"You certainly frightened Slug. You were the perfect Nazi. You frightened me; I thought I was going through it all over again."

"Poor little Schnoodie."

Fingers strayed to the girl's mouth.

"Schnoodie," she murmured, "Schnoodie; I . . . I haven't," tears welled into her eyes and she swallowed as though her heart had come into her mouth; "I haven't been called that since . . . since Toni went. Oh, Peter, you sent me back for a moment to those normal days of long ago."

Her head drooped and the words came hesitantly.

"Oh, dear God, if only I could live a normal life again just for one day. Why can't I be like other people? Is it asking too much of God? For years I've had no friends, no one to turn to. Forgive me, Peter, when I say this, but I see so many people in this country self-satisfied and smug, that I can't understand; I try, Peter, honestly, I do, but I can't understand . . . I wouldn't have said any of this if you hadn't called me Schnoodie, then it . . . well, the dam just broke."

Gently, very gently, Mohune raised her chin.

"Chin up, my dear. You're doing great work. Work that only you could do."

"I know, I know, but I can't go on alone. Can't you see that I can't go on? Any day I might make a slip." She swayed forward and clung to Mohune desperately.

"Courage, little Schnoodie. We're nearly out of the wood now."

"We're not. I know we're not. We are only at the beginning and if they should succeed, can't you imagine what will happen? Everyone seems to be thinking that because it hasn't happened to England yet, it never will. They say 'We've got a grand Air Force' and go on with their normal lives content to leave it all to the fighting Services. It won't do, Peter, it won't do. Everyone has got to work to their utmost capacity or you'll have the same thing happening in these English villages as happened in France, Poland, Greece, Norway and everywhere else. Why can't they see it, Peter? It will be too late soon, too late for them to do anything but submit to serfdom. Oh, Peter!"

She was crying now, great sobs which shook her body like a tempest; all the pent-up emotion of years under the Nazi heel was breaking through in a flood and Mohune, with his arm about a slender waist, let those tears go on unchecked. It was better so and as they stood there, close in each other's arms, he thought again of the fate that would descend upon this fair land, should the beast of Berlin ever drag his slimy trail across England's fields. Women raped and murdered, children struck down; he thought of Juno and her brother; men tortured; his mind turned to that night in the barracks at Berlin; the whole nation reduced to slaves without hope, without protection.

Minutes passed and then gently he eased her from him.

"It's time for us to go," he whispered; "can you bear it?"

She nodded; "I feel better now, but keep with me, Peter de L'Epee; just hold my hand now and then."

"That's a promise and an easy one."

Abruptly she turned away and pushed the foam of lace into its suitcase and snapped down the catch, while Mohune collected the bags from the closet.

"I must take them all," she declared; "Killinger's A.D.C. would never stoop to menial work."

"Miss O'Regan," Mohune's voice hardened; "you

forget that I, Hauptman Freidl Brandt, give orders in this country."

Together they descended the wide staircase; halfway down she paused and laid a hand on his arm.

"Tell me, why did you come out of that cupboard when you did?"

"I thought the situation was getting out of hand and perhaps . . ."

"Yes?"

"Perhaps I was a little jealous."

The grip on his arm tightened.

"Peter Mohune, you are a darling."

"Sure, sure," he answered.

CHAPTER FOURTEEN

IN WHICH HE REAPPEARS AS HAUPTMAN BRANDT

"How long will it take?

Mohune, seated beside the soi-disant Miss O'Regan in the back of the large Buick, addressed the driver.

" 'The Towers?' " questioned Mike. "Sure and it will only take about foive to eight minutes."

"The Towers."

Peter's memory flashed back to the local topography provided by Davis. Who was it that lived at "The Towers"? The hard-drinking Major? No, that had the very apt name of "Taverners." The Austrian brain specialist; no, that did not ring a bell. The author bloke who wrote pornographic stuff; that was the man. What was his name . . . what in Hades was his name? Fearnley something . . .

The tires hummed over the road's hard surface, the dark line of the hedgerows flashed past. Fearnley Derbyshire, Fearnley—Fearnley Davenport; getting warmer—it's Daven . . . Davenley, Daventry . . . damn it, it's not Daven at all, it's Davy . . . Daveyjones—Davigore, that's it! Fearnley Davigore. God bless the Security Officer.

The car crunched over a gravel drive and came to rest. Mohune helped the girl to alight and followed O'Regan into the darkness of a porch.

Within three minutes the heavy door was opened and a voice bade them enter. It was a strong melodious voice and Mohune wondered what kind of man possessed it; he had not long to wait. The door was closed, a light switch snapped and Mohune was facing a tall man in a well-fitting dinner jacket. Tall, with a mass of tawny hair, close-trimmed Spanish beard and two brilliant green eyes that regarded Peter with casual bewilderment.

"Evening. You Davigore?"

Mike's eyes opened wide and Schnoodel placed two fingers over her mouth to stem her gasp of astonishment.

"That is my name. I . . . er . . . O'Regan, er . . . Introduce me."

"Brandt is my name."

"Really; South African?"

"No."

Davigore turned again to the Irishman.

"Mike, frankly I do not understand. You were to meet your sister"—he appeared to see the girl for the first time—"You must be Mike's sister; charming, charming, so pleased that you could come, my dear. I'm afraid you may find my house a little primitive," he shrugged his wide shoulders apologetically. "You see, I am a bachelor and I have no maid-servant. However, we will do our best. We must have a long talk together later on, a long talk. And now, O'Regan," the green eyes changed their direction again, "your sister is rather early, is she not? I thought . . ."

"If you are referring to your orders that we should not arrive before midnight," cut in Mohune, "I cancelled them."

"Really, my dear fellow. Really, but don't you think

I am entitled to some explanation? Now, Mike, what is it all about?"

"He came with the girl."

"So I perceive."

"What I mean is, he came all the way with her."

"All the way? You amaze me."

"I would suggest we're getting nowhere," put in Peter. Brandt's monocle was now screwed firmly into his eye.

"The Fraulein's baggage is still in the car. I will give you all explanations. You must have had word that I was coming."

"Warned, my dear fellow; I know nothing about you whatever, but there it is. Mike vouches for our charming young friend. You do, don't you, Mike?"

"Sure, sure."

"And she in turn vouches for you. Is that so?"

"Yes," very quietly, this.

"So who am I to worry? Now come along. Just throw your coats down there. Piero will have collected your bags by now. Come along and meet my staff. We are to have our final conference."

"All eggs in one basket?"

"If you put it that way, yes."

Davigore led the way across the hall into a library, a comfortably furnished room, where four men in evening dress lounging in deep armchairs, were grouped around a merrily-blazing fire. Decanters and glasses were handily adjacent. They looked up and rose to their feet as Davigore ushered his small party into their presence.

Davigore raised a hand.

"Don't get up, gentlemen. I want to introduce Miss O'Regan from—well, shall we say, who has been touring abroad—and Mr. Brandt, who is not a South African."

He turned to Mohune.

"My dear fellow, you really are a bit of a mystery. Will you not help us just a little?"

"Who are these men?"

"Friends of mine."

"High operatives?"

Davigore's eyes closed slightly; "Very high operatives."

"All right. I'm General von Killinger's Aide de Camp."

A tension struck the occupants; all eyes were focused on the haughty face before them.

"My dear fellow," murmured Davigore.

"My credentials."

From an inside pocket Mohune produced Brandt's wallet and handed it to the author, who studied the contents thoughtfully.

"Is it wise, Hauptman, to carry such incriminating documents about with you?" he asked as he returned the wallet.

"I am the best judge of that. You are satisfied?"

"Perfectly, perfectly."

"Good. Now as to the purpose of this meeting?"

"I was giving my final instructions to my staff. They are Area Commandants. They already knew what they had to do, but had not been told the reason for their operations. I have explained that war, the oldest pastime known to men, has varied but little through the ages. That is to say, until the present conflict, which will unite the free-thinking peoples of the world and will finally stamp out the despotism of so-called Democracy."

Davigore was now standing with his back to the fire, resting his shoulders against the high mantelshelf. There was a fanatical gleam in his green eyes. From time to time as he made a point, the fingers of his left hand clutched at his tawny beard. The four men had sunk back into their chairs. Schnoodel had seated herself on a settee, over which Mike leaned possessively, while Mohune was perched on the corner of a large radio-gramophone.

Davigore continued, "War is the continuation of National Policy by resort to force. In the past, nations at war surrounded themselves with a wall of might, behind which their forces were arranged and their vital interests guarded. It was the task of the armies and the navies to break down the walls of the opposing side and to destroy the enemy's forces. To-day things have changed; aircraft have proved their worth and what is more important, that walls of force do not exist as far as bombers are concerned. An aeroplane moves in three dimensions; it is unhampered by the configuration of the world's surfaces. Thus it was that the gallant pilots of the Luftwaffe were of the opinion that when they attacked this home of Jewish capitalism, their task would be an easy one.

"They knew, such men as we ourselves had told them, that England's fighter force was not large enough to maintain standing patrols."

Davigore paused.

"O'Regan, get drinks for our new guests."

"Sure, sure," muttered Mike, and leaving his sister

with obvious reluctance, he moved across to a cocktail cabinet to collect glasses.

"You didn't make it clear why they couldn't use standing patrols," put in one of the men by the fire.

Davigore nodded, "I will do that now," he conceded.

"A fighter aircraft," he went on, "is a machine that stays in the air for a very limited time. It has to come down to refuel, and when it's down, another patrol must take its place and furthermore, when it is refueling, it must be protected, for a plane without petrol is as a crab without a shell—useless and highly vulnerable. We hoped, gentlemen, that when we attacked, we would catch many aircraft on the ground; we were unlucky, but more of that anon.

"Miss O'Regan, to your very beautiful eyes. Hauptman Brandt, your very good health."

Three glasses rose.

"To continue. Fighter patrols have other disadvantages. They must be large enough to tackle a determined enemy formation and even the dull-witted English realized that the Germans would be determined. And every aircraft on patrol lessens the defending forces. Do you wonder, gentlemen, that in September, 1940, the pilots of the Luftwaffe thought their task would be an easy one?

"That it wasn't was due to one thing—Ground Control. The English had realized that a vertical wall of force was of no use to them, so they devised with a cunning for which they are famous, a lateral network of nerve centers of information, and this network was perfect. However much you may dislike the English, and no one hates them as I do," the fanatical gleam crept back, "you will have to admit that their defense organization has reached a degree of unbelievable perfection. All these nerve channels fed their information to their Operations Room. Our planes were watched by a thousand eyes, our every move was known."

"Do you mean to say that we didn't know of this organization?" put in another of Davigore's staff.

"Of course we did. But we ourselves were not organized in England to smash as we will in the near future. Germany, gallant Germany, had to depend on her valiant pilots. No sacrifice was too great; they struck and struck again, but in every instance their blows were foreseen and parried by the damnable Ground Control. What matter how many aircraft we had, what matter what risks we took or what courage we displayed, so long as one man in an Operations Room could reveal our tactics by radio telephone to his pilots in the air.

"That is past history. We are now prepared. You, gentlemen, are the leaders of the German Army in England. O'Regan has organized the transport details for our action. His lorries are at your garages, doing normal jobs of work. Before long you will STRIKE."

Davigore's voice rose and he screamed that last word.

"No longer will you be oppressed. You will be free, free now to think as you wish to think, act as you wish to act, live as you wish to live. To-night you will return to your Headquarters. You will be at action stations. When the word comes, you will act. Some of us may die, but we will die paving the way for the final victory of Nazi Germany. You must not fail, you will not fail. The Ground Control of the Royal Air Force must be exterminated ruthlessly and completely. Think, gentlemen, of the glory and the honor that awaits you.

"And now, gentlemen, it is time for our evening broadcast. O'Regan, turn the set on."

"Sure, sure."

Complete silence fell upon the room while the valves in the radio-gramophone on which Peter had been sitting warmed up. An atmosphere of tense expectancy had fallen on the company.

A voice spoke in German; nothing startling, just an ordinary voice announcing a commonplace program of gramophone records. For a second Mohune thought an anti-climax had been brought to the proceedings; then he noticed that Davigore had turned his back to the room and was writing copious notes into a book upon the mantelshelf, but still the announcements conveyed nothing to Mohune, and from the expression on the faces of the other listeners, they were all similarly placed.

The voice went steadily on, giving a list of records and their catalogue numbers, which were about to be offered for the approval of his listeners.

Mohune drew out his cigarette case and offered it to Schnoodel. Their eyes met, mutely questioning. The announcements came to an end; the strains of a symphony orchestra filled the room.

"That appears to be all for this evening," commented Davigore. "I'll leave you gentlemen to enjoy the pretty music while I work this out. Come along, Miss O'Regan, and you, my dear fellow, you too, Brandt."

Peter and Schnoodel followed the author from the library across the hall and into a study, a long narrow room this, with bay window at each end. Down the center was a clear space about six feet wide, covered with fiber matting.

"My study and exercise room. I do a lot of fencing," explained Davigore. "Piero Nadi, my manservant, is an expert with the sword; he also throws a pretty knife. Please be seated; I won't keep you long."

Davigore crossed to a wall safe of ancient pattern and twirled the combination. Mohune watched intently and although the distance was too great for him to obtain the slightest inclination as to the coding of the combination, he saw something which interested him greatly.

The author, having set the dial, did not pull the door fully open; instead he merely gave himself sufficient space to slip his hand into the safe. There his fingers fumbled for a moment; then, withdrawing his hand, he pulled the door wide.

From the cavity Davigore produced a deed box and from this he in turn drew out a small book.

"You know this code?" he asked, glancing at Mohune, who was by now looking in an entirely different direction.

"I should not think so. Not in my line."

"Oh, of course not. Incidentally, later on you must tell me exactly what your line is; in the meantime you will excuse me."

Davigore seated himself at a desk in one of the bays and switched on an Adipoise lamp, while Mohune and Schnoodel moved quietly about the room, studying the various trophies which adorned the walls. At the far end of the room from the author was a rack containing foils, epees and sabers, neither better no worse than those to be seen in any salle d'armes, but on a ledge close to them lay a pair of swords of most excellent craftsmanship. Taking one from its resting place, Peter made a few idle thrusts and circular parries to test its balance.

Davigore looked up from his work.

"You are a fencer?"

"I know a good sword when I see one."

"If we have time, we will have some play together, you and I."

"I am here to work."

"Perhaps it's as well. I am very good."

There was no conceit in this statement; it was a plain statement of fact, which Peter was prepared to accept as the truth.

"I have finished now; would you care to read the message?"

"I would."

Mohune and Miss O'Regan walked over to the desk. upon which Mohune laid the sword, and took the sheet of paper which Davigore handed to him.

"Invasion commences within seven days. All to be at readiness for instant action."

"What's the basis of the code?" inquired Mohune. drawing deeply at his cigarette.

"The numbers of the gramophone records; but the message—doesn't it thrill you to the marrow?"

"I already knew it."

"Then why in Heaven didn't you tell me before, my dear fellow?"

"You didn't ask me."

"To be sure. I've asked you very little as yet. Tell

me one thing; why are they indefinite? It's not like them. Generally everything is cut and dried. The day, the hour, the minute; but within seven days!"

"Does it interrupt your plans?"

"Not a bit. My men will be ready by mid-day to-morrow. They will need no further signal from me. That will go to them direct. But this delay? Why? I ask you; why?"

"I think Miss O'Regan has come over for that express purpose."

Davigore whirled round to face Schnoodel, his tawny beard jutting aggressively, his hands palms upwards in supplication.

"Why? Why? Why? I don't like it; I don't like it at all. It's out of the norm . . ."

Mohune, knowing that the girl had not the slightest idea of what she ought to say, broke in upon the torrential flow.

"I gather that the English Bomber Command more than interfered with our High Command plans. It was the night before last the big blow fell. Am I not right, Fraulein?"

"Correct in every detail."

"Le Havre, Dieppe, Boulogne, were heavily raided."

"But," expostulated Davigore, "I understood that this was to be an air invasion."

"At the outset, yes. But heavy tanks need ships."

"I see. Well, it's good to know that it's not cancelled. That's some comfort. They say within seven days. Now tell me something about yourself, my dear fellow . . ."

"Do you mind if I go to my room?" interjected the girl. "I . . . I have had a rather trying time during the past forty-eight hours and now my report will keep until to-morrow."

"Of course, my dear, of course. Top of the stairs. First floor, turn right; second door along the passage; next to our friend here. I expect Piero will have laid your things out for you. Can't offer you dinner; these confounded rations; but you'll find some sandwiches in your room. Ring for Piero if you want anything. Goodnight, my dear, good-night."

"Good-night. Good-night, Herr Hauptman."

"Good-night, Fraulein."

Davigore crossed to the door, flung it open, watched her mount the stairs, closed the door and returned to Mohune.

"Pretty girl; pretty girl. Now then, as we were saying; tell me your story. What a pity I can't put it all into a book. When did you arrive?"

"Shall we say," returned Mohune, glancing reflectively at the tip of his cigarette, "that I took silk over England the night before last."

Davigore threw back his head and laughed.

"I like that; you're a droll dog, Brandt, I like you. And Miss O'Regan?"

"I don't know; submarine, I expect. I met her by chance; saw her with O'Regan. We're not in the same line, but we ... well, we know each other."

"I understand. I quite understand, my dear fellow. I wouldn't mind knowing her myself."

Mohune's fingers itched to catch hold of that pointed beard; instead:

"What I cannot understand is why you were not warned of my coming."

"Neither can I. Look here."

Davigore returned to the open deed box and pro-duced a paper from which he read an excerpt.

"Expect a senior intelligence officer; arriving air night 5th."

The author looked up; "That's to-night."

"They must have made a mistake in the date. That must refer to me."

"No, no, no. A later signal gave his name—Major von Rinck."

Not a muscle twitched in Mohune's face.

"Oh, von Rinck. I can explain that. He'll never take another trip."

"You mean . . ."

Davigore's thumb pointed downwards.

"Exactly. You must know that there have been cer-tain differences of opinion in the Party lately. He, fool-ish fellow, was on the wrong side."

"And you were on the right?"

"I am the Shadow's Aide de Camp."

"Of course. That, my dear fellow, brings us back to your—what did you so aptly call it?—line?"

"Insecticide."

Again that head was thrown back and again that explosive burst of laughter echoed along the long nar-row room.

"Insecticide! You grow on me more and more. I think I shall have a job for you."

Another paper was produced from the deed box.

"A list of insects for you, my dear fellow."

The paper changed hands. The list was a long one, and headed by the name of the Austrian brain specialist at "The Trundle." This name was underlined in red ink. Mohune tapped it with his long forefinger.

"Enemies of the Reich, and that particular one, an enemy of mine," announced Davigore.

"I suggest you liquidate him yourself, then."

"My dear fellow, I can eat mutton, but I cannot kill the sheep."

"You're too squeamish. That's a crime in Nazi Germany."

"I'm not squeamish, but I loathe noise."

Davigore's green eyes narrowed into slits.

"But if I could have him before me, with a sword in my hand . . ."

A clenched fist with extended forefinger moved forward suggestively. The purpose in the movement was bestial. Mohune laughed and immediately the author returned to normal.

"Well, I must put Pandora's Box away. The Security Police would give a lot to get hold of this. The whole bag of tricks. Invasion scheme, the only one in England; my code book, action signals. What a prey!"

"Aren't you rather unwise to keep it here?"

"It's as safe as houses—or as houses were before the Luftwaffe came to England."

"But a search party?"

"Would find nothing, my dear fellow."

"But if they opened the safe?"

"They'd still find nothing."

The metal door closed with a clang. Davigore corrupted the combination and moved across to the door leading to the hall. Mohune had noted that the dispatch box was unlocked when Davigore put it in the safe and had noted that peculiar fumbling through the half-closed door, and was then watching the light steps and well-balanced movements of the author.

"Help yourself to a drink, Brandt. In the bottom of the bookcase. I'll just give my staff their orders and then I'll join you. We might listen to the wireless later on. If they should send a substitute for von Rinck, it will be nice to know that he arrives safely."

"How will you know that?"

"By a curious freak of chance I can pick up a harmonic of the local Air Force Stations' frequency. We'll hear them talking to their aircraft in the air. We shall know if a plane does come and if it's intercepted."

The door closed and with a lithe step Mohune was at the safe. And combination locks were a hobby of his.

CHAPTER FIFTEEN

IN WHICH HE HEARS A HUN SHOT DOWN

WHEN Davigore returned to the study, he found the Shadow's A.D.C. reclining in a chair, gazing at the ascending bubbles in his whisky and soda.

The safe had been examined. It was, as Mohune had hoped, of ancient pattern, and he had decided that an hour would be ample time in which to wrest from it its secrets.

"Come along, my dear fellow. Let's go into the library; the boisterous O'Regan and his minions have left us and we can have a drink in peace, while we listen to the radio."

Five minutes later the two men sat on either side of the jovial fire. Davigore had replenished the glasses and produced some quite excellent cigars.

"Are you not going to turn the set on?"

"Not yet. We will know in good time should it be necessary."

"How?"

"The air raid warning will go; that will give ample warning."

Mohune nodded.

"Your schemes are all ready? No possibility of a breakdown?"

"None whatever, my dear fellow. This is the chance I have been waiting for. Do you think that I would make a mistake now? O'Regan, thug though he is, is competent. The plans are foolproof. As soon as the word is given, we shall act and even your High Command will be astonished at our efficiency. Power, Brandt, power! That's what it means to me; unlimited power. I . . .".

The undulating notes of the siren echoed across the peaceful fields. Davigore raised a finger.

"Our one."

He crossed to the wireless and turned one of the bakelite knobs.

"Hello, Bellboy; hello, Bellboy; Pluto 17 calling. Any further instructions?"

Mohune shut his eyes and was transported into the transparent nose of the Beaufighter. He could see the bulky figure of the pilot straining his eyes into the night, a night that Dulac could have painted, a scene of varying shades of blue. The cherry red glow round the exhausts, the moon shining in palest blue upon the whirling airscrews, the dark sea where capes stood out like white pointing fingers, the occasional wink from a flashing beacon, and solitude.

"Hello, Pluto One Seven, One Seven; Bellboy answering. One Bandit. Vector one four zero. Over."

"Understood. Out."

Good, this pilot; no unnecessary verbiage to fill the air with sound.

Mohune visualized the dip of the main plane as the Beau turned on to its new course, a flash of light as the moon penetrated the cabin.

"Steady on, one four zero."

"O.K. One Seven; he's ahead of you now."

"Oke; out."

The Beaufighter was after its prey. In his chair Davigore tugged at his beard; the suspense was playing upon a weak spot in his armor.

Minutes, silent minutes which seemed like hours, went by. Mohune's eyes were still closed; he knew what those minutes meant to the pilot. A Hun was ahead, but was he straight ahead? Was he to port or to starboard? Was he above or below?

He knew how easy it was to overshoot at night or to pass within thirty feet and not see the objective at all.

"Hello, One Seven, One Seven," the Controller was calling again. "You are very close to him now."

"Understood; out."

Mohune saw the pilot wriggling into a more comfortable position as he stared about him.

The stem of Davigore's glass snapped between his fingers.

"O.K. Control; I can see him now. I'm closing in steadily . . ."

"Well done, One Seven. Slap him down."

"O.K., Control; I'll do my best."

The pilot's voice had not altered; still calm, very calm.

"I shall give him a burst soon."

The gloved hand was on the cannon's button.

"I say, Control. His rear gunner's a damned bad shot; he's been firing at me for five minutes and hasn't hit me yet. Colored stuff, like fireflies; very pretty."

The Nazi's black silhouette ought to be discernible now.

"I'm giving him a squirt. Now!"

The Beau would shake a little as the cannons sent their shells through the air as the pilot pressed his button.

"Yes, Control, yes; I hit him then. His gunner's stopped firing . . . Yes, his port engine's on fire . . ."

Still no excitement in the pilot's voice; quite calm.

"He's burning nicely now. Yes, he's going down all right. Got anything else for me?"

"Well done, One Seven, but don't be greedy."

With a bound Davigore left his chair, leapt at the wireless set and switched it off. Mohune opened his eyes and saw a white face above him. Beads of sweat glistening like pearls in the firelight stood out upon the author's brow. Mohune said nothing.

"You—you heard?" he repeated.

There was a gurgle as Davigore poured whisky into a fresh glass.

"You heard?" he repeated.

"Every word."

Mohune rose to his feet and put his glass on the mantelshelf.

"Take a grip of yourself, Davigore. That's war. Nothing unusual about that."

"Maybe not for you. But . . . but . . . I can't stand that sort of thing. I'm an organizer, not a fighter."

"Well, whatever you are, it doesn't look as though your messenger will arrive now. I'm for bed. Good-night, Davigore."

"Good-night . . . good-night."

Mohune left the author huddled in his chair and mounted the stairs to his room. Everything had been prepared for him. Flame-colored pajamas were laid out on the bed, a silk dressing gown was hanging over a chair. A plate of sandwiches, a decanter, a syphon and a glass had been deposited on the bedside table.

He undressed, placing the Luger with its corded harness beside the sandwiches, and went into the adjoining bathroom.

For half an hour he soaked his long body, and it was as he was pulling his dressing gown over those brilliant pajamas that he heard movement in his bedroom. Lightly he crossed to the door; without sound it opened. Someone was about to be surprised.

The lights were still on; the mirror over the dressing table displayed the room to Peter; a smile flickered over his face and he tiptoed forward. His arms shot out.

"Got you, my proud beauty. Got you."

The girl, seated on the bed with her back to him, fell back into his arms.

"Oh, how you frightened me."

He lifted her and set her on her feet.

"Don't you know that it's an act of a brazen hussy to visit a man's bedroom?"

"I am a brazen hussy."

Peter held her at arm's length. Here indeed was a picture to dispel the thoughts of the sadistic Davigore.

Her fair hair hanging down to her shoulders gleamed with its own luster; her lips, slightly parted, allowed a glimpse of dazzling teeth.

"Schnoodie, you are very, very beautiful."

"You told me that before, Peter."

"I know I did and I shall quite probably say it again. Why have you come here, child?"

"To say I'm sorry."

"What in the world for?"

"I was a beast to you."

"Don't be silly. Have a sandwich?"

"I was a beast."

Those white teeth bit into the white triangle.

"I was simply horrid to you."

"You shouldn't speak with your mouth full; it's very rude."

"I said you had mucked things and you're doing so well. I couldn't have coped without you."

"Have another sandwich?"

"But you might have told me that you knew Davigore."

"I didn't. Here, sit down and I'll explain."

Peter crossed to the hand basin and collected the tooth glass. Two whiskies were poured out.

"*Na zdravi*."

"You speak Czech?"

"Only that much. Now I'll tell you all that I know."

In short staccato sentences Peter told the story of Dettmer, Davis and the Forest Patrol.

"I have decided," he went on, "that I must open that safe to-night. I'll give Davigore an hour to go to sleep and then I'll start."

"But we don't know the Zero hour or day, for that matter, of the attack."

"Immaterial if I can get my hands on that Code Book. Dettmer's radio sleuths can listen for the broadcasts. Now, this is the plan. If I can get that safe open—and I don't think it will be difficult as it is a hobby of mine—I'll make what notes I think pertinent, and you must take them to Davis to-night. Tell him to get them to Vye at the Air Ministry immediately. I'll hang on here and deal with Davigore should he smell a rat. Understood?"

"Understood."

"Good."

Suddenly Mohune leant forward and whispered:

"Follow my lead."

"But every girl since Eve has thought her lover to be the finest man on earth."

The ball was tossed back promptly.

"Eve hadn't much choice, had she?"

"Exactly; that's what I've always thought. Adam has achieved an undeserved reputation as the perfect lover. He had no competition. What chance have I to go down to posterity as the perfect lover?"

"Is that your ambition?"

"It wasn't until now."

"Darling."

Gently he pushed her back to the bed and leaned across her; their lips met and at that moment the door opened and Davigore in pajamas and brilliant dressing gown was framed in the doorway. Mohune and Schnoodel jumped to their feet.

"Don't—don't let me disturb you, children."

The author raised a hand.

"Beautiful," he went on, "beautiful, the blending of the colors; delightful, truly delightful."

"What the devil is the meaning of this intrusion?" flared Peter. "Am I to have no privacy? Is it your custom to burst into your guests' bedrooms, uninvited and unheralded?"

"Brandt, my dear fellow. You misjudge me."

"Misjudge you, you . . ."

"Now let me explain."

"I don't want your explanations; I want to be alone."

"Alone? Really, my dear fellow, you surprise me; with a charming companion and you want to be alone! I—er—went to Miss O'Regan's room. It was empty; the bed had not been slept in. I was worried. I thought it best to inform you without delay. But I see that my fears were groundless. I am sorry for the intrusion; I will inconvenience you no longer. Good-night, children, good-night and—er—pleasant dreams."

The door closed behind him.

"You must have ears like a cat; I didn't hear him."

"I did."

Schnoodel looked into Peter's eyes.

"You're a very good actor, Wing Commander. You made me think it was real."

"Perhaps it was."

A flood of color seeped upwards through her white throat and Mohune turned hurriedly away to replenish the empty glasses.

"One more little drink," he announced, "and then back you go to your room, Baggage. Get dressed and when I think the coast is clear, I will call for you."

"So be it. Er—Peter . . ."

Mohune raised an eyebrow.

"Kiss me, Peter."

"I won't be acting."

"I know. I want it as medicine."

"Baggage."

An hour and a half later, two figures descended to

the study. Mohune, despite his size, moved as silently as a cat and seemed to have an instinctive knowledge of the presence of obstacles which he circumnavigated without appreciable hesitation.

A small pencil of light from a torch led him to the wall safe. Schnoodel waited at his side in silence.

The minutes sped by. Only Peter's long fingers moved as he twisted the dial, a stethoscope aided his highly-trained sense of hearing.

Now and then the girl altered her position to ease her cramped legs. Once she started as a clock chimed the quarter.

It was nerve-racking work for Miss O'Regan, who had nothing to occupy the dragging minutes, but strain her ears into the darkness for the approach of unwanted intruders. The creaking of the old timbers, the fall of an ember from the dying fire, the sigh of the wind in the drive, all magnified themselves into a ghostly and terrifying chorus, but oblivious to all around him, Mohune worked on.

Suddenly he straightened his back.

"Got it," he announced, and glancing at the luminous dial of his wrist watch, "Forty-seven and a half minutes. I allowed an hour; not too bad."

The stethoscope was slipped into his pocket and he patted Schnoodel's shoulder reassuringly.

"Won't be long now."

The safe door was pulled four inches open and Peter's questing fingers explored the cavity behind. A light chain connected the back of the safe door with the lid of the deed box. Very gently this was detached and the safe door opened to its full extent. The deed box was removed and taken to Davigore's desk. With extreme care Peter raised the lid, placing his pistol on the desk.

"Neat," he murmured, "see this, Schnoodie; the lid is in fact a tank, which I suspect is filled with a corrosive liquid or possibly creosote. A chain is attached to this knob, which in turn is hinged to a plug. The other end of the chain is attached to the inside panel of the safe door. Get the idea?

"If the safe door is opened to its full extent before the chain is detached, the knob is pulled and the plug is withdrawn, so that the liquid goes into the box . . ."

"And destroys the contents?"

"Exactly. Full marks for uptake."

The box revealed its secrets as Peter removed them one by one and placed them on the desk.

"This is going to be a long job, Poppet," he announced. This invasion scheme alone will take some wading through, let alone the code."

At that moment all the lights flashed on.

"Don't move, Brandt," said Davigore. "Piero here can throw a knife with extreme, yes, extreme accuracy at this range."

Mohune blinked first at Davigore and then at Piero, an undersized man with pronounced Italian features, olive-skinned, blue jowl and dark smoldering eyes, who was holding a gleaming throwing knife by the point.

"What's the idea, Davigore? Can't you sleep?"

Davigore smiled.

"What's the idea, my dear fellow? Isn't that rather cool? I find you examining the contents of my safe and you ask me why I am interfering. No, my dear fellow, that won't do. It won't do at all."

Mohune stiffened. The Prussian bully was on parade.

"I will not admit your right to question me. I am satisfying myself that your work had been up to standard."

"That won't do, either, Brandt. You could have asked me questions and I should have answered."

"With lies, maybe."

Davigore's hands moved expressively.

"Perhaps, perhaps not, but I await your explanation."

"You have had it."

"Not accepted, my dear fellow, not accepted. I need another."

"If I have no other?"

"Piero will demonstrate his skill."

Mohune had been playing for time. His schemes had gone awry and new ones had had to be formulated. The intercourse with Davigore had provided that essential time. He knew that one false move would release the knife in the Italian's hand. The Luger was hidden from Davigore by the deed box, but he knew that Piero would act before he could seize it, raise it and fire. Quite casually, Mohune lifted the invasion file and put it down again, as though undecided as to his next action.

"All right, Davigore," he said, with a despondent shrug of his shoulders. "It seems as though I have underrated you."

The file was picked up again and holding it at an angle of forty-five degrees from the floor between thumb —which was visible—and forefinger, of the left hand, he moved round the desk and walked towards the author.

"No funny business, Brandt. One false move and Piero's knife goes sliding into your kidneys."

"I'll be careful," smiled Mohune, "but I think you ought to see this file; someone has been at your safe before me. Pages are missing."

"What!!!"

Davigore snatched at the file, tearing it from Peter's fingers, but it was not the green cover which held his attention, but the Luger which had been covered by it.

"Well, my friend, I don't think Signor Piero had better move now, do you?"

Davigore's face was ashen, his eyes wide with fear.

"Don't point it at me; turn it away from me. Don't point it at me! Piero, Piero, do something, Piero do something!"

"I would not advise him to do anything. You were talking of kidneys just now; perhaps you'd prefer to receive my bullet in your stomach. It takes three days to die, I'm told. Davigore, tell your thug to drop his knife."

Mohune's voice had an edge to it. As a rabbit will stare at a stoat, so Davigore's eyes were fastened on the knuckle of Peters second finger curled about the Luger's trigger.

"Drop your knife. Brandt, I'll do anything, but don't point that gun at me."

"Piero," Mohune did not take his gaze from Davigore, "Piero," he commanded, "stand by your master. I dislike Wops at a distance. A whiff of Wops is a miasma. in my nostrils. Fraulein, gather those papers together.

Davigore, drop that file. Fraulein, pick it up, but don't get in my line of fire."

Mohune's orders were promptly obeyed.

"Now, Fraulein, you know your instructions. Act on them."

"Yes, Herr Hauptman."

The three men stood motionless until Peter heard the front door close behind Schnoodel; then he heaved a sigh of relief, but the pistol barrel did not move an inch.

"Now, girls, you can loosen your corsets and lie back easy like. Davigore, in that chair. Piero on the floor at your master's feet."

Peter withdrew his cigarette case, noticed the gleam in Davigore's eye and laughed.

"No, *mon vieux,* you're going to be disappointed again. I can do it all with one hand. Watch."

The case was opened, a cigarette extracted, the case replaced, lighter produced, flicked into action and returned to its pocket, without the slightest tremor of that unnaturally steady left hand.

"What are you going to do with us, Brandt?"

Mohune sat on the edge of the author's desk and regarded the couple before him. He inhaled deeply and expelled twin jets of smoke through his nostrils.

"I haven't made up my mind yet; but still, there's plenty of time. Let's have the door open; it's getting a bit stuffy in here. Piero, what the devil do you bathe in? You smell like a courtesan's boudoir. No, don't move; I can manage the door quite easily myself."

Still facing his captives, Mohune reached behind him and with his right hand threw the door open wide.

Immediately there was a diversion.

"Drop that gun or I'll drill you."

The voice was unpleasantly close to Peter's unprotected back; he was quick to obey the order and the Luger fell with a thud to the ground. Piero bounded forward and retrieved it.

"Step forward and turn round; I want to see your face."

Obediently Mohune took a pace forward and pivoted to face the newcomer. The shock he received was not apparent as he spoke.

"Good evening, von Rinck," drawled Peter in conversational tone; "you certainly have a gift for popping up at inopportune moments. I thought I'd killed you. I see you have Miss O'Regan with you."

The German's amazement was undisguised.

"Mohune," he gasped, then laughed. "No, I'm not dead, yet. Your bullets only nicked my shoulder. It was a flying brick which knocked me flat. I had a narrower escape to-night."

"So you were in that plane. You certainly have a charmed life and, my, my, you have no gun with you. I thought I was too old a bird to be caught with a buck like that."

"What is all this?"

Davigore was himself again now that the menace of the pistol had been removed. It was von Rinck who answered.

"I'm von Rinck. You are Davigore? Yes? You had notice of my arrival?"

"Brandt said you were dead."

"Brandt!" von Rinck laughed. "Mohune, I admire your nerve."

He turned to Davigore: "May I introduce you to Squadron Leader . . ."

"Wing Commander," murmured Mohune.

"Congratulations. Wing Commander Peter St. Maur Beverley de L'Epee Mohune, a very clever and intriguing young man."

"Who has just walked off with my papers; but I see that you've caught his messenger. How did you find her?"

"She ran into my arms and gave herself away by blurting out my name. So I brought her along. Now let's have a look at you."

Schnoodel, whose wrist had been imprisoned by the German, was thrown forward. She stumbled and fell against Davigore, who, seizing her by the shoulders, spun her round to face von Rinck, who stared at her in amazement.

"It can't be. Surely not Pegler's secretary. How your looks have improved. Now, don't you think you had better hand those papers back?"

"I haven't got them." She faced the German defiantly.

"Then where are they?"

Davigore's hands moved forward over her shoulders into the open neck of her dress.

"Perhaps you've hidden them, my dear," he murmured.

With a jerk she tore herself free.

"You beast!"

One hand slashed at his face, the other gathered her ravaged dress about her throat.

"I think I shall kill you for that," suggested Mohune.

"Now I think of it," said von Rinck, "a small boy passed me on a pony. She may have handed the stuff to him."

"One of those whelps," muttered Davigore, who sprang to the wall and seized the dueling sword, the point of which he forced into contact with a point behind Peter's ear.

"Piero," he ordered, "get after that brat. Take that pistol with you. Kill him if necessary, but get those papers. Take the Buick. You should be able to cut him off before he reaches his home. You know the place, 'Tintagel,' an Air Force Security Officer lives there; it's their H.Q. If you don't, follow him into the house. Shoot the place up, but get the papers. Get going."

Piero left the room like a brown streak.

"And now, von Rinck," demanded Davigore, "what do we do with this excrescence?"

Von Rinck's reply was directed at Peter.

"It looks as though it's curtain for you, my friend."

Mohune shrugged.

"That's okay, but I wish he'd take the thing away for a moment. It tickles. Schnoodie, my dear, it's curtains for me. I like the idea."

"You want . . ." began Davigore, and then everything seemed to happen at once.

Mohune's hint had not fallen on stony ground. With a lithe spring she leapt at the heavy black-out curtains with the obvious intention of tearing them aside, thereby allowing a flood of light to stream across the countryside. Even Brag's Home Guard would not allow that to pass unchecked. At the same moment, von Rinck leapt forward to intercept her and Mohune, jumping forward, seized a soda-water syphon from the table and with a wide swinging sweep, slashed at the Nazi's head. Down went the girl flat on her face and down went von Rinck unconscious from the powerful blow on the base of his skull. Davigore sprang forward in pursuit of Mohune, who wheeled round with his back to the desk.

"You're out of luck, by dear fellow," he snarled, but Mohune, somersaulting backwards, landed on his feet on the far side of the desk and in his hand was the rapier that he had so casually deposited on the gleaming surface earlier in the evening.

The sword flashed up in salute.

"I'm ready, Davigore."

"All right, come out and fight. The end will be precisely the same."

"We shall see."

With complete confidence in his heart, Peter moved round the desk, pausing to assist Schnoodel, who was rising to her feet. She looked at him and smiled, while ruefully she rubbed a bruise which was discoloring the whiteness of her forehead.

"We'll have those curtains drawn, Poppet. I'd like an audience, and if the gallant Major shows signs of returning from the arms of Morpheus, just put him to sleep again. Davigore, I'm ready for you."

The author, who had been waiting with the point of his sword resting on the matting, came on guard as the curtains rattled away from the windows and a wedge of yellow light cut into the unresisting night.

Having made one or two passes to left and to right to loosen his muscles, Mohune, moving with a lightness unusual for his size, stepped on to the matting and prepared for Davigore's attack.

Both blades were parallel to the ground; they met with a sibilant hiss and parted again.

"You know, my dear fellow, I am enjoying this."

"Jamake," smiled Mohune; "you have told me that you are good. Your exhibition of cowardice this evening was not impressive."

"Cowardice, my dear fellow, cowardice? Rubbish! It is that I cannot bear the sight of firearms; I'm allergic to them."

"Allergic! I like that. Shall we—er—get down to the matter in hand?"

There was a flash of white teeth through the tawny beard.

"Here it comes!"

A feint in the low lines from Davigore, Mohune gave ground, collected up the ensuing lunge in a circular parry, riposted at the author's heart; tick-tack, tick-tack, points thrusting in, being parried, returning to guard.

A rapid one-two attack high from Davigore; again Mohune was forced back. The bearded man had not exaggerated when he said that he was good. He was a master of the art of fence. In again; Mohune on the defensive, alert, watchful, making neat parries which, to Schnoodel, watching spellbound from the window seat, appeared to be dangerously late.

Suddenly out went Davigore's arm to its full extent and he threw himself forward in a lightning flèche; only just in time Mohune gathered the blade and deflected it from his heart. Davigore's impetus carried him on past Mohune, at whom he aimed a vicious kick as he passed. They faced each other afresh, having changed sides of the tapis.

Again and again the author flung himself at Mohune. A lunge at the eyes was beaten down into the low lines by Peter, whose riposte scratched Davigore's sword arm.

"You'll have to hurry up, *mon vieux*. They'll take a dim view of your illuminations."

Davigore replied with a string of obscenities; his nerve was going; his supreme confidence was battered; sweat stood out on his forehead; his breathing was coming with less regularity.

"Why don't you fight, you mealy-mouthed dancing master? Fight!"

"Perhaps I will," replied Peter, giving ground before a determined attack. "On the other hand, perhaps I'd rather see you taken alive."

Another stream of lewdness was directed at Peter.

"All right, Davigore. I said that I would kill you for your action just now. Here it comes!"

Blade rasped against blade; a feint attack from Mohune was followed by a bind and cut over at the heart. The tempo had changed. Davigore's fencing became wild; his neat circular parries became wide and erratic; twice in as many seconds he was forced to give ground to evade the growing menace of Mohune's attack. His breathing was now labored, his eyes were staring and a trickle of saliva escaped on to the tawny network of his beard, and to his evident dismay, his opponent was still fresh and light of foot.

Steadily Davigore was forced back until his left foot came in contact with the window seat at the far end of the room. At that moment he realized that death was already rubbing shoulders with him. He gathered his strength and calling upon a final effort from his over-taxed muscles, hurled himself forward in an Italian lunge aimed at Peter's stomach. The parry was effort-less; the riposte found its target. For a second Davigore remained taut in the lunge, his green eyes staring up into Mohune's; suddenly the beard jerked upwards and the heavy body rolled over with a thud on to its side, twitching spasmodically.

Mohune's sword rose in salute.

The gangster, fifth columnist, sadist and renegade had fought his last fight.

"Come, Schnoodie"; Mohune had crossed to the girl, who had averted her face when Davigore had made his lunge.

"Is it ...? Is he ...?"

"Yes, my sweet. He is ..."

"Now run along and get your things together; we must be on the move."

"Sometimes," answered the girl, making for the door, "I don't believe you're human."

"Sometimes, my dear, I do not dare to be. Now be off."

Left alone, Peter drew the curtains over the windows.

Their message was no longer necessary; in fact, in-truders at that moment would have been an unpleasant encumbrance.

His next move was to sit at Davigore's desk and put through a call to Dettmer. While this was coming through he phoned Davis.

"Davis? Hello! Who? Oh, Mrs. Davis! Wing Com-mander Mohune here. Everything all right with you?"

"Yes, yes. Arthur has left as instructed."

"Bolt your doors and windows. Open to nobody until I come. Be with you in ten minutes. Bye."

Mohune replaced the instrument.

What had happened to Piero? Had he flunked it? Or was he following Davis to London?

Peter stared at the motionless bodies on the floor. Von Rinck had not stirred since the syphon had crashed against his skull. Peter thought that he must be dead and was about to investigate, when the phone bell broke the silence.

"Yes? Evening, Pomposity. The moon's rising. Put me through, will you? . . . Hello, sir, Isis here. Yes; all Sir Garnet. This is an open line. The whole bag of tricks is on its way to you now."

"What?"

Even Dettmer was shaken.

"The whole bag of tricks? That's amazing. Anything else?"

"I'm afraid there is, sir. I've been a little untidy. I've had to kill the Big Shot . . . Yes, he's dead."

Dettmer's voice crackled angrily.

"Just a moment, sir. It had to be done, but it won't interfere with their plans. The machine is working and they will not refer to him until after the show starts; but the point is, I need your help. I must get away from here; if the Police or Home Guard turn up and find these bodies . . ."

"Bodies! What is this—a massacre?"

"Not quite. Von Rinck walked in at the wrong moment and walked into a spot of trouble. Now, sir, I want to get on to the Security people and hush everything up. If this gets bruited abroad, I shall have wasted my time."

"All right. Address?"

"Fearnley Davigore deceased. 'The Towers.' Brag."

"Leave it to me. As for you, proceed to your new Group H.Q. and I'll make contact with you there."

"Jamake."

The phone went dead.

CHAPTER SIXTEEN

IN WHICH HE GOES TO GROUP

Schnoodel and Peter, the latter driving, swung out of Davigore's drive and turned the car towards Brag. The author's body had been left behind, but the still unconscious von Rinck sprawled across the back seat of the author's car.

"Only one thing worries me," commented Peter.

"I should have thought that worry was a malady you never suffered from."

He patted her arm.

"Quiet, Baggage, quiet. Piero worries me a lot. You heard his orders. Why weren't they carried out?"

The solution was quickly solved.

As they turned a corner, Mohune applied the brakes for across the road straggled a crowd of men. A red lantern had been waved as the car approached. A man appeared at the window.

"Take it easy, sir; been a crash. Glass all over the road. Hit the road block, he did. That Buick won't be much good for aught but scrap."

"Buick?" Mohune's tone was quite casual.

"Yes, that's the make, that was; they say the driver was the butler from 'The Towers' back yonder. Funny thing, I was just going up there to see the occupier 'bout his black-out—or lack of it—and I ran into this mess. Some crash! Took place quite a bit since, I reckon.

Yes, he's bin dead quite a while. All right, sir. Good-night, sir."

"So Piero has joined his master," mused Peter as the car moved forward. "That's one Wop less in the world."

The next stop was the local Police Station, where they found an Air Force officer in converse with the local sergeant.

"Evening," said Mohune.

The two men looked at him in silence.

"Has there been a phone call for me?"

"This isn't the Post Office," commented the sergeant.

"I know, but I generally get more civility in a Police Station. I find that the Post Office are seldom Civil Servants. So there has been no phone call; what a pity, what a shame."

"Would you be Paul Marjoran?" put in the Air Force officer.

"I would."

"Then there has been a call from Davis. He's been called away. I've taken his place."

"Security?"

"Yes."

"You've moved quickly."

"I was on the spot."

"Good."

Mohune produced his identification card and in return accepted the officer's wallet.

"The moon is rising," said the latter.

"Correct. One body is still at 'The Towers'; the other, still alive, is in the car outside. Can you deal with him?"

"Certainly."

"I shall want a fast car."

"You can take mine."

"Thank you. That it outside?"

"Yes. I was instructed to inform you that you are to take the girl with you to Group."

"I'm on my way."

"Very good, sir."

A brief halt was made at "Tintagel," where he learned that Davis had left for London as soon as the boy had arrived with the files. The explanation of the boy's presence in the vicinity of "The Towers" was simple. It was in no way connected with Mohune's activities, but the senior members of the Patrol had been having a night exercise.

Off again, heading west; a five hours' run before them. For a while they kept up a desultory conversation, then the fair head fell on to Mohune's shoulder. The fragrance of her hair captivated Peter's senses. Schnoodel slept.

Mile after mile sped past. The quiet fields of Somerset, bathed in moonlight, peacefully sleeping, were left behind them and then two hours before dawn Wing Commander Mohune and Schnoodel Holech reached their destination.

"Where are we, Peter?" she murmured, as the car came to a halt before an old manor house.

"Journey's end, my Poppet."

"And now?"

"To find a W.A.A.F. officer who will provide you with a bed, my dear. Two hours' sleep, bath, breakfast, and ..."

"I'm not tired, really I'm not."

"Child, you'll do as you're told just for once."

Fifteen minutes later, Peter, escorted by a Staff Officer, was entering the sanctum sanctorum, the brain or nerve center which controlled the fighter defenses of South-West England. They entered a small room, the far wall of which was of glass, through which the Group Controller could look down into the Operations Room itself.

The Controller was speaking into a telephone, ordering aircraft into the air at a sector many miles away. Mohune looked over his shoulder and saw that a blitz was in progress over a large dockyard.

The Controller turned.

"Why—Mohune! The Old Man ... just a minute"— another sector was demanding his attention. "Yes, yes, all right, put two more up. It's easing up a bit now. They seem to be going home now. As I was saying, Mohune, it's good to see you again. We all thought that you'd gone for good. Congratulations on everything; being alive, promotion, D.S.O., and thank God you've come into this Group. We need a few wing leaders."

Mohune bowed.

"Thanks. I'm glad to be here. Is the A.O.C. about?"

"Flew to Command four hours ago. He said you were coming. He'll want to see you as soon as he gets back."

"Jamake. I'll leave you to it. You appear to have got your hands full."

"I certainly have. The blitz has started again in earnest. London, Southampton and Bristol have all been attacked tonight. We've got twelve down so far."

"Good show! I'll be seeing you. Can I doss down in your room for an hour or so?"

"Surely. You know where it is?"

"First block on the left, isn't it?"

"On the right, old boy. The left is W.A.A.F. officers."

"My mistake!"

At eleven o'clock Mohune was summoned into the Presence. The A.O.C. sprang to his feet as his new Wing Commander entered the room and grasped Peter's hand.

"Glad to see you, Mohune. Sit down. Cigarette? You've just done a grand job of work. Heard all about it at Command. Just got back. Things are banking up, Mohune. The night blitz has started again. But that's not all—for some time now Jerry has been moving his Air Forces. From Stavanger to Brest they're lined up. Fighters and Stukas near the coast; troop carriers, gliders, long range bombers inland. And that's not all. Take a look at this."

The Air Vice Marshal pushed his chair back and crossed to a map on the wall and jabbed repeatedly with his finger.

"Barges, barges, everywhere. In the docks, in rivers and in canals. They're going to try it this time, my boy, and remember this—in the Battle of Britain they were beaten back; this time they must be annihilated, crushed.

"As we see it, there will be four attacks: Scotland from Norway; Suffolk from Holland and Dunkirk area; Kent from Calais, Le Treport, et cetera; and Cornwall from Cherbourg, Le Havre and Brest. Thanks to you, Mohune, we've got an inkling as to their plan of campaign: One, a fighter screen to lure our fighters into the air. Two, sabotage of Operations Rooms. Three, the main attack; fighters, Stukas, long range bombers. Four, at dusk, paratroops and gliders. It's the old story, troops landing at nightfall and consolidating. But this time it's got to fail. The S.A.S.O.* is sending out my orders now. The forces are at stand to. Tonight the Bomber Boys will smash at the invasion ports and will go on smashing until the show starts. I want you to get down to Blake as soon as you can. You've got three good squadrons, as good as any in the command.

"There's one other thing. When the attack comes, we'll let them think that our Ground Control is out of action. We'll do the luring; we'll try and make them offer us their Stukas on a plate.

"That's all, Mohune. Good luck to you. Group Captain Wirrell is expecting you."

And yet again Mohune was traveling, but this time it was the girl who drove and Peter sat beside her in silence, his brain active with thoughts of the coming blitz.

Southwards towards the English Riviera, a three-hour journey. A new station. Mohune lit a cigarette and handed it to Schnoodel. A new station, with all the peculiarities of a new school. New faces, new ideas, a new countryside to learn, new controllers to get to know, new problems to tackle. There was one bright cloud in the sky—a third of the pilots were his own pilots, pilots he had trained and led for the past six months. He lay back in his seat and closed his eyes. The sun-bathed fields sped by.

Group Captain Wirrell looked up from his desk as his new Winko Flying stopped before it and saluted.

* S.A.S.O.—Senior Air Staff Officer.

"Mohune, sir."

"Howyah, Heard lot of you. Never met before, eh?"

"I don't think so, sir."

"See plenty of you from now on. Sit down. I'm giving you a free hand. The flying side of this sector is your pigeon from now on. Keep me in the picture as much as you can. Understand you've been enjoying yourself lately. Take it not much time before the bubble bursts. Good thing, put a stop to all this bumph. A.O.C. tells me you know the inside story. Have arranged conference in the Card Room of the Mess for twenty-thirty hours. Had any lunch?"

The staccato utterances came to a full stop as though a foot had been taken off an accelerator.

"We had some sandwiches on the way down."

"We? Not married, are you?"

Mohune laughed.

"No, sir, quite fancy free. I brought a girl with me, though; a secret agent."

"Phillips Oppenheim stuff, eh? What are you going to do with her? Don't like women on the Station."

"I concur, but this one is slightly different..."

"All women are the same."

Peter raised an eyebrow.

"I am inexperienced, sir, but as I was saying, this girl could give a very excellent lecture on Germany."

"H'm. Where's she now?"

"Ladies' Room, taking a dish of tea."

"Safe enough there. Let's go and look at the aerodrome. Join you for dinner."

The G.C. jumped to his feet and seized his hat.

"In the Ladies' Room, with girl friend."

"Sounds good to me."

"No pilots here today. Away on a show. Back before dusk. You can see dispersals and hard standings. Show you your office. Best on the Station. Whole of the top floor of Watch Office. Full view of runways."

For two and a half hours the two men toured the camp. The Station Commander, short, dapper, very much on his toes, kept up a flow of descriptive conversation and Mohune, taking it all in, felt satisfied with life and at peace with the world. He, with his experience of the Service, could find no faults. The Station was excellent in every way. Every man they met was alert and obviously supremely keen on his job.

The sun was setting over the sea as they turned towards the Officers' Mess and paused as a squadron broke up above the aerodrome in preparation for landing.

"They're the Czechs," announced Wirrell, "Kabratil leads them. Good; keen as mustard. You'll meet them later. The Jerries bombed Exfleet this morning. Lost a couple for their pains. No damage."

"Things are looking up."

" 'Bout time too. We're getting stale. Want action. Now let's go and see your girl friend. I'm thirsty."

In the Ladies' Room, a comfortably-furnished annex to the main Ante Room, they found Schnoodel having tea.

The Group Captain bowed over her hand and Mohune raised his eyebrow.

"Wirrell, my name."

Schnoodel smiled up at him.

"Will you have some tea?"

"Hate the stuff. Peter, it's ... " he glanced at his watch, "Yes, just on time. Join me in a drink."

"Never been known to say no, sir."

The Group Captain pressed a bell, but before the waiter had a chance to appear, the loud-speaker over the door sounded a preliminary crackle and gave notice.

"Hello, hello, Operations calling. Will the Station Commander please telephone Operations. I will repeat that. Will the Station Commander please phone Operations. That is all."

"Drink'll have to wait. Order me a pink gin, Peter."

"Jamake, sir."

The Group Captain departed and Mohune seated himself on the arm of the girl's chair.

"Well, my Poppet? Enjoying yourself?"

"It's ... it's ... Oh, Peter, it's indescribable. I can't believe I'm safe and that I don't need to be on my guard against everyone I meet."

"But you do, my dear. Pilots have a reputation."

Schnoodel laughed.

"Peter, you're a fool, but you know what I mean."

Mohune gazed at her and saw the tears welling into her eyes.

"You've been so kind, so good to me and I ... I was a little beast to you. I feel so big, there's something," her hand rested on her heart, "there's something here that's going to burst very soon."

"I think I'd better go and find that waiter ..."

She sought his hand and held it firmly.

"You're a darling," she whispered.

"Rubbish."

With his free hand, Peter patted the fair hair and

then as she released him, he left the room in search of a waiter. In the corridor a pilot officer was standing studying a notice board with his back to the Ladies' Room. It was a back that Mohune recognized immediately. Silently he moved forward and spoke into the pilot's ear.

"Oh, Beacon . . ."

The pilot officer went rigid; he knew that voice, but the voice of a dead man was the last thing he had expected to hear.

"Could you tell me where I could get a drink?" continued Mohune.

Like a ramrod, Pilot Officer Bright turned about. His eyes were wide, his mouth gaped.

"I . . . I . . ." he stammered. "It can't be true. It's . . ."

"All done by mirrors," grinned Mohune, as the pilot's hand touched the Wing Commander's sleeve tentatively.

"It is you! Great snakes, it is you, sir. Jumping flying fish, you frightened me, sir. I thought you were dead. Where have you sprung from, sir? How did you get here, sir? Great snakes, it's good to see you. Do the boys know you're here? A drink, sir? Great snakes, we'll have a barrel. How long are you staying for, sir?"

Mohune threw back his head and roared with laughter.

"Steady the Buffs, Beacon, one thing at a time."

"But the boys, sir. We must have a party, a regular jamboree. Come along, sir, they're in the ante room. We've just got back."

He seized Peter's arm and shepherded him towards the ante room.

"Just a moment; I have a guest."

"Oh, he can wait for a moment."

"It's a she."

"Well, we'll get someone to act as stand-in for you."
Bright flung the doors open.

"Gentlemen," he announced in a voice which he
fondly imagined was imitative of a toastmaster, "I give
you Wing Commander Peter St. Maur Beverley de
L'Epee Mohune, the man from the dead."

Sixteen heads turned as one. Spellbound with amazement, the pilots remained motionless for fully two seconds; and then the dam burst and a wave of bodies rushed
to the door. Above the commotion could be heard
Batchy Salter.

"Fan me, what is it I see before me? Question, is it
a dagger? Answer, no, verily it is our Commandant, our
Wing Leader; I mean to say, old sir and what not, are
we not amazed? We are. Drinks I demand. Drinks.
Ginger, see to it."

Flying Officer Rogers hurried away willingly.

"Now, Batchy, cease blathering for a while and introduce me to the other blokes."

"Surely and indeed. Here on my left with my back to
the refreshment room is Rudolf Kabratil, the leader of
the Czechs. The bounding Czechs. Fan me, how they
bound."

A dark-eyed Squadron Leader clicked his heels and
bowed.

"This is 'Bungy' from Sixteen-sixteen; a poor squadron, my Commandant, but we're teaching them slowly.
This is 'Cripes,' leads 'A' Flight of the same perfidious
squadron. 'Watty,' their I.O., cooks their combat reports

in a most shameful manner. Fan me, I mean to say, it's
disgusting; makes us quiver, positively quiver, with in-
dignation and whatnot. Tonda, another from wilds
afar. Where the hell has Ginger got to? I have a thirst,
a palpitating affliction of my larynx. Fan me, I could
drink a cask. All right, all right, don't say it. I know
your nasty minds. Here we have another Peter. He's
the Senior Ops. B; a hefty man who lays us low at
squash. Does nothing else, fan me, if he does."

"But ahead of you as always. Your drink, sir."

A glass was thrust into Mohune's hand.

"There you are, Batchy," laughed Mohune, "that's
what I call co-operation."

The tour of introduction continued until at last they
returned to Rudolf Kabratil.

"Now," announced Peter, grasping a foaming tank-
ard, "there is someone I want to introduce to you."

"To me, sir?"

"To you, *mon vieux*. A very gallant lady from Prague
who has been working for the Allies in Berlin. Excuse me."

Mohune disappeared through the doors leading to
the Ladies' Room.

"Hello, Schnoodie. I want you to come and meet
the boys."

"Peter, I can't; I'm—I'm frightened."

"Rubbish, you don't know what it is to be frightened.
Come along."

He took her arm, but still she hung back and then
from the ante room came the sound of voices raised in
song.

> "Zivio, Zivio, Zivio, Zivio.
>   Mnoga Ljeta, Zdravi Byli
>   Mnoga Ljeta, Zivio.
>   Mnoga Ljeta, Zdravi Byli
>   Mnoga Ljeta,
>   Zivio, Zivio, Zivio, Zivio."

The girl's eyes brightened, her chin went up.

"What is it, Poppet?"

"My own tongue, Peter—

> "Cheerio, Cheerio, Cheerio, Cheerio,
>   For a long life and good health,
>   For a long life, Cheerio,
>   For a long life and good health,
>   For a long life,
>   Cheerio, Cheerio, Cheerio, Cheerio."

"Not frightened now?"

"No, but keep near me, Peter mine."

Arm-in-arm they passed through the swing-doors and the singing burst out afresh. The pilots, with the Czechs in the foreground, had made a semicircle; at the back a violin was being played by a master.

"Zivio, Zivio, Zivio."

Louder and louder until it seemed that the song could no longer be contained by the walls of the ante room.

Glasses were forced into their hands.

"To you both," said Kabratil; the glasses were raised; then came an interruption.

"Schnoodie! Schnoodie! SCHNOODIE!!"

A figure forced its way through the crowd of officers

and the Flight Lieutenant whom Batchy had introduced as Tonda, burst into the open semicircle.

"Schnoodie!"

"Toni!"

Holech was about to leap forward again, but instead he halted and faced Mohune.

"Excuse, please. My sister."

Then and there did he seize the girl in his arms, while the song broke out for the third time.

Mohune whispered into Tonda's ear.

"Take her into the Ladies' Room. You'll have a lot to tell her."

"No, no. Everyone, everyone must be 'appy all to-gether."

Suddenly his eyes caught sight of the grim swastika scar; his jaw set into a hard line.

"My little Schnoodie. They to do this to you!"

He swung round to face the pilots, holding his sister's wrist up for all to see and broke into vehement Czech.

Peter edged away. Schnoodel was with friends now and he had much to say to Batchy Salter.

"Well, Batchy . . ."

At seven o'clock a message came to Mohune from the Group Captain saying that he would not be in to dinner, but that he would see Peter at half-past eight as arranged. Then came Tonda with an urgent summons from his sister, and together Peter and Batchy returned to the Ladies' Room.

"Well, my Poppet?"

Peter looked into the dancing eyes.

"They've only laid the table for two. Can't Toni eat with us?"

"That is for Toni?"

"But you, Peter; you must be here too."

"You won't want me."

"I do want you"; she sprang to her feet indignantly. "Of course I want you. How dare you be so stupid?"

Peter shrugged his shoulders.

"Don't believe a word, not a solitary word he says. Positively he was born with a lie in his mouth. I mean, fan me, he goes off on these jaunts of his, leaving good types like your very humble servant, to get themselves out of the mess, the squalor, the what will you, that he leaves behind him, and what does he do? Answer, he comes back with a beauteous and divine damsel. Each one positively more beautiful than the last and even more alluring. Fan me, but it's unfair. What is there left for men like me to do but seek solace in the barrel, and then what happens? Answer, he sleeps the sleep of contentment and dreams of pretty dancing eyes, while I sleep not a wink, and all I get for it is little woolly jumpers on my teeth in the morning. Fan me, it's unfair."

Schnoodel laughed happily.

"Is all this true, Peter?" she demanded.

"About the woolly jumpers, I should say definitely yes."

"There he goes again, avoiding the point at issue. Waiter! Drinks!! And lay this table for four. I feed in here!"

As soon as the meal was over, Batchy and Peter left Toni and Schnoodel to themselves and made for the room where Mohune was to address his Squadron Leaders.

The walls were covered with maps; a few easy chairs had been arranged in two straight lines facing a small table, upon which the Station Commander was sitting talking to the officers before him.

"Ah, Mohune. Expect you know most of these fellows by now. Belland, my Senior Controller. Colonel Burns, my Defense Officer. Rowley, Sector Intelligence Officer. Kabratil and Kenworthy of Sixteen-sixteen. Won't keep you fellows long. This is the man who knows the story. Incidentally, Zero Hour—Dawn to-morrow. Came through when we were talking to your girl friends."

Mohune's eyebrow jerked up.

"Sooner than I expected, sir."

"Sooner the better. Now carry on."

"Well, chaps, here's the dope. Jerry Hun is going to have a crack at us once more. This time it's the Big Thing. He's not going to waste time trying to smash the fighters down, he's coming straight in. But—there is a but and it concerns you, Colonel . . ."

Colonel Burns readjusted a single glass before his eye and leaned forward intently; Mohune continued:

"They have built up an elaborate scheme of saboteurs who are to strike at Fighter Command Operations Rooms throughout the country at a given time."

"Eleven hundred hours to-morrow," put in Wirrell.

"Their plan is this: a wave of fighters will approach the coast in force. Our fighters will take off and be lured out into the Channel. Then comes the attack on the Operations by fifth columnists. Our Spitfires will be out of touch with Ground Control and will either stay in the air, useless to man or beast, or they will return to land and refuel. The Hun is banking on hearing our aircraft announce their intention to return and that will be his signal for fighters and Stukas to come in. He hopes to catch the Spits refueling and dive bomb them and their aerodromes to high heaven. Long range bombers will follow to attack communications, disrupt the Army supply lines and then at dusk will come Ju 52's, gliders and parachutists. That's the plan, gentlemen, as far as it concerns us. The Navy will attend to the barges if Bomber Command don't do it tonight."

"They won't," snapped Wirrell. "Fog, thick fog, tonight on the French coast. Not rising before dawn."

"So be it. There'll be a job for the Navy and Coast Defenses. Now; some of those fifth columnists should have been roped in by now. Others will make their attack. That's your department, Colonel."

Mohune looked across at the two rows of medal ribbons and Burns nodded.

"We will cope."

"Just leave one for me," pleaded Wirrell.

"Now, Belland," continued Peter, turning his attention to the Senior Controller, "here's where you come in. You will take the normal action with regard to the first raid. We shall take off and you'll forget your training and fill the air with orders. Just the normal type of interception stuff. Then at eleven o'clock you will shut up abruptly and we'll start screaming at you. You know, the usual type of thing—'Why the hell don't you answer?'—'Are you receiving me?' et cetera, et cetera. Then I shall announce that the whole thing's a washout and that we're turning for home. We won't turn, of course, but we'll stooge about waiting for the Stukas. Hold your horses, Belland, for as long as you can with safety and then give us the gen. I'd like to intercept them twenty miles off the coast. Now for formation. The wing will be stepped up in sections of four. Thirteen-twenty will lead at eighteen thousand feet. Sixteen-sixteen, two thousand feet above them and behind, and the Czechs up another two thousand as upper guard. Kabratil, you'll get the One Oh Nines."

"That is good."

"And you, sir?"

Batchy had momentarily forgotten his persiflage.

"I'll lead your Squadron. We'll make a section of four; you and I, Ginger and Beacon; Jamake?"

"Okey Doke, it is."

"Any questions?"

It was the loud-speaker then answered. The Controller's voice from Operations was casual and unhurried.

"Hello, hello, Operations calling. Action Stations, Action Stations."

"Fan me," muttered Batchy, "I shan't get a drink now."

CHAPTER SEVENTEEN

IN WHICH HE SEES DEATH IN THE AIR

THE night passed without incident; moonlight cold and austere flooded the western aerodrome at Blake. There were no alarms or excursions, although further east the Beaufighters of the Night Flying Squadrons of Fighter Command grappled incessantly with the bombers of the Luftwaffe, who had returned with all the fury they had displayed in the latter months of 1940.

Out in the night Colonel Burns was busy. His Battle H.Q. was in readiness, his strong points and gun positions had been visited, an air of expectant calm hung over the environs of the aerodrome.

Burns removed his monocle and polished it. He was ready; for months he had perfected his defense plans and now it appeared that at long last they were to be tried out. Two figures approached the soldier, who replaced his glass.

"Halt!"

"Station Commander."

Wirrell advanced, preceded by an airman carrying a tommy gun.

"Hello, Burns. Grand night."

"Broad, sir, very broad."

"Going the rounds?"

"Everything in order."

"Good. I'm relying on you. Patrols out?"

"Yes, sir. Interlocking with Home Guard."

The Station Commander looked up at the sky, who was wearing her full galaxy of stars and decorations.

"Weather lousy over Invasion Ports," he announced. "Bomber Boys won't get much of a look in tonight."

"That's bad luck."

"It is. Coastal Command report naval activity in North Sea. I must push on. Want to get an hour's sleep before show starts. Thank God I've got a Wing Commander Flying and an excellent Operations Staff. That helps a lot. 'Night."

"Good night, sir."

The two figures moved away and were swallowed in the night.

In the Ops. Room the Duty Controller was talking to the Sector Intelligence Officer.

"Quiet, isn't it?"

"Calm before the storm?"

"Maybe. There's a stream of orders coming through. Teleprinter is red hot."

"It'll quieten down when the fun starts. Who's on tomorrow?"

"Belland's controlling. Peter Delafield'll be Ops. B. Those two seem to get all the fun. I've got nothing up at the moment. Have a cup of tea?"

"It's an idea."

The two men left the dais and repaired to the Controller's Rest Room.

A W.A.A.F. plotter whispered to another.

"Wish it was our watch on tomorrow."

In a strong point two airmen were talking.

"I feel griped. Standing about for hours on end staring into the darkness. Why the hell can't they let us play at soldiers in the daylight?"

"This is probably the real thing."

"Real thing, my gum boots! I tell you I feel griped."

He patted his machine-gun affectionately.

"If I could get a chance to let little Daisy here spit a few blurry bullets at a blasted Jerry, I'd be satisfied. As it is I'm griped."

"Less talking in there."

A sergeant in tin hat and full war regalia dropped into the post.

"Gun loaded?"

"Yes, sergeant."

"Well, keep your eyes skinned. The balloon's going up."

The sergeant left the post. The two airmen stared into the darkness.

"Still feel griped?"

"Just gimme a chance, that's all I ask; just gimme a chance. Yes griped; don't be blurry silly."

In his bunk Mohune lay asleep. Schnoodel had gone to stay the night with Peter Delafield's wife, some five miles away. The day squadrons were released until dawn. The night was undisturbed. The weather which had prevented Bomber Command from operating had also grounded the Luftwaffe in north-west France.

In the towns, dance bands blared out synthetic music, a sympathetic accompaniment to the consumption of equally poor liquor. The wise men nodded their assurance that the blitz of the previous nights had been nothing more than a flash in the pan. Invasion; the thought was absurd; even Hitler knew better than to try that on England. The leaders of the Black Market thought out new plans for their battle in the field of commerce. A colliery contemplated another strike. A farmer wrote a letter to his solicitor complaining that the Forces had taken a piece of his waste land to build a pill-box. In short, it was a normal night.

"Your tea, sir."

Mohune woke at the touch of a hand upon his shoulder. In his dreams he was back in Berlin and von Pegler was offering him a cup of tea. Error had crept in.

"One hour before first light, sir. Your bath is ready," continued Pegler.

Peter's eyes opened and the Grand Inquisitor hurtled back through space, while the prosaic figure of a batman materialized in his place.

"Have you roused the others yet?" Mohune demanded, taking the teacup and wondering why it was that batmen always managed to spill at least half the cup into the saucer.

"Not yet, sir. There isn't much hot water. Thought you'd like first plunge."

"Jamake."

First light. The Station was at readiness and at Action Stations. There was nothing to betray the fact that this was not just another morning which would commence with the usual routine inspection.

Seated in his office, Peter called Operations.

"Controller, please. Wing Commander Flying here . . . Who's that?"

Belland announced himself.

"Anything doing?" asked Mohune.

"Nothing, sir. Dead as a dodo at the moment, but Group are flapping a bit."

"Jamake. I'm going round the flights. Give me a shout over the Blower if anything starts."

"Righto, sir. We should get plenty of warning."

"Good show. Bye."

Leaving his office, Mohune climbed into his staff car and began a tour of the Perimeter track, a wide carpet of camouflaged concrete which encircled the aerodrome, connecting dispersal bays with the runways.

Outside the low wooden hut which now housed his old squadron, Mohune stopped the car as he saw Salter standing in the doorway of "A" Flight dispersal. The Squadron Leader's salute was smart and correct.

"Good morning, sir."

"Morning, Batchy. All set?"

"Verily we are all set. We are as hounds straining at the leash . . ."

"Mastiff, greyhound, mongrel, grim
    Hound of spaniel, brach or lym,
    Or bobtail tyke or trundle-tail?" quoted Peter.

"As You Like It, sir."

"No; King Lear."

"Fan me, your erudition is amazing, but I mean to say, here we are like falcons tugging at the wrist to soar and . . ."

"Remember Macbeth. 'A falcon towering in her pride of place was by a mousing owl hawk'd and killed.' "

"You're being very Eton and Harrow this morning, sir. I mean to say, quotations and whatnots simply bubbling out, like a geyser with the gas on full, but what I mean to ask, sir, and leader, is—what's to do?"

"Haven't heard anything yet. Just been talking to Ops. All's quiet."

"Hope to hell those blighters don't rat on us, fan me, after getting up so nice and early and shaving and making up; it'd be, well—Question, would it be cricket if they wouldn't play? Answer, it would not. After all, there must be a rule somewhere just now and then as a what-you-may-call-it."

"Quite, Batch, quite."

"By the way, old sir, have you seen the charming Snood this bright morn?"

"A snood is a hair net or . . ."

"She's a net all right. It would catch me if the net wasn't already full. It's damned unfair actually. You Wing Commanders come stalking along, clanging your gongs and flashing your wide stripes, and we humble people, bashful and tongue-tied, with mere scraper ring to show that we're not still Flight Lieutenants, have to fade miserably away. But as I was saying, have you seen her this morning?"

"Not a chance. She's five miles away and I expect still peacefully sleeping."

Batchy, who had stooped to adjust the strap of his left flying boot, looked up into Mohune's face.

"That's where you err, O Commandant. She is up, verily she is up and not that it would interest you, of course, should you want to find her, it might be worth your while to beetle around to the Czechs, but as I say, of course, you wouldn't be interested."

Batchy's attention was returned to the recalcitrant strap.

"On the aerodrome? Don't be so damned silly . . ."

"That's right, that's right, call me a liar. Fan me, for eight years, man and boy have I worked for you and now," Batchy shrugged his shoulders and ran a hand through his fair hair; "I will not argue. I will not plead, but this I do say. This is what I mean to say, she is not so far away, and if with her you want with her to play, look for the car of the Y.M.C.A."

"Thanks for the tip. I'll go and send her home; this spot will be no place for a girl when the show starts. See you later. You know the gen?"

"Answer verily I know the gen."

Mohune moved on for another half-mile and there in the center of a seething crowd was the khaki-colored canteen car, bearing the ubiquitous red triangle, but the arrival of Peter's staff car proved a greater attraction, and as Mohune stepped out on to the perimeter track, he was surrounded by the mass of eager pilots.

"Any news, sir?" demanded Tonda, Schnoodel's brother.

Mohune shook his head. His eyes swept over the crowd; all young, but with determination born of bitter experience stamped on every feature; they were harder these boys than men of their age were expected to be. An implacable hatred had been burned into them, into the very core of their being.

"It's early yet," said Mohune apologetically, as he made his way through the throng to the open hatch of the car. Laughter sparkled in her eyes.

"Good morning, Peter de L'Epee."

"Good morning, Baggage. You've no right to be here."

"A cup of tea, Wing Commander?"

Her golden-guinea colored hair hung down in its shimmering wealth past the soft contours of her face to her shoulders. Its beauty fascinated him; he fought down an almost irresistible desire to stretch out his long arm and touch its fair beauty. Instead he murmured:

"I said you were a Baggage and I still mean it."

"Tea?"

"Please, miss."

She pushed a steaming cup towards him and he turned to face the pilots. Those boys in their short fur-lined Irving jackets, fleecy-lined boots.

"I'm sorry it's not a stronger drink for this toast."

He raised his cup.

"Na Sdar!"

"To Success!"

The cry was taken up on all sides and at that moment the loud-speaker brayed a message.

"Attention, everybody. Operations calling. Preliminary warning. All pilots to stand by, stand by. That's all."

Cups were hurriedly set down. Pilots pulled up their zipp fasteners; some adjusted Mae Wests, others pulled on their flying helmets, leaving microphone and oxygen mask hanging free, and all began the short walk towards their aircraft. Only Mohune was left by the canteen car. A voice was raised in song, a song in which the others quickly joined.

> "Tri sta Trinact,
> The might of the Czechs appearing.
> Oh, when shall we turn?
> Aye, homeward turn?
> The pain in our hearts is searing,

Yet still, because of the savage Hun
From house and home remain we,
And still because of the savage Hun
No peace or leisure gain we.

There were four more stanzas before they reached the
concluding one:

"When first our country tortured on the rack
The young shoots green were growing;
Now we're strong. We'll drive them back.
A blast from the West is blowing,
Vision of Victory comes at last.
Lift up your heads,
Lighten your hearts,
Victory will come;
Tri sta Trinact."

Throughout the song, Schnoodel gripped Peter's fingers tightly, as his arm lay across the open hatch of her
van. There was a mist of tears before her eyes as the
singing ended with a mighty shout, and Mohune covered those clutching fingers with his free hand.

"Won't be long now," he murmured and as if in
answer, the loud-speaker's brazen voice spoke again.

"Wing Take Off. Wing Take Off. That is all."

"That's me, my Poppet."

The girl threw herself forward; her arms went around
his neck.

"Take care of yourself, Peter," she whispered.

"That applies to you too, Baggage."

Then he was gone; with the back of her hand pressed
against her teeth, she watched the camouflaged car

sweeping away towards the Watch Tower, saw the tall
figure climb out and sprint to his waiting Spitfire, saw
an airman throw a parachute harness about the wide
shoulders, saw a hand wave, and the plane move forward.

In the Operations Room an expectant tensity had
fallen upon the watch. The Senior Controller, Squadron
Leader Belland, had taken over control of the sector and
was standing rocking gently on his heels, staring at
the table before him. To one side, his Operations B,
Peter Delafield, lay back in his chair, his head held
slightly on one side, and he was smiling as a father will
at the antics of his small son, a tolerant, happy, posses-
sive smile. He had trained that particular watch then on
duty and was satisfied and proud.

In the Senior Controller's office, Group Captain Wirrell was speaking on the telephone to the A.O.C. at
Group.

"Yes, sir, my wing is off. Airborne about three minutes ago."

"Good show, Wirrell. It looks as though Mohune's information is going to bear fruit. I've just been speaking
to the C.-in-C. Altogether there are ten raids, each of a
hundred and fifty plus, approaching our coast line. The
west coast is clear. Cover has been arranged for to-day.
There should be no chance of your boys being pounced
upon while refueling."

"Thank God for that . . ."

"Exactly. Ground defenses? You're on the top line?"

"Absolutely."

"Good show! If Mohune's story is correct, the attempt

to wreck our Operations Room should start in twenty minutes."

"We're ready."

"That's about all, Wirrell. Best of luck. There's no need for me to tell you what will happen if they establish a bridgehead in Cornwall."

"We'll do our best, sir. I'm going to my Battle Headquarters now."

Wirrell replaced the telephone on its cradle and leaning back in Belland's chair stroked his smooth chin.

Battle Headquarters; his mind flashed back to France in the early days, to Norway, to Crete. Would the English population panic, would they fill the roads, a seething mass of uncontrolled bodies? Would the Home Guard come up to expectation? Would their oft-reiterated statement, "Oos'll be there when Germans coom!" prove to be a reliable forecast? Would communications stand up to the strain about to be enforced upon them? Could he hold the aerodrome? Rifles, Tommy guns; were there enough?

Wirrell flung the chair back and stamped along the corridor to the Operations Room, above the door of which the illuminated sign was a fiery warning: "Silence. Interception in Progress."

Belland was studying the large horizontal map from his vantage point on the dais; a telephone handset was against his ear and fingers pushed a red switch. He was "on the air."

"Hello, Isis, Isis. Walleye control calling. Understand formation made. Over."

Back came Mohune's voice, loud enough in Belland's earpiece for both Wirrell and Delafield to hear.

"Hello, Walleye. Correct. Listening Out."

Belland laid the handset down on the counter before him.

"Something's about to happen, sir," he remarked. "There's more activity than there's been for months and months. Looks like the big thing."

Wirrell nodded.

"Relief crew here?"

"Yes, sir. In the rest rooms."

"Spare Controller? Who is he?"

"Blades, sir. Downstairs seeing to emergency rations."

"Good. I'm going to Battle Headquarters now. All lines been tested?"

"Yes, sir."

"Good. Who's that girl down there? The one on the Exfleet line."

Belland looked down at the "floor," at the large table map with the plotters seated about it.

"Stokes, sir."

"Stokes. Tell her her lipstick's too bright."

Wirrell nodded to Belland and after a final look at the "board," strode out of the room.

In the Guard Room an airman armed with a tommy gun came to attention, while another saluted and flung open the door.

"Know your orders?" demanded the G.C.

"Yes, sir."

"Not to open this door to anyone, sir, until further orders are received."

"Good. See that you carry them out. Not only the lives of everyone in this block may depend upon you, but the fate of England itself. Sounds melodramatic, but

isn't. Truth. Keep the grille closed. Don't want a hand
grenade thrown in here."

"We'll look after ourselves, sir."

"Don't give a damn what happens to you. It's the
Ops. Room I'm thinking of. Clean those buttons to-
day?"

"Yes, sir."

"Well, clean them again when you're relieved."

Group Captain Wirrell departed.

Throughout England, Fearnley Davigore's fifth columnists were converging on their objectives. In the air
the leaders of the German formations consulted their
clocks. The large formations split and diverged. Each
formation of a hundred and fifty became three of fifty,
each one headed for a sector aerodrome. It was to one
of these that Belland passed instructions to Mohune to
intercept.

South of Morlaix on the north-west coast of France
a group of German signalers were seated before a bat-
tery of wireless receivers, earphones clamped to their
ears. Staff officers stood in a group behind them, smoking incessantly, and from time to time casting anxious
glances at their watches. Zero hour was approaching,
10.50 A.M.; in ten minutes the advance troops of Nazi
Germany, the fifth columnists, Hitler's secret weapon in
the past, would strike at the very heart of the British
Fighter Command.

Not again would Germany have to waste valuable
time and lives in smashing or attempting to smash down
the English squadrons before launching the invasion.
The head would be struck over and then although the

squadrons would be left intact, their efforts would be but that ineffective flapping of a decapitated hen.

Ten fifty-five. The German formations turned and flew south-east and south-west. The British squadrons followed in pursuit, being lured away from their bases and leaving a right of way for the Stukas to fly through and wreck their havoc on the unprotected aerodromes.

Eleven A.M.

A large petrol tanker drew up at the closed gates of Blake Aerodrome.

"Open up, chum. I'm in an 'urry," demanded the driver.

Quite nonchalantly the sentry stepped forward, a tommy gun hung in the crook of his arm.

"Identification card, mate?"

"Sure thing. 'Ere you are, chum."

The man beside the driver handed down two cards, which the airman scrutinized and returned.

"O.K. mate. Seems all right."

"Course it is. Open up."

The sentry shook his head.

"Sorry; you'll 'ave to wait a bit. Can't allow anyone through just yet."

"Nark it, chum. We're in a hurry."

"Sorry, you'll have to wait."

"Blimey! An' blokes talk of 'old ups in the factories; it's your ruddy red tape wot causes the ruddy bottle necks. Come on now, open up."

"Can't be done, mate. Got me orders."

The driver's elbow banged against the back of his cab and one of the heavy round covers on the top of the tank itself fell back with a clang. A head popped out.

A sub-machine gun laughed sardonically and the sentry's eyes widened in astonishment; his tommy gun dropped to the ground, his hands clutched his stomach, his knees folded and he fell forward on to his face.

Instantly the man beside the driver was out on the road racing towards the barred gates; the lorry moved forward.

"Ha-ha-ha-ha-ha . . . Ha-ha . . . Ha-ha-ha-ha."

A Lewis gun spat its messengers from the shelter of a Cornish wall. The driver twisted in his seat, his right side shot away. Sub-machine gun and Lewis spat at each other for a second. The lorry stopped. The driver lay dead across the wheel and his rear gunner collapsed into the dark interior of the tanker.

A clergyman climbed a cliff path to the aerodrome, a benign elderly man with stooping shoulders; in his left hand he carried a suitcase which seemed to be too heavy for him. His right hand was thrust deep into his overcoat pocket. It was a large aerodrome which it had not been found possible to surround with wire, and the cleric was within the boundary; ahead lay the Operations Room. Another twenty-five yards. His eyes, surprisingly youthful for his age, held a smile of satisfaction and success.

"Just a minute, mister."

The clergyman turned and bowed to the young soldier who had accosted him.

"Ah, my deah young man. Perhaps you can be of assistance to mah. I am searching for the Station Chaplain. I find that age is creeping upon me and this little walk has wearied me."

"It is a bit of a climb, father, but you're going the wrong way."

"My son"—twenty-five yards and with but this one man in sight; the right hand moved slowly in the pocket —"I am too tired to journey further."

"No you flaming well don't."

In the nick of time the soldier had caught a glimpse of a revolver, but he leapt in and a balled fist cracked home under the cleric's jaw, who rocked on his heels. In vain he tried to disentangle his gun; another fist caught him at the side of the ear; sickening blow landed in the plexus and he collapsed unconscious, dropping his case to the ground.

"Phew," muttered the soldier, " 'e'd a 'ard jaw for an old 'un."

"Not so old, I think," commented a new arrival, who stooping jerked off the man's hat and wig. "I'd treat that bag gently if I were you. Probably contains a bomb."

"Cor!" muttered the Tommy.

At the north gate of the aerodrome, an Air Force lorry laden with crates demanded admittance, a request that would normally have been given, as the driver's papers were in order, but a member of the ubiquitous Security Police noticed that despite the mud-stained condition of the lorry, the number plates were spotless. A small point, but one which led to investigation and the discovery of the human contents of the packing cases, with the result that two dejected fifth columnists were marched with lifted arms to the nearest cell.

Precisely at eleven, Mohune had called Operations.

"Hello, Walleye, Walleye. Isis calling. Any further instructions for me? Isis over to Walleye."

Two seconds passed without reply.

"Hello, Walleye, Walleye. Isis calling. Any information for me?"

Another pause.

"Hello, Batchy. Are you receiving me?"

"Hello, Isis, Isis. Receiving you loud and clear. I'll give them a shout. Hello, Walleye, Walleye. Are you deaf as well as blind? Pull your finger out. Over."

"Hello, Isis, Isis"—it was the Czech Squadron Leader calling—"I am receiving you ver' well. Shall I call Walleye? Dagger Leader over to Isis. Over."

"Hello, Dagger Leader. Isis answering. Don't think it'll be much good, but you can have a try. Over."

The air became full of nattering; everyone was calling the Controller without response.

Round the coasts of England the story was the same. The fighters were cut off from the ground.

In the wireless station south of Morlaix, a German signaler sprang to his feet and stood rigidly at attention before an officer.

"It works, mein Herr. No. 1 Area is silent."

"No. 2 also, mein Herr," added another.

"And No. 3."

The officer stubbed out his cigarette and seized a telephone.

Further along the coast other wireless stations flashed similar good news to Headquarters.

A Generalfeld Marschall rubbed his hands together.

"Very good. Now we shall see. Dive bombers to move forward according to plan."

He turned to his assembled staff.

"Tonight, gentlemen, the first of our troops will be

established in England. In a week . . ." he flung his arms
out in an embracing gesture and brought them together
across his massive chest.

In the Operations Room at Blake, Belland had been
listening to the pilots nattering; his long solemn face
broke into a smile as he turned to his Ops. B.

"Well, Peter, my friend, we've done it. The question
is now, will they bite?"

Peter Delafield lay back in his swivel chair; his
massive form seemed to be out of place. He conveyed a
thought that he would be more fitted to the Regency
period. His fair, loosely-curled hair, his pink and white
complexion, was that of a Corinthian rather than that
of an officer in the Second World War; his manner was
genial and expansive, and although Belland had known
him for a number of months, he still expected him to
produce a snuff box from his top pocket.

"That is certainly the question. I hope . . . sir . . . that
for your sake they do walk into the trap . . ."

"Surely, Peter . . ."

Delafield, still at ease and retaining still that tilt of
his head, lifted a hand in deprecation.

"I welcome the return to the blitz, but for one thing
. . . sir . . . do I take great dolor. I am entered for a chess
competition. I had hoped to solve this week's problem
during this watch, but of course, this may prove equally
entertaining."

"It may, it certainly may. By Jove, it's worked a new
plot. Two hundred plus heading our way. Time I got
busy."

Belland reached for the handset microphone.

"Hold it!!"

An airman who had snatched a tommy gun from its rack, stood with his back to the far wall, threatening the occupants of the dais. The W.A.A.F. plotters stared thunderstruck at the tense figure whose shoulders pressed against the Squadron State Board. They stared in awe at the tight-drawn lips in a dead white face, a pair of eyes drawn down to slits, which held the lack-luster stare of a snake, and above all, the menace of that venomous muzzle. This was not the airman they had worked with for so many a long week. It was something foreign, something vaguely unclean.

"Now, Mr. Bloody Belland, you think yourself so mucking clever. Cheated the Germans, have you? Cheated them, you poor mucking swine? You with your putrid rat-shaped brain! You? You to cheat Nazi Germany! In six hours they will be here. Here in this cesspit of a country you call England. But you, Mr. Bloody Belland, won't be here to meet them. You'll be dead. It's not so mucking funny to feel death coming to you, is it? It's easy enough to sit here and send people out to fight, but when death comes to meet you, that's another story, isn't it?"

Belland stood immobile; his fingertips rested on the desk counter; neither had Delafield altered his position; his long legs were still outstretched, his head still held slightly on one side. He still grinned that patronizing smile of complacency.

"See them coming?" went on the airman. "You! You who thought you could lure them into a trap! Well, you're in the mucking trap yourself and now you can take what's mucking well coming to you."

The muzzle of the tommy gun came up and was

trained on the dais. The gunman became even more rigid; the pupils of his eyes were almost hidden behind the close-drawn eyebrows. A finger tightened about the trigger.

Three sharp staccato reports; the tommy gun crashed to the ground; the airman's hands clutched spasmodically at his collar. He swayed forward on his toes, paused for a moment and fell forward, his head striking the corner of the plotting table. A raid block jumped with the chock of the impact, from Land's End to the Bristol Channel. Still in his same recumbent position, Peter Delafield held his Smith & Wesson to his mouth and blew the smoke from its muzzle.

"I'm most terribly sorry... sir..." he murmured. "You must forgive my unpardonable temerity, my unspeakable presumptiveness, but I've always wanted to fire a pistol in anger."

Belland bit his lip.

"Thank you, Peter."

"Please."

The pistol was returned to its drawer.

"You've broken the clock, sir," put in the Floor Supervisor.

"What a pity. I didn't even aim at it."

Belland picked up the handset.

"Hello, Isis, Isis. Walleye control calling. One hundred and fifty bandits approaching from the south. Angels two-seven. Vector one-seven-zero."

"Jamake, Walleye. We're on our way."

CHAPTER EIGHTEEN

BATTLE, MURDER AND SUDDEN DEATH

THE Air Officer Commanding in Chief of Fighter Command handed a sheaf of teleprinted forms to The Civilian at his elbow.

"These are the latest reports, sir," he remarked. "The fifth column plot was a complete failure with the exception of Neethley."

The Civilian removed his famous cigar.

"Neethley?" he demanded. "What happened at Neethley?"

"A dispatch rider was allowed admission to the Operations Room Guard Room. His dispatch bag contained a bomb. He went up with the Ops. Room. They will be off the air for two days, but the control of their Wing is unimpaired; it has been handed over to the next sector. We had a close call, sir. If the plan had come off . . ."

The Air Chief Marshal shrugged his broad shoulders.

"They used imagination," commented The Civilian. "Converted petrol tankers, clergymen, greengrocers' carts, dispatch riders, our own lorries. I see that at Exfleet they tried to smuggle men in in coffins being delivered for the funeral of three pilots. Somebody must have talked very carelessly. Any reports through of the actual fighting yet?"

"Sparse, sir. I have just come from the Operations Room. All the raids came in split into three, like Prince of Wales Feathers and curled back towards their bases. The Stukas then followed the original tracks and the fighters having turned in a complete circle, overtook them and covered their approach to the English coast. Battle has been joined."

Battle had been joined. Twenty miles south of the Lizard, Mohune's wing had met the Luftwaffe. The two English squadrons had pounced upon the Stukas, smashing their formation and throwing them into confusion. Three thousand feet above, the Czechs had met the escorting Messerschmitts and taken the fight to them. For twenty-five minutes the planes twisted and fought; then the Stukas, a broken remanant of an arrogant formation, turned and fled. The first round was over. Independently the English aircraft turned for home. In twos and threes they came in to land.

Mohune climbed out of his cockpit and looked at his watch; noon. Only half the day gone. Pulling off his harness, he walked across to Batchy's dispersal, but an Intelligence Officer greeted him expectantly.

"Can I have your report, sir?"

"In a minute"; he turned to the telephone operator. "Get me Operations . . . Hello, Ops.? Mohune here; are we all back?"

"Three Czechs adrift, sir. Otherwise all accounted for. How did you get on, sir?"

"Oh, so so. Just so so. Let me know if they turn up. I'll be in my office."

"Very good, sir."

"Hello, hello, Operations calling. Squadrons to refuel

and come to readiness as quickly as possible. Squadrons to refuel and come to readiness as quickly as possible. That is all."

"Can I have your report now, sir?" pleaded the Intelligence Officer.

"Oh! We met about forty Ju 87's at eighteen thousand. We shot up and attacked."

"Squadron Leader Salter says you got three, sir."

"We all had a whack at 'em. I saw three break up, but divide 'em between Beacon and Ginger. What's the total bag?"

"Sixteen Ju 87's destroyed, four probable and five damaged is the claim, sir. The Czechs bagged three One Oh Nines and they lost three."

"Hm! They had the harder job. Get on the phone for me. I want to see all Squadron Leaders in my Office right away."

"Ha, Mohune. Good show! Taught 'em a lesson. Think they'll call it a day?"

"Frankly, no, sir. They didn't alter their plans when they were thrashed in 1940 and I don't expect they'll alter them now. Any news from the other sections yet?"

"Little enough. Betlowe was bombed; not badly. A few stragglers got through. Bofors shot one down, I'm told. We'll hear later. How did the Wing shape?"

"Very well, considering. I'm going to alter my tactics next time. I'll take Batchy's boys up top. I'm going to brief the boys now in my Office."

"I'll come with you."

Ten minutes later the new plan had been explained and Wirrell had spoken to Group.

"Marsden caught a packet," he announced as he replaced the telephone, "but the Hun is the fellow who has paid in full. Perhaps he'll learn that Stukas can't be used until the fighters of the other side are out of action . . ."

"Hello, hello, Operations calling. Wing take off. Patrol base at eighteen thousand. Wing take off. Patrol base at eighteen thousand. That is all."

"Here we go again," said Mohune, grabbing his Mae West.

"Back to Buk-Buk," murmured Batchy.

From her tea-car, Schnoodel watched the Spitfires skim the runway and climb into the sky. One Squadron after another until all three were circling the aerodrome, catching up the leaders and taking up formation.

"Hello, Walleye, Isis calling. All set. Over."

"O.K., Isis. I'll have some customers for you shortly. Listening out."

There was no doubt that the Hun meant to push ahead with his plan. Raid blocks were appearing on the "board" at an unprecedented rate. Short concise orders were passed by the Controller to his aircraft. The Wing turned south-east to meet the enemy.

"Hello, Isis, Isis. Walleye calling. A hundred bandits will cross you from starboard to port in about three minutes. Keep your eyes skinned."

"Thank you, Walleye. My eyes are skinned. Hello, Batchy; keep a look-out above for One Oh Nines."

"O.K., Isis. Ginger, you mug; get off my wing. Fan me, this isn't an air display. Keep your distance."

"Sorry, sir."

The Wing forged ahead. The minutes passed quickly.

"Hello, Isis, Dagger Leader calling. Ju 88's below; Ju 88's below. Over."

"O.K., Dagger Leader. I can't see them yet."

"To starboard and below."

"O.K., O.K. I've got 'em now. Prepare to break. Prepare to break."

"Hello, Isis. 109's ahead. Fan me, swarms of the blighters."

"Hello, Dagger and Fortune Leaders. Ju 88's are for you. In you go. Up, Batchy, up."

The Czechs and the other English squadron peeled off and screamed down after the bombers. Hell was adrift over the placid sea.

"Here we go, boys."

"Going down. Ladies' underwear and bargain basement."

"Don't talk so much, Batchy."

"O.K., sir, O.K."

Down went the Pimpernels and 109's in a mad scramble, twisting, turning, guns roaring. One 109 turned over on to its belly and spiraled down with black smoke pouring from its cockpit. Another flashed across Mohune's sights and it, too, had fought its last fight. Then to one side Peter saw a Spit stagger, saw the nose jerk up, pull over and plunge downward towards the sea, twenty thousand feet below. Mohune's eyes narrowed. Ginger Rogers had gone. The sky was full of those twisting aircraft. Another Me 109 was dead ahead of Peter, who closed in rapidly, gave it a burst, turned on his side and dived away after yet another who was closing up on a Spitfire; another burst, another sheet of flame. The battle went on.

Back at the aerodrome the Controller had broadcast a "take cover"; another raid had come in from the west. Aircraft from a neighboring sector were hurrying to intercept, but at that moment only two sections remained to deflect the Huns from the target.

Gallantly the Spitfires met the bombers, attacking them head on to break their formation. Three bombers went crashing to earth, followed by two of the Spitfires.

Bomb releases were jerked back. Stick after stick screamed down at the aerodrome; the earth shook and quivered. A dispersal hut soared into the air. A petrol tanker burst into flames. The front of Mohune's office was clutched at by an unseen hand and flung to the four winds. The Operations Room rocked as a beach hut will rock in a high wind, but the Controller remained impassive and his crew unmoved.

"Hello, Isis, Isis. How are you getting on?"

"Hello, Walleye. Nicely, thank you. The bombers have turned back. The One Oh Nines are not putting up much of a show now. Over."

"O.K., Isis. Take care on landing. There may be a few holes about. Listening out."

At that moment, relief arrived over the stricken aerodrome and the bombers turned for home. The second action was over.

"Hello, Isis, Isis; Walleye calling. Return to base. Over."

"O.K., Walleye. It's about time. I've no ammo left."

"Hello, Walleye," a plaintive voice was calling Control. "Fortune Green One calling. I have some ammunition left. Have you a customer for me? Over."

"Hello, Fortune Green One. Green One. Don't be so damned greedy. Return to base."

"O.K., Walleye."

Once again the aircraft trickled in to land, once again eager ground crews ran forward to inspect their charges and refuel the tanks. Once again Intelligence Officers clamored for reports.

Six Ju 88's destroyed; three probable, five damaged. Seven Me 109's would never return and the score against? Another Czech was missing. 1616 Squadron had lost two. And the Pimpernels? Ginger was gone. Nobby, the Bloater, and young Steve had failed to return.

With his flying jacket slung across his shoulder, Mohune strode along the perimeter to his Office, an Office that was now an open cavity. Mohune fingered the hole in his ear. There was something else missing. He stared about in perplexity. What was there when he had taken off, but which was now absent? The ambulance and fire tender were still in their places. The Y.M.C.A. van? A sudden weight pressed against Peter's chest; the van had gone. At the double he made for the nearest telephone.

"Ops.? Ops.? Where's the tea-cart?" He forced his voice to be casual.

"Blown to blazes," cames the reply.

"And the . . . the attendant?"

"No idea. We haven't had a casualty report yet. The bodies are in Practice Flight. That is, what's left of them."

"You'll find me there."

"Who's speaking?"

"Mohune."

Peter slammed down the receiver and ran for his car.

"Schnoodel, Schnoodie . . ."

With screaming tires the Snipe was jerked to a halt; long strides conveyed Mohune to the hangar. A doctor looked up from his work as Mohune entered the building and watched him moving impatiently among the pitiful heaps.

"Can I help you, sir?"

"Looking for a girl."

"It's difficult . . ."

"Hello, hello, Operations calling. Will Wing Commander Mohune phone Operations please. Will Wing Commander Mohune phone Operations please."

Peter grabbed the doctor's arm.

"Doc!" Mohune's fingers bit into the medico's forearm. "I . . . Find that girl for me, if you can. There's . . . She's fair-haired . . ."

"Any distinguishing marks, sir?"

"A scar; a swastika scar on her left wrist."

Sick at heart, Mohune hurried away. His thoughts for the moment were full of Schnoodel. The happy eyes that had welcomed him that morning. He shook his head as though to jerk the misery from his brain.

"Mohune here."

"Oh, Wirrell. Mohune, I've just heard from Group. It looks as though the Hun is going to throw everything in and at us. Reconnaissance have reported Ju 52's and gliders on the move. Group will deal with all wing formations. Our function is to act against troop carriers. Bomber Command," continued Wirrell, "have been out today and have done some damage to the invasion

fleet. There is an invasion fleet this time. Barges massed
everywhere. They'll come, but that's the Navy's job. For
us, the parachutists. Dusk and dawn, usual times. Rip
into 'em, Mohune. You're at thirty minutes for an hour.
Get some food into you. Mark this, it will mean landing
after dusk. Choose your men carefully."

"Jamake, sir."

Thirty minutes available. Mohune strode out to his
car and headed for the Station Sick Quarters, where he
was greeted by the senior Medical Officer.

"What ho; what do you want? Pink Pills for Pale
Pilots?"

"Thought I'd see how you were getting on."

"Getting on?" demanded the medico. "Getting on?
I'm going mad. All my beds are full and damme if I
haven't got a civilian thrown on my hands as well."

"Haven't seen a girl anywhere about, have you?"

"Girl? Girl? Don't be fatuous. I'm working for once."

A door opened behind Peter's back.

"Hello, darling."

Mohune swung round on his heel.

"Why, Peter, you look as though you'd seen a ghost."

"I . . . Schnoodie . . . I . . ."

"Hurrump," grunted the medico. "Don't waste the
time of my staff."

"Your staff?" Mohune's brain was numbed. "What
are you doing here, Baggage?" he demanded.

"My van was blown up. I . . . well, I wasn't in it at the
time, so I . . ."

"Came along here to make herself useful," put in
the doctor cogently, "which she is doing, or was until

you arrived. We're about to have some food. Join us?"

"Too true."

For half an hour the world was back at normal, then the "blower" summoned Peter to the telephone. It was Wirrell again.

"Things are blowing up again. I'm calling the Wing to readiness."

"Very good, sir."

"I don't want you to go or the Pimpernels ..."

"But ..."

"No buts. The two squadrons, if they do take off, will work independently. I'm keeping your boys for the next part of the program."

And so once again the Spitfires took the air, but this time Mohune was forced to watch them go and then to wait impatiently for their return. From the dais in the Operations Room he watched the two Controllers move the squadron across the board, saw the separate track of friend and foe converge, watched the squadrons split into disconnected units and saw them turn for home, their task completed.

More Huns were down, more still would never reach their bases, but as the minutes passed, the full story was related. The Czechs had lost two more and the English squadron had one missing. Group reported that more aerodromes had been bombed and that all along the English coastline the Hun was maintaining his pressure.

"Serial One Four Zero." The Operator on the Group tie-line was taking down an Operational Order. "Squadron 1320 patrol base seventeen thousand feet. Time of Origin, Sixteen thirty-five."

"Patrol base." Mohune grabbed his hat. "My cue again. See you later, chaps."

He left the building and drove like a fiend possessed towards his waiting aircraft, but already the Pimpernels were airborne and heading south-east. Jacket, harness, Mae West, helmet, were pulled on with practiced rapidity, then he too was off, screaming after the squadron at full boost.

"Hello, Batchy, Batchy. Isis here. Make way for a youngster."

"O.K., Isis."

The leading section re-formed; the squadron climbed steadily.

"Hello, Isis, Green Two calling. One Oh Nines above at three o'clock."

"O.K., Green Two. Prepare to break. All right; they're Spitties. Keep together, boys."

"Hello, Isis, Isis. Walleye calling. Bandits approaching you from south-east."

"Jamake. What height, Walleye?"

"Don't know. Can't see them from here."

"Oh, you funny little man. Fan me, what a sense of lovely scintillating wit."

"There they are, Batchy, straight ahead below. Hello, Walleye, Isis calling. Gliders, my beamish boy; calloo, callay. Listen out."

Four thousand feet below was an amazing sight. Heavy two-motor bombers, each towing a string of six gliders, were headed for the English coast.

"Down we go."

"Look out, Isis. 109's above and behind."

"I think they're Spitties. Anyhow, I want a glider."

Down went the Pimpernels, their cannon belching out death and destruction. Slap into waves the bombers in a beam attack; in vain the heavy Junkers tried to forge ahead. Batchy's guns raked one, blowing the tail clean off, and the six attendant gliders, breaking loose, spiraled downwards. Into Number Two tore Peter; a plume of smoke poured from an engine cowling; pieces of wing flew in all directions; the engine itself tore away and another bomber was plunging down towards the sea. Up above other Spitfires grappled with the Messerschmitts' umbrella and then as suddenly as it had started it was all over. The Pimpernels turned for home.

"Too easy, fan me, it was positively child's play," murmured Batchy, divesting himself of his flying clothing, "but Question, would I like to be towed over the sea in a glider? Answer, verily I would not."

"Pretty grim," agreed Peter, pouring himself out a cup of tea from a large thermos.

"Cigarette?"

"Thanks"; Peter's lighter flickered into action. "Anyone seen Beacon yet?"

"Nope. He'll be all right. He'll turn up."

"Of course he will. I was just asking," agreed Peter, blowing a smoke ring at the ceiling.

The first day had made a hole in the Wing; good pilots who would be hard to replace; the first day, and that not yet over.

"Tell you one thing, sir and commandant. Those Huns were devoid of sense sending gliders over by day. I mean to say, not one of them could hope to make land when their puff-puff had gone off the rails."

"True enough," assented Peter, helping himself to

more tea, "but had we missed them, had not our worthy Controller put us on to them with his customary skill, the loss of their prime movers wouldn't have mattered a hoot."

"You could have shot them down as they glided in, couldn't you?" put in a man who had been busy with a Primus stove.

"There lies the rub, Bishop"; Mohune turned to the Station Padre. "I did attack one, but he spiraled down inside me. I had the devil of a job to catch him. Got him in the end, though."

The padre nodded thoughtfully and placed a kettle on the hissing stove.

"Shoot them down from the ground I suppose, is the only answer. I used to be a good shot with a twelve bore in my young days."

"Hark to Methuselah," said Batchy.

"Anyway, Jerry seems to be giving us a rest for the moment."

"Only two hours since we landed. It'll be getting dark soon. They'll have a shot then."

Mohune's words were prophetically accurate. At dusk raids appeared in large numbers. Spitfires were ordered off. Fighting recommenced. Waves of Stukas plodded forward; some were interrupted, some got through. The whine and screech of falling bombs rent the stillness of the evening air. Buildings crashed and toppled to the ground. A water tower swayed and collapsed. A section of the roof of Sick Quarters sailed away into the dusk. Then night; heavy bombers droned overhead, singing "War, War; War, War." Beaufighters whistled as they curved into pursuit. The crash and shudder of the bombs became heavier. The Germans were un-daunted.

Mohune and Wirrell stood side by side in Battle Headquarters. Messages were coming in thick and fast; arrows and flags and miniature aircraft were growing into a fine crop upon a large wall map of the surrounding countryside.

"Parachutists landing on Bodmin Moor."

"Predalzion Aerodrome heavily bombed."

"Gas reported at Trebalen."

"Troops landing at Mendennis."

Colonel Burns removed his monocle and polished it thoughtfully. A bursting bomb caused the lights to flicker and swing violently.

"They're trying," he murmured.

"Number One Post in action. Report small party of enemy."

A quick burst of Bofors fire added to the confusion; Vickers and Lewis guns took up the story.

"One Ju 52 in flames on the aerodrome."

The door was opened and an officer stood in the entrance.

"I have a prisoner, sir," he announced, saluting.

Wirrell looked at Mohune.

"You'd better interrogate him."

"Very good, sir. I'll see him alone in your office."

Casually he removed his pistol and placed it on the table and, with an airy wave of his hand, left for the next room. There was a pause and the prisoner, a German Major, was ushered in by his escort, a grim-looking soldier who held the point of his bayonet in the small of his captive's back.

"All right, I shan't want you."

"But ..." began the soldier, looking at Mohune's empty holster.

Peter nodded. "I can take care of myself—or at least I think I can."

The soldier forgot discipline, shook his head and withdrew, and Mohune, throwing a leg over the corner of a table, smiled at the German.

"Cigarette?" he asked in German.

The prisoner made no reply and Mohune, selecting one for himself, continued. "That won't do you much good, my friend."

There was a pause while the Player was ignited, then—

"Three or four days ago I was in Germany. I was a prisoner of the Gestapo. I ..." he studied his knuckles thoughtfully, "I learnt quite a lot from them and, *mon vieux*, I'm slightly different from the average Englishman. I believe in Total War. Do you get my point?"

"In an hour you will be dead."

"What a pity, what a shame, but never mind, we can have our little talk first. I shan't kill you, but I shall certainly hurt you ..."

Fifteen minutes later, Mohune returned to the Battle Headquarters; his uniform was as spotless as when he left, but he sucked at his knuckles reflectively.

"The gentleman has apparently fainted from the heat. He couldn't tell me much. He was in command of a party, but they didn't join up on landing. He reckons that they'll have Cornwall by dawn on Thursday."

"Forty-eight hours, eh?" Burns smiled confidently. "Well, we shall see, we shall see."

At nine o'clock the Prime Minister spoke to the nation, urging them to be calm and steadfast, reiterating his statement that we would fight on the beaches and in the streets.

In the news which followed, a brief account of the day's fighting was related. Two hundred enemy aircraft had been accounted for. Gas had been used and casualties were high. The people were ordered to keep off the roads and carry on.

The hellish symphony of war carried on throughout the night and the next morning. At dawn more parachutists were dropped on England. British troops were in action. Mohune's Wing took off, fought, landed, refueled and took off again.

At midday the news that the aerodrome at Trebalen had fallen; a counter-attack was in progress. A fleet of private cars had jammed the main road at one point. The village of Polnen was in enemy hands.

A mechanical brigade passed through Reith. Advancing, yes, advancing to prearranged position.

At one P.M. a burnt and battered figure staggered into Battle Headquarters. His face was blackened, his hair burned away, clothes hung in smoldered shreds. He staggered forward; Colonel Burns caught him as he fell and eased him into a chair.

"Beacon, sir. Flying officer Bright. Shot down . . . God, when was it? Yesterday sometime."

A flask was put to the boy's lips; he drank deeply.

"Polnen . . . the swine killing—killing everything, everybody. Flame throwers on children . . . Dear God . . . Women stripped and dead . . . The village is burning —burning like a beacon . . . just like a beacon. Passed a

kiddy." Bright placed scorched fingers over his eyes ...
"Gas—Lewisite," he went on. "Roads blocked with private cars ... expensive ones ... hell of a tax, big horse-
power. Saw Cornish miners lug the people out ...
kicked up the bottom into ... into ditch. Manhandled
the cars round ... and were off ... armed with knives,
axes, butchers' cleavers ... off back to that ... Hell of
Polnen. Saw a woman kill a Hun ... pitchfork ... he
squealed like a pig. Tell—tell the Winko ... I'm back."

The head fell forwards.

"Better get him to hospital," suggested a Captain.
Colonel Burns polished his monocle again and turned
away.

In the Ops. Room, Wirrell was talking to Mohune; in
front of them the Controllers were still on the job.

"... that seems to be the situation. We're holding the
Boche everywhere. Only that one aerodrome and one
village are in their hands. Everywhere else we are masters of the situation. It was a close call and it may get
worse if we don't retake that aerodrome. Command think
the Hun has shot his bolt. The Navy have killed them
in their thousands. The air is ours, but get that aerodrome we must. It's up to you and the other Wings."

"We'll do our damndest."

The battered but still valiant Wing took off twenty
minutes later; flying at tree-top height, they screamed
across the captured aerodrome. Twelve wrecked Ju 52's
showed the desperate fight the defenders had put up.
Crashed gliders were everywhere. Germans dived for
cover as the Spitfires dived upon them. Down in line
astern, up, up, over, down again; in between buildings,
round the smoking stump of the ruined watch tower,

spraying death, leaden death, not the foul blistering agony of gas.

"Hello, Isis, Isis. Bandits approaching from south-east. Angels twenty."

"O.K., Walleye. We're on our way."

The Hun was making a stupendous effort. Beaten back in the north and in the east, they were throwing everything into an effort to take and hold Cornwall at all costs. An armada was approaching The Lizard.

Belland wiped the sweat from his eyes and worked out a course for the fighters.

"Wind at twenty thousand? From 273°, 60 miles an hour."

He twirled the dial of his computator.

"Hello, Isis, Isis. What are your angels now? Over."

"Hello, Walleye. One six. Over."

"Hello, Isis. A black mass of bandits ahead. You should see them any minute now. Vector one seven zero."

"Jamake, Walleye... Steady on one seven zero. Climbing. Hello, Dagger Leader; come in a bit. Hello, Fortune Leader; close your squadron up."

"Hello, Isis. Batchy calling. Ain't life grand?"

"Whatcher, Batchy. Sea looks cold, though. There they are, Batchy; there they are. Verily a black mass."

"Fan me, the whole of the Crooked Cross."

The battle was on. Mohune flew straight at the leading formation, meeting them head on. He saw the glass cover of the German's cockpit smash into a thousand pieces as he skimmed over the top of it. Over on to his side, full rudder, a feint, followed by a quick dive up again, guns chattering. The wings from other sectors were now in the fight, the greatest air battle of all time. Messerschmitt, Heinkel, Dornier, Ju 52, plunged down to the ever open arms of the sea below.

In Battle Headquarters, Colonel Burns, D.S.O., M.C., was addressing his staff.

"Look at that notice."

On the far wall indicated by the Colonel's long arm was a facsimile of that famous order found in a recaptured pill-box at Passchendaele in 1916:—

"1. Special Orders to No. 1 Section dated 13.3.16.

"2. This position will be held and the Section will remain here until relieved.

"3. The enemy cannot be allowed to interfere with this program.

"4. If the Section cannot remain here alive, it will remain here dead, but in any case it will remain here.

"5. Should any man, through shell-shock or such cause, attempt to surrender, he will stay here dead.

"6. Should all guns be blown out, the Section will use Mills grenades and other novelties.

"7. Finally, the position, as stated, will be held."

The notice was signed with the boyish signature of a Second Lieutenant.

"That, gentlemen, is our example for today. Your men know the importance of this aerodrome. They know now that apart from the ear-splitting, heart-melting nose, a dive bomber is an innocuous adversary. There is nothing else for them to learn. All they will have to do now is fight."

He thrust a hand deep into his pocket and produced

four lapel badges which he placed on the table before him.

"Look at these; they are the badges of a doctor and a clergyman ..."

In the Operations Room, the converging armadas of Nazi Germany were being plotted across the large "board." Every person in that room realized only too well that the colored arrows were headed directly at them and that unless they could be diverted, death would rain from the skies in an unprecedented torrent, but no uneasiness showed on the W.A.A.F.'s faces. The loud-speaker from the Watch Tower broke the silence.

"One Moth taking off."

"What was that?"

Wirrell standing behind the Controller grabbed a telephone.

"Did he say Moth? What the hell? With every plane in the German Air Force headed this way, some fool wants to do circuits and bumps. Ops. B! Did he ask permission!"

Peter Delafield shook his head.

"Exchange!" demanded Wirrell. "Exchange! Exchange? Give me the Watch Tower ... Look-out? What's this about a Moth?"

A Cockney voice answered.

"Yus. A Moff 'as just gorne orff. The Doc's aflyin' it and the God-botherer's gorne as passenger. Taken a tommy gun wiv 'im 'e 'as. Took their badges orf 'fore they went. The Colonel's got 'em—the badges, sir. The Doc says as 'ow 'e an' the Padre'll put paid to them ruddy parachutists. Says as 'e can turn inside 'em."

Wirrell replaced the handset and stared at the far

wall. A doctor and a clergyman in a Moth, flying to meet the Huns. He turned to Delafield.

"Tell the Observer Corps I want that Moth plotted and carefully plotted."

"Very good, sir."

"Twenty enemy aircraft approaching the aerodrome from the southeast at eighteen thousand," announced the lookout, and as the loud-speaker clicked into silence, the bombs began to fall.

"I'll be back," announced Wirrell, making for the door. "Oh, and Belland..."

"Sir?"

"That W.A.A.F. is still using that lipstick. It's a foul color."

Mohune's Wing had split in all directions. They had gone headlong through one formation, throwing it into confusion, had been pounced upon by 109's and had fought their way out. Bombers and troop carriers were their targets. Spitfires had plunged downwards, spinning to destruction. Once Peter had seen Batchy diving on a Ju 88 and had lost him in a haze of cloud. He was alone. Out of the corner of his eye, he saw an aircraft screaming towards him and jerked away. The transparent roof above him shattered into fragments, near, unpleasantly near.

He slewed round in a vertical bank and coming out, a Hun was in his sights. His trigger button went down, as did the Messerschmitt. Round again. Another fighter on his tail. The Spitfire shuddered and a hole was jabbed into his wing.

"My, my," murmured Mohune, jerking away. "Too bloody close."

The sky seemed to be full of fighters, all attacking him. He twisted and turned, rolled and climbed, banked and dived again with a Hun full in his sights.

"On your tail, Isis. Guard your tail."

Mohune swerved away and a 190 shot past with Batchy attached to its tailplane by invisible ropes.

Then from the sun another pounced on Batchy, which in its turn was chased by Peter. The Hun rolled over on to its back with smoke pouring from its belly.

"O.K., Batchy?"

"Not so O.K., Isis. Fan me, they've hit my ruddy Glycol. Question, is that cricket? Going down, Isis, going down. Fan me, the kite's starting to burn."

At the moment Peter was engaged again, but even as he turned into the attack—

"How's it going, Batchy?"

"Burning like a Roman candle. Fan me. Can't . . . can't get this . . . bloody hood open. It's . . ."

"Batchy! Batchy!"

Mohune went berserker; he dived on to his target until it seemed that he would ram it and blasted it to the four corners of the earth, pulled away and saw a Dornier 217 four thousand feet below. Over in a stall turn and down.

Another score against the Hun. Suddenly all was strangely quiet. An icy wind was blowing across Mohune's face, an icy wind which blew a sticky moisture across Mohune's forehead.

Not an aircraft was in sight; the upturned bowl was empty save for that solitary damaged Spitfire.

Mohune shook his head to clear a numbness that had

settled on his brain. He raised a hand and touched his lips. His lips! His lips!

"Where in hell's my oxygen mask?" he muttered, shaking his head again. The sticky moisture was crawling across his face, seeping into his eyes and sprawling in red tentacles over his chin and neck.

His aircraft was sinking. The airscrew had ceased rotating, but of this Mohune knew nothing. His mind had drifted from the narrow confines of the cockpit to the untrammeled depths of bygone memories.

He saw again a formation of eighteen Dorniers appearing through a blood-red haze, heard himself say, "Bombers right. Turning in." Saw the wing now inside his own orbit and saw at least six of the bombers burst into flame and fragments at the first attack.

He saw Schnoodel and Madeline. Saw bombs bursting among a row of thatched cottages and heard pitiful cries as tanks crushed hapless civilians beneath their tractors, but as a beam of searing light, he heard Batchy saying, "I'm going down, Isis. Going down. Ladies' underwear and Bargain Basement."

To all intents and purposes, Mohune was unconscious, but his hands remained on the tick, his feet on the rudder bar. Subconsciously he tried his undercarriage release, without result. As a pigeon in its death throes, the Spitfire approached the aerodrome, watched by a group of spellbound pilots.

A thousand feet, eight hundred.

"Why the hell doesn't he lower his legs?" demanded a pilot.

Five hundred, four hundred feet.

"He's going to make a belly flop," muttered another.

Three hundred.

The Spitfire lurched and shuddered; the tail unit fluttered. There was a long drawn out sigh from the spectators. The tail shuddered again and broke away from its parent fuselage; the plane whipped over on to its back and dived at the runway. Disobeying all aerodrome regulations, a crowd of pilots ran forward as the first tongue of orange flame licked the crisp air.

Seven days later a Squadron Leader and a girl approached from behind a wheel chair.

"Dear Peter," Schnoodel called quietly, "I've brought someone to see you."

The chair spun on its axis, a pair of extremely dark blue eyes stared in amazement.

"Batchy! My God, I thought you were a goner."

"Only the good die young, Peter . . ."

"I quite agree. Upon my soul, I'm glad to see you both. What's the news? How are the boys? Schnoodel, you baggage, sit down on that chair and let me look at you."

"Shall I come back later? I mean, fan me."

"Don't be an adjectival idiot. Tell me the news."

"Firstly, O Commandant, you ought to be dead. How you got out of that fiery chariot beggars description . . ."

"But the war? They've told me nothing."

"They've kept you in the dark literally and figuratively. Feared concussions, but all is well. I was at the helm. The war goes on as usual." Batchy's voice adopted the unctuous tones of a B.B.C. announcer. "A man charged in London today with stealing four tons of rations and selling it in the Black Market was slapped on the wrist and told not to be a naughty boy. Mrs.

Allfor-Quietlife has protested against the noise of firing. Less hours and longer pay rolls have been granted to several grades of so-called workers . . ."

"But the invasion, you chuckle-headed chump!"

"The invasion? Fan me, he asks of a slight detail like that. Mrs. Hearnothing-Donothing has expressed the opinion that it never took place and that the Services are overpaid and underworked. In short, England's watchword remains the same—'Sugar you Charlie. I'm all right.' "

Mohune made an effort to leave his chair, but was immediately forced back again by Schnoodel.

"Will no one tell me about the invasion?" he grumbled.

"It's over, Peter; at least for the present. For a whole week it was touch and go, but it's over now. The Hun," the beauty left her face momentarily, as it always did at the mention of the Nazi regime. "The Hun banked everything on the fact that the Ground Control would be smashed and refused to believe that his plan had failed. Everything was thrown in, everything he had. Gas, flamethrowers, everything, but he didn't change his plan by one iota. It was a near thing, Peter de L'Epee, a very near thing."

"And Blake?" demanded Peter. "Did the aerodrome fall?"

"Question, did it fall? Answer, it did not. They attacked it, fan me, how they attacked it, but the Brown Jobs did their stuff. The gallant Colonel had the whole thing buttoned. The Doc and the Bishop shot a couple of gliders down!"

"What!!"

"Verily, the Doc did the flying in a Moth, mark you, and the Bishop popped off with a tommy gun from the back seat."

"Stiffen the crows! And the lads, how are they all?"

Batchy evaded the question and replied, "Young Schnoodie's brother is leading the Czechs now. Incidentally, he'll be in to see you soon. There's a party of 'em here visiting the halt and the maim."

Schnoodel took a cigarette case from her bag and offered it to Peter; a lighter flicked into action and Mohune, leaning back in his chair, blew smoke rings at the ceiling.

"The Doc tells me you'll be out of here in a week," she announced.

"Let him out, fan me, that's the worst news I've heard since Auntie died. I suppose I'll have to hie my weary legs to a florist and order a wreath of orange blossoms. Schnoodie, my sweet, this man Mohune is a constant disappointment to me. Time and time again have I squandered my hard-earned shekels in the useless purchase of orange blossom and what will you, but has the dirty dog ever taken the wench to the altar as in honor bound? He has not. Have I ever had the golden opportunity of heaving a hobnailed boot at my Commander's head. Have I, hell! All that happens is that my blossoms, those tender insignia of blushing matrimony, are handed to the Mess Steward to garnish his green salad. Fan me, but it's a miserable man I am, I am."

Mohune and Schnoodel did not appear to have heard Batchy's lamentations. Peter had never considered marriage with any degree of seriousness; it had meant ties, and ties that he was afraid of, but suddenly those ties did not seem to be so burdensome. He stroked that small hole in his ear as he considered the matter. Schnoodie? He shook his head. War-time marriages were often poor agreements, and yet—Schnoodie. His mind flashed back to that night at Davigore's. Would she think it a good idea? He inhaled deeply and stubbed out his cigarette. Then very gently he took her fingers and for a moment sat staring at the swastika scar. Their eyes met.

"Batchy," began Mohune diffidently, "we would be alone."

"Fan me, he's gone all Garbo. But to hear is to obey. Silent obedience has always been the motto of the Salters. Any message for the boys, sir?"

"Thank them for me. I'd like to see them. Tell them that as soon as the medicos finish with me, we'll have a party, a veritable celebration, and then we start a training program."

"Training program!" Batchy's voice rose to a squeak. "Did you say training program? Well, I'll be horn-swoggled! Fan me! Fan me!! Fan me!!!"

Batchy's long body stalked towards the door, at which he paused and regarded the girl bending over the wheel chair. A shaft of sunlight caught her hair; he sighed deeply.

"Poor clown," he murmured, beating his chest. "I'm always unlucky."

The door closed quietly and Mohune's left eyebrow quirked up quizzically; his grip tightened; he pulled Schnoodie forward on to his knees; her arms went about his neck.

"Monsieur de L'Epee," she whispered.

"Baggage."

For a moment they remained motionless. Then Schnoodel rose to her feet, pushed her golden guinea hair away from her eyes. Mohune watched her intently as she crossed to the high window and stood with one hand above her head, holding the curtains, while she gazed into the gardens.

A party of Czechs who had been visiting the hospital passed beneath her, singing quietly; the words of their song filtered into the room as they passed the window—

> "When first our country tortured on the rack,
>> The young shoots green were growing.
>> Now we are strong. We'll drive them back;
>> A blast from the West is blowing.
>> Vision of Victory comes at last.
>> Lift up your heads,
>> Lighten your hearts;
>> Victory will come.
>> Tri sta Trinact."